CHAPTER ONE

THE ADVENTURE BEGINS

Bjork awoke with a start. As he hurriedly sat up in his bed the book that was lying on his chest went crashing to the floor. Ah yes, he remembered now, he had been reading The Tales of the Wimpet King. He also had a vivid memory of the monster in his dream and shuddered. I really must try not to eat too much before retiring to bed he mumbled to himself.

It had been some time now since he returned from the Land of Lox with Naomi's cure. He had been very anxious indeed to return home. But lately especially since reading this book he felt bored with his daily routines. He found himself envying the adventures of the Wimpet King, and longed for one of his own.

Today in particular he felt very tired and out of sorts as he shuffled around his kitchen waiting for his teakettle to announce it was ready for a new day. Even the thick slice of berry pie that he snuck home after last night's Hork feast looked strangely unappealing and unappetizing to him. He pushed it around his plate with his fork, as he slowly pushed his chair back and rose to the sounds of the shrill whistle as the kettle reached its boiling point upon his fireplace grid. He carefully brought the pot to the table where his empty cup and tea leaves lay. He poured the steaming water into the cup over the tea leaves and set the kettle down. Then he scooped the leaves out and slowly raised the cup to his lips as he thought fondly of Naomi. He hadn't paid her a visit in awhile. Just what I need to cheer my spirits he mused. So he quickly finished his tea, left his pie sitting uneaten and began to carefully groom his appearance. He trimmed his beard and brushed his hair and splashed splendid smelling cologne onto his face. He went to his bedroom closet and withdrew his magical cloak. Quickly he proceeded in putting it on. He was whistling to himself happily as he raised his arms in splendor and thought deeply of Naomi's Meadow.

Within seconds he was there. What a hubbub was occurring. Fairies were scurrying and flying hither and thither. They were all excitedly chattering. The din of their voices was loud and their words were unclear. As Bjork stood there trying to take it all in, he remained completely unnoticed by the fairies. They were far too busy to pay him any mind. He observed Naomi as she stood with her wings outstretched and her fingers pointing this way and that as she gave hurried orders to the others. Straining his ears he found that her words too were still unclear. As she stood there in all her fragile beauty he felt the usual excitement at just seeing her again. He was a bit shy and embarrassed for not notifying her of his intentions; as he usually let her know when he was stopping by.

Naomi continued to give orders and when the last fairy had left in a hurry and flurry of wings, it was at that exact moment that she noticed Bjork standing there alone. He appeared to be a bit forlorn she thought. He carried his age rather well, which had left him handsome and rather distinguished looking.

She found him to be very attractive. It was as if she had just met him as her heart still made that little flutter and she fell in love once again. He looked impeccably groomed today. She could smell a very nice masculine scent as she flew to his side.

"My dearest Bjork, what brings you here unannounced?" she inquired. "I had a strong urge to drop by," Bjork said as his face reddened. "Please forgive my intrusion; I see you are in the midst of something very important. I can come back again some other time," he added.

"Now don't be silly Bjork," Naomi said as she gently touched his arm. She had become Hork size as a courtesy to him, to speak easier with him, more or so at his eye level. She sat herself down upon the ground and folded her legs and placed her fairy wings behind her. Then she clasped her hands and placed them in her lap.

"Bjork, just last evening my Father ordered Nimrod, Mahew, Jeziah, Jacor and Ryob to go out in search of Syncore the Sailor." They have heard word that he was seen in the dreaded land of the Cyclops to the east. He has much experience as a sailor and surely must know the way to Leprechaun Isle. It is here that my Father feels my Mother Geneva must be. He has been so lonely for so very long. It breaks my heart to see his pain. I hope that my brother and his brave fairy men can be as successful in their journey as you were in yours, (Which I may add I will be forever in your gratitude.") Then she did something much unexpected and very sweet as she stood up, turned to him and placed the sweetest kiss directly upon his lips. Then she backed away and said, "I will always love you Bjork, with all my heart."

Bjork's heart swelled with sadness as he gave her a smile and said, "I also shall always love you." It was just then that Nimrod who was hurriedly fluttering by, upon seeing Bjork stopped, turned and gracefully landed upon his feet in front of them both. He too assumed the Hork size as a gesture of courtesy and respect.

He extended his hand in greeting. "Hello Bjork! What brings you here today?"
"I felt a visit was long overdue," Bjork said as he winked at Naomi.
"Naomi has told me of your plan to seek Syncore the Sailor. A very dangerous and very adventurous plan it is. You will be traveling to the unvisited land of the dreadful Cyclops. I envy you my dear friend."
Nimrod looked very serious as he spoke.
"It was just last night that my Father cast this decree upon us and now I must honor his wishes and take up the search for my beloved lost Mother. It is my duty as the son of King Calliope and it is a subject that is very near and dear to my own heart. This quest is one that I must travel and these dangers are ones that I must face, I would never dream to cause you peril by asking you to take these huge risks by joining me. In my heart I would love to have you, for after our successful journey, your presence would give me a sense of succeeding in this one. But I dare not ask this of you my dearest friend."

"Although I am not a Nimbus fairy my heart will always belong here, as you very well know, "Bjork said. He looked lovingly at Naomi, "It would bring me dishonor to not go along, to not try as hard as I tried for Naomi to find her Mother and return her to her rightful home. I would do this not just for Naomi but also for you my dear friend and your Father the King whom I know and admire so well. I may not have anything to offer you but my heart and soul. I have no magic powers of my own but only what this cloak may possess, although I do have love and determination to not fail." Bjork looked pleadingly at Naomi first and then at Nimrod.

"I am firmly convinced my dear Hork friend, you are a distance relative to the Nimbus fairies, for you speak and feel with your heart as we do. I cannot deny you this right; I can only welcome you along for another adventure. I will be proud to have you at my side along the way. Hurry home and make haste to depart very soon. I will come to you when we are ready. I am grateful that you chose today to surprise us with a visit," Nimrod spoke with a smile as he vigorously shook Bjork's hand.

Bjork raised his arms and thought of home and instantly he was back inside his house, standing in his living room. The cloak had the power to transport him to the Fairy Meadow and back along with anywhere within the confines of Horkland but beyond that his ability to transport was nil. He also knew that he could only transport alone. The cloak did possess other powers as well which Bjork was not too familiar with. I must hurry, and this time I will not forget to carry the scroll of spells for the cloak. I am sure I will find them quite handy he mused. He began to gather all the necessary provisions. He carefully placed the Tales of the Wimpet King back on his bedside table. "I will return in victory to read you once again my friend, "he said. He then went to the library, took out a notebook and pen and wrote a brief message for his Hork relatives and friends. I have been called away suddenly, do not worry, I shall return soon and tell you all about it he wrote. He looked at it and thought that's not right it's not what I want to say at all. He crumbled it up and threw it in the waste can. He was just about to start writing a new note, when Nimrod appeared.

"Are you ready? We shall await you at the eastern edge of Hork Land. We must make haste; for word is that Syncore may have already set sail. My friend you must muster courage and travel light for we make our passage through the Land of the Cyclops under the cloak of darkness."
Bjork watched as Nimrod disappeared in a flurry of wings. He would reach the others soon Bjork thought, as fairies flew at a great rate of speed within Horkland and the neighboring Fairy Meadow. Beyond these areas their magic was lost and they would be left helpless and could succumb to many diseases and perils. There for they rarely left these parts of the Lands of Nod but when they did they were in the company of guardians. The Nimbus fairies were allies to many peaceful clans and had been so for a long time. They were not such allies with the likes of some of the warrior clans and it was of these that they were protected. They also

needed protection from the beastly things that dwelt in the various Lands of Nod.

Bjork looked at the empty paper set his pen down and thought. He didn't have time to tarry with this now, besides he didn't quite know what to write anyway. He simply wrote I shall return and signed it Truly, Bjork.

"I am ready now I must not keep the others waiting any longer," Bjork whispered to himself. He grabbed his scroll of cloak spells and tucked them safely inside an inner pocket as he raised his arms and thought of the Eastern border of Hork Land.
 Within seconds he stood in the darkness looking for signs of his fairy friends. He felt a bit uneasy, as he had no idea what lay ahead across the border. He had heard many horrifying tales about the Land of the Cyclops. How frightening their massive muscular torso was, with the enormous head that appeared much too large for their body. These Cyclops were hideous beasts towering over seven feet tall, their arms slung low at their sides (their huge hands almost scraping the earth beneath them), causing them to look in appearance as if hunched over. They had massive backs and thighs, spindly little legs and cumbersome feet. It was surprising how agile they were and how quickly they could scale a tree, or jump over an obstacle in their path. Their enormous round bald heads were bordered by massive pointed ears and long protruding noses. One huge eye was placed in the middle of their forehead, (which often scanned hurriedly from left to right). They had a very keen sense of smell for Hork in particular. So naturally this

made Bjork very nervous, yet excited at the same time.

Needless to say he was suddenly startled when Nimrod appeared beside him and whispered, "Hurry Bjork, we must meet up with the others." He tugged at Bjork whose heart had ceased beating quite so rapidly and off they went through the thick foliage until at last Bjork could see the other fairy men beneath the pale moonlight standing in a small clearing.

Just ahead was the border behind a dense thickly wooded area. The woods were eerily quiet as Bjork and the fairy men entered. It seemed very odd to not hear the sounds of its inhabitants which consisted of many nocturnal beasts. It was as if this dense dark forest was long abandoned by any living creature. The forest was much darker than he could have ever imagined.

If not for the fact that fairies have excellent night vision, Bjork would have easily gotten lost. But Nimrod and Jacor remained on each side of him, guiding him through the winding twisting paths. The only audible sounds he heard were of his own feet walking upon the fallen leaves and once in awhile the sounds of his own heavy breathing. Mahew, Jeziah and Ryob held up the rear, watching and listening carefully for any signs of imminent danger.

Bjork thought it would be a welcome sight to finally leave this horrible darkness and step out into the moonlight, even though the Cyclops were waiting on the other side. He knew he would rather face danger in the light than in the total darkness. The Cyclops were very heavy sleepers and did their hunting by the light of day. It seems they had rather poor peripheral vision, due to the fact of the placement of that one large eye in the middle of their forehead. They slept now, wherever they could find comfort. They didn't sleep in the shelter of caves or beneath the cover of bridges or cliffs unless the torrential rains began. These rains occurred frequently and gave the land a lush thick green foliage, and steamy gurgling foggy bogs and swamps.

The Cyclops simply lay upon the ground and the echoes of their deep snoring would fill the night air.
They must be careful not to step on one. But they could easily walk right by without waking the beast. Therefore any other inhabitants of the Land of the Cyclops did their hunting, foraging and all traveling at night.

Since so very few foreigners had traveled the path they now followed they had no idea what other creatures they may encounter. This too put them all on constant alert. They could now faintly see the light from the moon as they were approaching the end of the dark forest. How oddly peaceful it seemed. The night air was calm and a pleasant breeze blowing, with the scent of night blooming jasmine when they finally emerged from the forest.
Bjork thought, none too soon and he shuddered as he looked behind him into the total darkness of the woods that he left behind.

Soon they were traveling in pairs across the meadows and along the winding paths of the foothills of this strange land. They were traveling quickly but quietly. Until in the near distance they heard the distinct loud snoring of Cyclops. They could see a strange mist rising ahead and a terrible acrid smell became more noticeable as they continued forward. They were moving ever so cautiously as the foliage turned to tall grass stems, or rather reeds and it was at that moment that Bjork stepped out and sank to the bottom with a loud splash! He soon rose, coughing, sputtering and blowing water from his mouth. "Help me please," he called as quietly as he could. Both Nimrod and Jacor grabbed hold of his arms and pulled him safely up out of the steamy rancid waters. A swamp Bjork thought. He had heard tale of these but until today he had not fully understood how horrid this place was. He looked around and could see no end of this terrible bog. Here and there were huge beds of floating lily pads. He could hear the sounds of bullfrogs croaking and the cry from what sounded like a whimpering pup. At that very moment he noticed two large eyes emerging from the water and realized with horror that this was no pup but a rather large alligator.

Nimrod and Jacor struggled to hold on as they searched for dry land. Off to their left there was a tall wall of some strange type of flowering bush; they decided to see what lay on the other side. As they passed over, much to their surprise they found it was indeed flat dry land. But they also saw many Cyclops lying on the ground, some lay fearlessly side by side with their alligator friends. They were relieved to hear them all snoring away peacefully, as Nimrod and Jacor set Bjork down.

"Don't fear they are heavy sleepers," Nimrod said. It was soon after that they noticed a windy path that lay ahead which crossed a small weathered wooden bridge. There was a little stream that ran beneath it. It was such an inviting path that it wasn't long before they all agreed to take it.

Very carefully they stepped out upon the bridge as it boards gently creaked. No sooner had they started to cross when they heard a small muffled voice call out "Help, please, I can't swim". They all stopped dead in their tracks as Nimrod looked over the side. Down below he could see a small lad frantically trying to stay afloat.

"Continue on", he said to Jacor and Bjork. I will meet up with you on the other side." Nimrod wasted no time reaching the lad and soon he had lifted him out of the stream and onto the creaking bridge. The child sat there as Nimrod patted his back and he began coughing out water. After a short while the lad was able to catch his breath and began to tell Nimrod his story. He had been out foraging with his father when a Cyclops had startled them both, and not thinking he had run on ahead, it was then that he stumbled over a rock in the path near the end of the bridge and found himself thrown sideways into the water. Desperately he had tried to tread water as his father had taught him but soon He became too tired to last much longer. It was at that exact moment that He heard the fairy men and Bjork walking on the bridge. He didn't know what they were, but the lightness of their steps told him they were small of stature like him. Perhaps other foragers he thought. He decided then and there to call out

and take his chances, as drowning now
seemed very eminent.

Nimrod asked, "Of what clan are your people?"
"We are dwarves", the lad said as he extended
his hand in friendship. "I am Allar, and me
Father is Windor."
"What brings ye to The Land of the Cyclops?"
are ye the Nimbus fairies we have heard tell
of? "Allar asked.
 Allar was a strange looking little lad. His head
was quite large with bright red hair, his body
small of stature but stocky, his hands and feet
seemed to be way too large for his body. He
stood roughly about two and a half feet tall
but the way he proudly stood and smugly
spoke gave him the delusion of being much
taller. "I do like a lad to be sure of himself,"
Nimrod thought to himself. Allar was dressed
in what appeared to be some sort of a green
smock and pointed green slippers. He sported
a small strange green matching pointed hat
upon his head, all of which were saturated
and dripping. His infectious smile exposed his
large shiny white front teeth.
Nimrod couldn't help but smile himself, as he
replied.
"Yes, my friends and I are Nimbus fairies; all
but one which is a Hork, Bjork is his name. I
suspect you shall very soon meet them on the
other side of this bridge. I myself am Nimrod
the son of Calliope the Nimbus Fairy King,"
Nimrod said proudly, with a bow. We have
come seeking Syncore the Sailor. We have
heard tales that his travels have brought him
to this land. Lad, do you know of whom I
speak?"

"Syncore! Why yes! I saw him but just the other fortnight. He was on his way to meet up with the Vashings clan. They were to set sail soon for distant lands of fortune."

"The Vashings clan? Forgive me my newfound friend but I am unfamiliar with that clan, "Nimrod said with a very puzzled expression.

"The Vashings are distant relations to the Vikings of yore," Allar said. They are a fierce and brawny clan. They are extremely seaworthy and take pride in their ability to hold their drink. They also have an insatiable appetite for beautiful women, and have been known to steal a few away. The women also find them oddly attractive and often are willing to leave their clan to take up with the likes of them. A few of our lady folks have met such a fate. I hear tell they are a handsome bunch, and stand nigh to five feet tall. Yet even for their roughness they are a likable bunch and Syncore has made many a friend and sailed with quite a few of the noblest of them .Ye mustn't tell me Father that I spoke to ye of these things, he thinks I'm far too young to carry on so, but many an evening I hid from view and heard me Father and Syncore swap tales," He said with a wink.

Bjork and the fairy men were long becoming impatient as they waited for Nimrod to return. He was taking such a very long time, so long in fact that they were beginning to start back over the bridge when the image of two tiny forms approaching them began to come into focus. "Alas, Nimrod and his drowning victim." Bjork said. Well my little lad whom may you be?" Bjork asked as Allar stepped off the bridge.

Nimrod then briefly told them Allar's story. "We must continue on for daylight approaches, soon the Cyclops will awaken." Jeziah reminded them.
"Yes please do come along, follow me,"Allar said. Me Father will gladly give ye shelter in exchange for rescuing me."
They were indeed all in need of shelter for the day. Not one of them relished the idea of being caught dead in their tracks by the likes of the dreadful Cyclops. Rest was very appealing now, as they were also feeling very hungry. They hadn't eaten in quite a few hours and the air had taken on a chill, so Bjork was very glad indeed to find somewhere to spend the day. He shivered as he hurriedly wrapped his cloak tightly around his body and quickly followed the Dwarf Allar down the long windy trail. Around the corner the landscape changed and became much more green and pasture-like. He could once again hear the sounds of birds in the trees that lie to the edge of the pasture and smell the rich scent of blooming flowers. How long they walked he did not know, but it seemed like only a few moments before they reached a small village. The homes were all made of clay bricks with thatched grass roofs. They were small homes, built for the dwarves, which only stood less than four feet tall at adult height. In each house he could see a candle burning and the light from the flames were gladly dancing on the walls. He also noticed the wisps of smoke that rose from the clay brick fireplace stack on the top of each roof.

A wonderful scent of delicious foods being cooked over an open hearth soon filled the air. Was that the scent of Huckleberry pie? His stomach growled at the mere thought.

Bjork suddenly felt extremely ravenous as they came to a large house that stood large in girth, not in height. There were two large doors in the center that Allar now approached. He grabbed the doorknocker in his small chubby hand and rapped on the door with surprising strength. It immediately was thrown open by a short stature older dwarf woman that was rather chubby and perhaps three and a half feet tall. She instantly grabbed Allar and kissed him on both cheeks. "Where have ye been Son?"she inquired. Father has been fretful worried and pacing frantically all evening. He was sure a Cyclops had captured his only Heir." Then Bjork noticed two fierce looking Wolverines guarding each side of her.

"Excuse me rudeness." she said, as she looked at her son, "Allar whom may these guests be?" Then turning back to the newcomers she noticed the worried look on Bjork's lined face. "Oh deary don't worry any about these critters they are friends to the dwarves and to all other wee people.Tis Cyclops that they hate. They've been known to rip them apart flesh by flesh and bone by bone. If it weren't for me Banshees, Boris and Bosco I would never survive a day in this land. A different pair of Banshees protects each dwarf family. All they ask for is love, affection, a cozy hearth to lie beside and the leftover food scraps from the table. Please do come in Allar and introduce these fine guests to thy Father."

"Father, Father, Allar anxiously called, "Come meet me rescuers, for they have traveled far and have much to report. "

Father Windor quickly appeared with a large smile and swooped his son up in his arms, and planted a kiss upon his forehead. "Me son I must hear all about thy guests, he turned to the others and spoke, "Please come eat, drink and take rest, me home is thine," he said as he looked upon the fairy men and Bjork. " Introductions were made all around and soon they were sitting at a large long table covered with many plates and bowls of delicious hot steaming food.
Bjork and the fairy men soon ate their fill. It was all so wonderful. There were deliciously prepared pastries and stews and bowls of fresh fruits and nuts. Steaming soups and shimmering puddings.

Three young dwarf women, in identical wardrobe, cheerfully served the food, and cleared away the empty plates. Servants I assume. Bjork thought. Windor's wife sat at one end of the table across from Windor whom sat at the other.
"My dear Lady, Bjork said, "How long does it take for you to prepare such a heavenly repast?" "Forgive me for not addressing you by name but Allar has not quite introduced us as of yet."
She blushed and placed her hand over her mouth for a second. "Kind sir, I must confess I did not prepare this fine meal. I must apologize for me son's ill judgment, me name is Wynneta." "Percy! Percy" she called, as a very portly younger woman appeared. "Yes me lady," Percy said.

Wynetta pointed her stumpy index finger in Percy's direction, and then swept her hand across the air palm up towards her, "This is me cook, Bjork, it is Percy and her fine staff whom prepared this elaborate meal."

"Percy, you are truly talented in the kitchen", Bjork said as he patted his overstuffed stomach."

"I hope ye have room left for Percy's special Huckleberry pie" Wynetta said with a wink.

"I have just enough room left for that, always room for that," Bjork said with a grin.

These dwarves were certainly very friendly people indeed and excellent cooks. I will enjoy my stay here he thought as he tossed a few crumbs to the Banshees. After they had finished eating them the Banshees approached nearer to Bjork and soon he was patting their soft furry heads while they licked his hand in gratitude.
It was hard now to imagine these gentle beasts as vicious Cyclops killers. But even so he felt safe knowing they were.

After they had finished the last piece of Huckleberry pie, Windor called to his servant girl Mariah to bring him the Dwarf ale. She soon reappeared with three small flasks and mugs for the ale.
It had a fruity sort of cider taste with a definite fermentation, and was very palatable and very potent. Soon Ryob was flirting with the servant girls as Jeziah, Mahew and Jacor were talking about past adventures. Bjork listened intently to Windor and soon learned that he

Windor was indeed the Dwarf King. So Nimrod has rescued the heir to the throne. How amazing is that? Bjork mused. It was many hours later when Windor called to the servant girls, who were enjoying Ryob's attention. "Girls, show me good guests to their rooms for the night. May ye all rest well until the morn. Tomorrow we will show ye the way to the seacoast where ye will find the Vashing clan. It is here we hope me friends that ye will meet up with Syncore the Sailor."

CHAPTER TWO

WINDOR THE DWARF KING

Bjork awoke extremely well rested after sleeping on the overstuffed mattress which had been placed upon the Dwarf size bed. He remembered the evening before with fondness and soon was up and out the door in search of his fairy men friends. He found them waiting patiently in the Windor King's immense library. They were reciting titles from the huge collection which was neatly arranged upon the library's many shelves. Bjork had never seen so many books in his entire life. Each one was categorized by genre and in alphabetical order. Not a speck of dust was to be seen anywhere. It must take the Dwarf King's servants hours to keep them so nice he thought. He found himself falling into a trance as he read the titles to himself. The one that really caught his eye was titled Leprechaun Isle. The words leapt out at him from the shelf and left him in deep thought, so deep that He didn't hear the footsteps approaching him from behind, causing him to be startled by the voice that spoke gaily near his left ear. "Good morning friends!"

He sprang around quickly to see Allar standing beside him. "Come enjoy the breakfast that Percy has prepared especially for ye. She was very pleased by thy kind remarks last night."

Breakfast Bjork thought, how curious He hadn't felt hungry until Allar mentioned it. But now he felt suddenly ravenous as he waited anxiously to taste Percy's feast. "Come fairy men, we must enjoy one last meal with our new friends, before we begin today's long journey."

They all followed Allar into the main dining room where the long wooden table was once again laden with steaming plates and bowls of food. There sat at each end King Windor and his wife Wynetta the Queen
In front of each place setting there was a small note placed in a card with each one of their names written in the most beautiful calligraphy Bjork had ever seen.

He sat down where his name was and picked up the card. Carefully He pulled out the note and read: To Whom It May Concern, also to all creatures near and far that are friends to the Dwarves, take upon ye Bjork as thy ally. Treat him with the love and respect of all thy fellow kinsmen. In return I King Windor will stand with ye in times of war and peace. Keep our pact of alliance to defend each other's peoples and lands forever and honor this pact also with Bjork the Hork. If he may need assistance from ye in his journey give it to him freely and with a glad heart. Signed Respectfully, Windor the King of the Dwarves.

Each note was identical only the names had been changed. "What a very thoughtful and special gift this is, I cannot thank you enough your Majesty, nor can I ever repay you for your hospitality, "Bjork said as he stood up and bowed.

"Nonsense Bjork I will always owe ye and the fairy men far more for rescuing me only son Allar. I am indebted to ye until me dying day, and so will be me son the heir, even long after me old bones have turned to ash."
They then began to consume the most delicious feast consisting of porridges, sweet breads and flap jacks all dripping with rich berry syrup. These were then finished off with a delicious hot drink, made from some unknown fruit nectar. "What do you call this delicious drink?" he asked.
"Ambrosia," Wynetta said. "It's made from the nectar of the passion fig, which grows wild in our fruitful land."

"Finish thy meal me friends and then I will personally escort ye to the edge of the caverns that lead to the shoreline. They are well lit by day, as there are many openings in the ceilings from past storms, where the rocks have come loose or may have been worn away. Ye must be careful though because they do tend to turn and twist, so always follow the hand painted symbols on the inner walls. One wrong turn and ye will be lost in the cavern's never-ending maze of twisting turning tunnels. It is said it is haunted by the spirits of the poor lost souls who perished trying to find their way out.

Once ye get to the end of the caverns ye will reach the shoreline where ye will see behind ye high upon a cliff the magnificent Vashing King's castle. It sits very tall and immense against the sky, facing the waves of the fierce blue sea. It is an ominous site with enrapturing splendor, which has stood upon that very cliff for eons. As ye round the right hand corner of the cliff the massive fleet of ornately carved wooden sailing ships that sit anchored near the shore will astound ye. Crews of very seaworthy and brave Vashings man each splendid ship. It is here that ye will find among these ships the largest of them all which belongs to Syncore the Sailor. His vessel is tenfold the size of one of the Vashing ships. It stands tall and true also manned by Syncore's famous crew. A crew that has weathered many a terrible storm at sea, and fought off evil pirates that tried to invade her. Ye will also see carefully carved out steps that lead up the side of the cliff to the bridge that stretches over the moat that lies before the castle's door. Here upon the bridge ye must present the Vashing guards with the notes that I have prepared. They will only then allow passage across the bridge to speak to the Vashing King Lore.

They soon had finished their breakfast and rose to prepare for the trip to the caverns. "Thank you my kind Queen for all of your wonderful hospitality, "Bjork said as he kissed the top of Wynetta's outstretched hand. "Be safe me friend Bjork, travel with the blessings of the Dwarves she said. " Me dear Nimbus fairy friends may ye also be greatly blessed in thy quest to find Nimrod's Mother.

May ye have a successful voyage, and safely return to thy homeland."

Allar stood sadly at her side as they all walked out the doors with Windor the King and his Banshees leading the way. Bjork turned his head and looked over his shoulder. He could see a longing for adventure in Allar's face, almost envy, as Bjork gave him a wave goodbye. That lad is destined for greatness, He will make a fine King someday, Bjork mused.

I hope that Syncore the Sailor is still visiting the Vashing King's castle Bjork thought. His heart raced excitedly as he thought of how wondrous this new adventure was becoming. So many more mysteries yet lie ahead.

They traveled lightly today with the gentle breezes blowing as the Banshees kept them safe from harm. This land was so rich with beauty; the Cyclops seemed very out of place he thought. The birds were singing and the sun was shining as they traveled along the winding dirt path. It was a well-trodden path that was lined with many trees on each side, which gave the travelers a constant comforting shade and a refuge from the sun. This path was so beautiful and peaceful, that they almost forgot about the dreaded Cyclops. It was then that they turned the last corner and to their horror, before them stood the most hideous site, two large Cyclops females and a small Cyclops child. The Cyclops shrieked in high piercing voices that set Bjork's nerves on edge, when they noticed the snarling Banshees. Windor struggled to keep them from attacking, as he could never harm any child, not even a Cyclops child.

He ordered," Leave this path now before I set these loose to feast upon ye!"

The Cyclops women looked at each other as one grabbed the child and they turned and ran between the trees to the right of them, leaving only the faint sounds of their frightened screams, as they grew farther away in distance.

"Hurry, they will soon warn their men that we are here, we have no time to waste", Windor cried.

They ran along the path that winded down now turning and twisting, being careful not to trip over the roots of the trees that filled the path. Down down they ran until Bjork felt his lungs would burst. It was at that moment that the path took its last turn to the left where it came to an abrupt and sudden end. Directly in front of them they saw the entrance to the caverns, very well lit, just as Windor had claimed them to be. In haste to escape the dreaded Cyclops they dashed inside. "The Cyclops won't enter here", Windor said. "They have poor vision but enhanced hearing and the sounds of the ocean cause them throbbing ear pain too great to endure." Once inside the cavern walls, they could very faintly hear the sound of ocean waves in the distance as they crashed upon the shore. This sound was so unfamiliar to them, as none of them had ever traveled to the shoreline before. They had read of the sea and seen pictures of it in books, but never heard its wondrous sound.

Bjork was frightened as were the fairy men as he spoke" What pray tell me awaits us that makes such an awful angry noise?"

Windor laughed, "That Bjork is the mighty sea; she calls to ye as she heaves her waves upon the shore. Stick to the path with the symbols and follow it's sound and ye will soon reach her in all her ageless splendor. Travel quickly me friends; please give Syncore and the Vashings me regards. Forgive me me haste me friends but I must hurry before the Cyclops return!" He cried. With that he gave a little bow as he turned quickly and raced out up the path with his Banshees at his side. "What a great and noble friend I have made", Bjork said. "I only hope to find the Vashing King to be as amiable."

"Yes, Bjork and I hope that Syncore the Sailor is waiting there still," Nimrod said. They began to follow the paths of the caverns, looking for the symbols and now carefully listening to the new sounds of the sea, as if she were a friend lying in wait, welcoming them to join her. "If we hurry we'll reach the end before dusk," Bjork said, "I truly wish to see these wondrous things in the light of the day. I think I'd rather meet up with a Vashing guard before night falls too", he chuckled. "They must be a little frightening in appearance themselves."

CHAPTER THREE

THE VASHING KING'S SURPRISE

Bjork was nearly out of breath as it became more apparent to him by the sounds of the

crashing waves that they were approaching very near to the seashore. It was at this time that he noticed a marking on the wall with an arrow that pointed to the left. He called over his shoulder to his fairy men, " Hurry lads I believe I see the exit ahead." The fairy men rushed up behind him just as Bjork was stepping out into the massive arch which formed a doorway beyond the cavern walls. Though dusk was upon them, they could now see what they had only once imagined in books. How wondrous and glorious a sight it was. There were no words to describe its splendor. The sky was a colorful reflection from the huge rising moon that lit up the ocean's waves. Bjork could now see very clearly by its illumination the majestic white crests of the waves as they pounded the shore. The sand felt cool and enticing beneath his bare feet as he playfully let them sink into it. It was welcomely damp and cool as the air was filled with sea spray and the smell of the ocean reached his nostrils. His long gray hair was blowing in the sea breeze as he stood in total awe. He was silent and frozen for a while, just taking in the moment, when he realized it was growing darker as he now fully could see the moon emerging from behind a cloud. "Night will soon be upon us thus we must hurry to the castle men," he called.
So he sat down and hurriedly put his boots on. Then he followed the others in haste.

Just as King Windor had promised, Bjork looked up behind him and saw the enormous Vashing King Castle. It was even more prestigious than he had imagined, as it stood proudly in watch over the Vashing Fleet. There were torches burning now that encircled the perimeter of the castle, as the sun had almost completely left the western horizon. He turned back and looked at the sea; she was suddenly less beautiful and more eerie, as she grew darker. The moon cast a brilliant light upon her waves, while the countless stars twinkled in the sky far above her as Bjork and the fairy men turned toward the carved stone path that led up the cliff to the Vashing Castle.

The climb was steep but Bjork was feeling a burst of adrenalin from the anxiety of meeting the Vashing King and in no time reached the summit. A Vashing guard was standing there protecting the bridge that stretched perilously across the moat. He looked very capable of defending his ground. He was short in stature yet very massively muscular. He wore Vashing armor, complete with the horned Vashing helmet, all made from forged steel. His long bright red hair was visible beneath the helmet's bottom as it hung down his back in a long braid. A bright red beard with a wide bushy mustache covered his face. He looked stern and showed no fear as he spoke, "Who goes there? What business do ye have with the Vashing King? "

Bjork very nervously reached in his pocket and pulled out the card that Windor had written upon. "I believe this will explain everything," he said as he handed it with shaking hand to the Vashing guard. The guard reached up and grabbed the torch to draw its light nearer, as he squinted and read the announcement card. "Very well Bjork, I will notify King Lore at once of thy presence."

"I am Darrel a castle guard and humble servant to King Lore, I'm very glad to meet ye me friend of King Windor," he said as he extended his hand. Bjork thought his hand would break, as it was shook very tightly by the strong Vashing guard. "Thank you Darrel, but there are more that accompany me," he said, just as one by one the fairy men reached the top and stood side by side in a line.

"Lads give him your cards," Bjork said. "That won't be necessary Bjork; I need to see only one of them for I am sure Windor has written the same on each one," Darrel said. Nevertheless Nimrod stepped forward and presented his card. Darrel read it as before and smiled as he said, "Welcome to King Lore's Castle the King of the Vashings, me friends."

He then turned and placed a horn to his lips, he blew it hard, to produce a deep resounding pitch, which echoed across the moat. There was an instant reply from another horn that came from the other side of the bridge. "I have notified the guard to let ye pass, he in return will notify the others that friends have arrived. Soon ye will be entertained by the King's best and ye will be feasting on the finest buffet in our kingdom. There will be tastes to tantalize any pallet from all over the world, from the farthest corners of the sea. Far east teas and spices, succulent tropical fruits, and more, all this awaits ye. Enjoy thy stay and may the good Lord return ye safe always from thy travels." Darrel then gave a little bow and extended his arm in the direction of the bridge, " Ye may now pass, don't look down, it's a far fall and there are no railings, stay to the middle, in a straight line one following the other as she sometimes sways a little from old age. There are sharp rocks below and dangerous spikes. Hurry now!"

With that Bjork stepped out upon the bridge and began to move quickly, staying toward the middle, the fairy men all followed, he was halfway across when he felt it sway. His heart raced and he picked up enough speed to soon reach the other side.

He could see the guard now, who looked in all appearances to be a close kin of the other. He too had the same attire and red hair. His facial hair looked the same also. "I bid ye welcome me friends, I see ye have gained the rite of passage from me brother Darrel. I am Jarrel his identical twin", he said with a very broad smile. He also extended his hand in friendship.

"Be gentle please, for you don't know your strength and your brother nearly broke it," Bjork said with a blush.

Jarrel roared with deep laughter, "Aye me friend, tis true we don always realize this." He clasped Bjork's hand between both of his and gave it a gentle shake.

"Enjoy ye, the night is nigh and the entertainment runs high." He again gave a true belly laugh, "The King has acquired many beauties from his fleet's travels. He has won a few too in battle or on a wager. But ye shall see," he said with a smile and a wink. He gave a different shrill sound on his horn that was echoed from deep within the walls of the mighty castle.

Bjork was startled as the castle door began its creaking ascent.

He could see the massive wooden gears turning around as it slowly rose. There on the other side stood a huge entrance hall with five Vashing guards on either side. They all were of small stature but shared a very muscular build. They each had the same armor as the other guards, and were carrying several weapons wielded from forged steel. They stood prepared for battle in an erect row as Bjork and the fairy men entered. They didn't physically move, but their eyes kept a constant watch of Bjork and his clan as they traveled through the entrance hall. Bjork felt unsteady about what they might do, as he slowly moved forward. He continued on until the hall opened upon a large acceptance room. The room was well lit with many torches blazing from niches in the stone walls. He was admiring the many fine statues and art pieces that were displayed when a group of five Vashing guards approached them. They too were dressed as for battle, but they carried no obvious weapons. They approached with their hands extended and said in unison, "We are King Lore's faithful servants, he awaits thy presence, do not be ye afraid, only follow me for he has much joy to share with ye tonight." They bowed in unison and pointed to an upper chamber and a larger spiral staircase, which led to it. They could faintly hear the music of flutes, laughter and voices as they began to climb the stairs. Along the way Bjork was amazed by the beautiful art, statutes and paintings that adorned the walls. He couldn't help but to pause on a few steps as he took it all in. The statues were so lifelike and they were etched in the finest of gold. The paintings were breath taking and they too were framed in gold. He had never seen such a fine display of art and wealth as this in all his days. He felt for perhaps the first time in his life that he was a small insignificant being. His treasures at home now seemed so worthless and plain. It was his first real taste of envy. He felt ashamed for feeling so. I must concentrate only on the issue at hand he thought; we must find Syncore and Naomi's mother. I mustn't indulge myself in such selfishness.

They continued their long climb as the music and laughter grew louder with each step. When Bjork finally reached the top he glanced behind him and took in the awesome grandeur of the castle entry hall, now dwarfed by the height he had risen. It still appeared so immense in size and the torchlight that danced upon its shadowy walls, gave it a warm and cozy appearance. It was indeed breath taking. He couldn't imagine how much more grand the King's ballroom would be. He took a deep breath in anticipation, straightened his cloak and stepped into a long hall that also was laden with bountiful exquisite sculptures and paintings. Large statues stood guard along the way, as he glanced at the far end of the tunnel, he noticed at its end there was a bright light emanating from a huge archway.

The fairy men kept in close pursuit of Bjork also taken by all the beauty. The chandeliers that hung from the ceiling seemed to have been forged from pure gold and the finest crystals adorned each leaf, from which a small candle now burned. This lit up the hallway as they approached nearer the archway and it became apparent that the two statues at the entrance that stood at each side were not statues at all. They were Vashing guards dressed in splendid gold armor. They had large plumes of ostrich feathers that draped from their helmets and the finest hair of a golden yellow. They wore beards that were neatly groomed and large trimmed mustaches and they bore the eyes of deepest blue. These were King Lore's bodyguards; it is told that they never have left his side, not even as he slept. They stood silently posted by whichever door that the King remained behind.

They gestured to Bjork and the fairy men that it was safe to enter, as they pointed to the open doorway and gave a polite bow. Bjork entered first and was soon joined by the others. Bjork took in the sounds of the beautiful music as well as of hearty male laughter mixed with the gentle voices of young women. In front of him was a long red carpet that wound past ornate statues that were spaced every few feet apart. They were statues of nudes, and lovers, in various poses, that were very lifelike in appearance and made Bjork embarrassed of the blush he now wore upon his face. Bjork didn't notice the young Vashing that stood to the right of his elbow until he spoke. "Is ye Bjork, the Hork which saved the Nimrod fairy princess? Me Father the King has heard tell of thy bravery and is delighted to meet ye at last." He then curtseyed and rose with extended hand, "Forgive me rudeness, I am Prince Lars, son and heir to King Lore."

He had the friendliest smile and eyes of the brightest blue, and a yellowish blonde braid that was draped very nobly across his back. He looked like a very young Vashing, as he had no signs of facial hair at all. He wore a suit of spun silk, burgundy in color with a dark crimson sash. He was obviously not a warrior, perhaps too young or inexperienced. At any rate Bjork took an instant fondness to him. "I am indeed much honored to make your acquaintance," Bjork said as he shook his hand.

"Follow me Bjork, I will take ye to me Father now."
"May my fairy men accompany me Prince Lars?" Bjork asked.
"Yes indeed ye mayst bring thy friends along", Prince Lars added.
They followed the young prince down the red carpet and around the corner, which turned, into a massive ballroom. To the right of them were enormous banquet tables bountifully laden with distant foods, some of which Bjork had never seen. Beautiful bowls and flasks of gold and large golden platters were covered with exotic fruits and vegetables, meats, cheeses, fish and the list went on. There were large kegs of ale and so very many bottles of wine. He then realized how extremely hungry he was.
His stomach growled a little nervously as he approached nearer the next turn and walked down a few steps, which led to the entertainment room. Here he saw many different beautiful women of all cultures and colors, dressed in elaborate exotic clothing. There were so many smiling beautiful faces that it made Bjork feel strangely self-conscious.
Gay music played while women belly-danced, spun and twirled in perfect unison with the music. They all were dressed in the apparel of

their distant lands; some also wore veils across their faces. The King's guests sat upon large pillows and drank ale laughing heartily at a young female as she slapped away their inquisitive roaming hands. The King's guests were also of different cultures and had apparently traveled a great distance at sea to attend. In the far right corner sat the immense golden throne with the finest embroidered silk cushions of a deep spun gold. The arms and feet of the throne were very ornately carved. Upon the silk cushion sat, a rather old Vashing wrapped in a yellow robe of spun silk. He appeared to be bored or simply tired from old age as he tried to keep from falling asleep. His hair was now a fine white braid that hung upon his back. His wizened face was covered with a well-groomed white beard and a small neatly trimmed white mustache. His head wore a simple crown of gold upon which was engraved in the front. "Lore". The crown was encased with rows of rubies and pearls. "Father, Father", Prince Lars said as he gently shook the King to get his attention." I have brought Bjork the Hork and his fairy men to greet ye"

King Lore sat up with a start and patted his son upon his head, "Please do come forth Bjork, I wish to speak with ye. I am an old Vashing King and too frail anymore to travel, I do wish to be amused by thy stories and adventures. In return thy friends and ye may feast, and enjoy a dance with me many wives."

Bjork blushed as the King gestured to a yellow embroidered cushion, which sat to the left of the throne.

He had never been offered a dance with a man's wife in all his days and didn't know quite how to accept this gracious offer. He had been quite the dancer in his youth, but as of late he was sure his dancing skills were rather rusty.

"My noble King Lore, I am truly honored to share my tales with you. I am also looking forward to your hospitality." Bjork said as he sat down.

Bjork soon had the King's full attention as he told him the tale of the quest for the cure for Naomi. Bjork's great talents at story telling amused the King. His gestures and his inflection relived each moment and brought his tale to life. The King and Bjork didn't notice that the fairy men were busy enjoying the food and gaieties. Nor did they notice that Ryob was quite immersed in ale and women. Nimrod was also enjoying himself; he admired beautiful women also and was deeply conversing with one from a far off distant land. Strange cultures were of the utmost interest to him. Mahew was busy trying to draw the likeness of one of the beauties; he himself had indulged in a little too much wine. Jacor was busy raising a flask of alc in competition with some foreign nobleman as three beautiful young girls looked on and giggled. Jeziah was arguing the point of if the world was round or flat with some rather stout peculiar swarthy male warrior.

It was strange but not one of them had thought to inquire of Syncore's whereabouts. The night was growing near its end when Bjork finished telling his story. King Lore was now looking in much need of sleep. His yawn confirmed it, as he then stretched and spoke, "I must soon retire me friend, I will see to it that thy friends and ye are given suitable quarters for the night. I am still puzzled as to why ye have traveled so far to speak with an old Vashing King. Although I did indeed enjoy thy story," He scratched his beard in deep thought.

"Oh my, I was so thoroughly enjoying myself I forgot to mention it. Forgive me my King; we have come seeking Syncore the Sailor. The Nimbus prince's Mother, (Queen Geneva), was captured a few years back by the Leprechauns. We believe they have taken her to Leprechaun Isle. We aren't a seaworthy bunch and are seeking a sailor with the means to take us there. We only but yesterday, heard he might be here. Now though I have to admit, I don't remember seeing anyone that matches his description tonight."

"Ah, me new friend Bjork, it is with deep sorrow I must tell ye, Syncore set sail aboard his vessel the Drakkar two days ago. He was after the scoundrel that stole the Vashing ship the Ægileif. The rotten thief set sail with her in the middle of the night a few days back. Syncore is on a quest to bring her back to the Vashings. I me self commissioned his services. He has taken more than a few of me best men with him. I shall sleep on this dilemma, and reach a decision for ye tomorrow. Take heart Bjork, Vashings are always open to problem solving, and anxious to meet a new challenge. But now I take rest upon it me friend."

With that King Lore arose, slowly walked down the red carpet and turned down a long well lit hall, his guards in pursuit.

This must wait until tomorrow Bjork thought. There was nothing neither he nor the fairy men could do. It was odd but he felt strangely relieved as he looked upon his friends. He knew that even the most well laid plans could go awry. I believe this wise old Vashing King will have an answer. He was getting ready to tell Nimrod, when the fairy men approached him, "Have you heard Bjork, Nimrod said. We're too late, Syncore has already sailed." Nimrod's face looked distraught. "I have spoken with King Lore," Bjork said as he grabbed his friends shoulder. "Apparently he will have a solution for me tomorrow."
"I've heard tell that he is a wise King full of surprises", Ryob said.

Two beautiful women now approached Bjork, "Come, we will show ye to your quarters."
"Thank you my ladies, Bjork said, I do feel a bit tired myself."
They followed along behind them. Bjork was in a sleepy haze, and the fairy men in a drunken stupor.
When they had shown the fairy men to their quarters, the two women rounded a corner and pushed open a door that had the largest guest room behind it that Bjork had ever seen. The bed was enormous, as were the shelves, which were laden with books. Books filled with wonderful information and stories. Torchlight danced on the walls. A fireplace stood upon the largest wall where a cheerful fire blazed. "This is far too generous," he said as he politely bowed. "I do thank you ladies and bid you a goodnight."
"Do ye require nothing more? They asked, with inquisitive looks. "No dear ladies only a goodnight's rest, I thank you once again."

When they had both turned and walked down the hall Bjork shut the heavy door. He lay down upon the huge bed and was wondering what solution will King Lore have for our dilemma? The bed was so comfortable and his eyes so heavy that soon he fell into a deep sound sleep, only the sounds of his snores filled the room, as the torches light grew dimmer, and finally the room grew black as the torch flames burned out.

CHAPTER FOUR

GENEVA WAITS

Geneva stood in a swirling sea mist near the edge of the shoreline looking intently out to sea. It had been so long now since she had been bore away by the leprechauns, and taken to this dreadful island. How she missed her homeland, her beautiful daughter Naomi, her handsome son Nimrod and yes her dearly beloved Calliope.

She sat down wearily now as her mind became a fortress of fond memories that soon overcame her. A silent tear slid gently down her cheek and sat glistening upon her breast as she thought back to the last day that she had spent with her precious family. It had been a grand day for a celebration, Naomi and she had been preparing all day for the festivities. They were celebrating the newfound peace they had made with the Gnomes. She had decided that the final touch would be a wonderful bouquet of wild flowers, which lay across the borders of Horkland. I will surprise them all she smiled and quickly fluttered her wings in hasty retreat. They won't miss me; I know Calliope has warned me of the danger of traveling alone. But I so do need a little time to myself she mused. It has been so long since I was able to travel unattended, before I wed the Fairy King. I miss those adventurous days she thought. Surely a quick trip beyond Horkland won't harm me. I believe the adventure will do me good.

 She was soon in a glorious meadow covered with the many wildflowers of the neighboring land. So vast it was and so beautiful, that she lost all track of time. She continued to harvest her bouquet, unaware of the small eyes that watched her. She looked so beautiful, her hair glistening and her wings blowing in the breeze as she bent to place another flower upon her now quite large bouquet pile. It was at that very instant that they swooped upon her. She felt one hand over her mouth as more held her wings back to prevent her flight. She tried to see who it was as they carefully wrapped a piece of cloth across her eyes. Then she heard a deep chuckle, as one spoke "Well I be , I have me a fine Lassie, she will make me a fine catch indeed! I've traveled far and wide for this, tis me lucky day, yes indeedy."
"Aye yes a handsome one she be," another proclaimed. It was then that she realized by the accent and the stature of her enemies that Leprechauns were kidnapping her! She couldn't fight back as her hands were now being bound also, as they stuffed her into a large knapsack and she felt herself being lifted and thrown onto the back of one of her captors. She trembled with fear as tears now freely flowed from her eyes. Her poor Calliope,

Nimrod and Naomi, she would miss them so, she must get word to them, and she must escape, but how?

Soon day gave way to night and she found herself being placed down upon the ground, as she could smell the scent of a campfire. Surely they don't intend to eat me? She could hear the other leprechauns as they began to settle in for the night. One of them said, "I suggest that early dawn we head out for the shore and return to our ships. We must set sail for Leprechaun Isle without delay. Our kidnapped cargo puts us on full alert. I'm sure the wee one will be missed and soon they will be sending out a search party. Well then we be voting on the agreement to leave first light". Then she heard a round of "ayes" and all went silent. She crawled up into a ball, as tears streamed from her eyes and terrible fear clutched her heart. Surely Calliope will search for me; surely he will come to her rescue she thought. Oh Calliope my dearest I am a fool I am so sorry I disobeyed you. I should have never gone searching for flowers alone.

The night soon passed and she was startled by the men rousing each other. She could barely make out a bit of light through the trees as the sun was on the horizon. The cloth that was wrapped around her eyes had slipped a bit out of place, and if she peeked underneath it she could just barely glimpse the leprechaun men. They were a rough looking bunch, shocks of red unruly hair, large nose, hands and feet. Their prominent features included dimpled chins, bright red rosy cheeks and green eyes. They all wore green overalls with brown suspenders and brown knee length boots. They all had large bushy moustaches and trimmed beards. Their hands were fat with stubby fingers and upon each head on unruly red hair sat a tall green top hat with a large golden buckle in the center. She lay still and watched them pack their knapsacks. Then one particularly burly looking one came over and reached to pick her up. She closed her eyes hoping he wouldn't notice that she could see a bit. He didn't, and quickly threw her in his knapsack, flung it over his shoulder and ran off after the others as they made their way to the shore. He soon caught up with them. "It will take us a fortnight to reach the caverns," one of them said. They hurried along the windy paths and through the bushes , up and down hills, all the while Naomi kept listening waiting to hear Calliope or Nimrod or any signs of the fairy clan. Little did she know that it would come far too late when her son Nimrod , his fairy friends and Bjork would set off to find her. She would be far away on a remote island, where time passed so slowly and each day grew into the other. Where she had to close her eyes and dream to remember the faces of those she left behind.

They were traveling through the Land of The Cyclops she heard and there lie danger around every corner. She had heard tale that leprechauns had magic dust that they carried in small cinched up sacks. This magic dust was so powerful a tiny little pinch could make an object invisible to the naked eye. The leprechauns were spry little fellows that hopped along from branch to branch, from tree limb to limb, with nary a sound. They were quickly reaching the clearing where King

Windor, his wife and son dwelled. Then all of a sudden they heard a loud thrashing off to the side of them in the tall hedges. It startled Geneva, and she stifled a scream under her breath. Just then she heard a gruff voice announce "Who goes there??"

The leprechaun whose voice she had heard give commands now spoke again. "It is Mighty McGillicudy and me leprechaun brothers. We will be on our way now thank ye, pay us no mind at tall, we be off to meet up with our kinsfolk, have been on a little holiday, now we will return to our home across the vast great ocean.

"Hmmmm, well then I figures I'll let ye pass ifin ye give me what is in that knapsack on this here fellars back," the gruff voice said.

"Oh no sir Mr....?? I believe ye didn't tell us thy name. Who might ye be? Who is it that gives ye the power to ask such a thing? Well? Sir???" Then Geneva heard the entire group of leprechauns chuckle.

The gruff voice then said. "It is I that gives me self the power to ask for such a thing. It be I Mr. McGillicudy, I ONE_EYED JACK!

"One-eyed Jack, where is it that ye hail from then? said McGillicudy."

"I hails from as far as the eye can see in any direction ye can go. I nary had a resting place; I'm always on the move ye see. For tis a pirate's life that suits me. I've sailed the seven seas in every kind of weather, from east to west, from north to south in search of buried treasure. Silver, gold, trinkets and pearls, and gems of every color. I'd gladly sell for any of these me own dear mother.

I have a dagger that fits in me sash along with a musket in me boot, I'm not afeard to slice or slash or point this gun and shoot. I have no concerns for where ye are going, or where ye ever been. So I'll ask ye one more time for the knapsack, me wee little friend."

Geneva's heart took a leap that she was sure her kidnapper felt. In a flash off his back the knapsack came and as she thought he was handing her over to the dire fate of this terrible pirate, she felt it soaring through the air. In an instant wham something caught it, and she was being bounced and jostled as her captor ran, faster, climbing, and bouncing along the way. It seemed like the longest time had passed when his pace came to a slow canter and he began to breathe very heavily. She lay in wait, not knowing who had her now. Then he stopped, and she felt herself being lowered to the ground. She could hear him now kneeling down beside her as the knapsack was flung open wide. She was huddled in a corner of it, with the cloth still upon her eyes; despite this she tried to squint beneath to better see his face. She tried to focus as her eyes slowly became accustomed to the light. Her vision was still a bit of a blur, yet slowly the face was coming into view. Yes, Yes. She could see clearly now, it was a leprechaun that peered into her knapsack. She had escaped the clutches of One-Eyed Jack after all. He leaned closer and asked. "Be ye alright wee lass? I hope I didn't jostle ye much. We shall be to the caverns by dawn if we travel tonight. Me kinsmen know the way, like the back of me hand and they will not tarry. They will meet us at the shore, where me sailing ship is moored. Twill not be long lassie and we be back on Leprechaun Isle. Me name be Dylan McSwane. The proud son of me dear Father Conor McSwane and me dear Mother Megan McSwane."

It was common knowledge that all Leprechauns were males and their wives were all fairies. Some of the wives had been captured, while others had been smitten and left home willingly. In some foreign lands they dwelled together sharing the natural resources, but on Leprechaun Isle they were only permitted to live together as husband and wife. "The Mcswane's of Irish Spring we be. The others they be me younger brothers, Patrick, Michael and Daniel. Ye see we leprechauns know the powerful magic that ye fairies possess. It is said that if a leprechaun has the rightful fairy, he has but to ask her to sing to find the pot of gold. It is only through the fairy magic that the leprechaun may find the pot of gold at the end of a rainbow. It has long been a curse on the leprechaun that not one of us will ever see it, only less a fairy's song reveal it. Our leader Mighty McGillicudy, a long time friend to the McSwanes had the misfortune of being the only living descendent of the victim of the witch Hagatha's curse. Tis the curse that for hundreds of years has kept the leprechauns from finding their rightful treasure. No lucky charm, no four leaf clover, no potion, talisman, nothing can remove the terrible curse. Twas Nathan McGillicudy whom she cursed, when he refused Witch Hagatha's affections. She cursed him and all his kind for eternity, or until a beautiful fairy, from across the seven seas, traveled to Leprechaun Isle. Only she could see it, only she could lead us to it, and once we reach the pot of gold, the curse be done. For many a year, we travel, from every corner of the sea. We travel seeking the fairy the one that will

set us free, of this terrible thing. Many a fairy
we capture, many a fairy we caught. We
brought them in from all around, not one of
them was she. Tis said she be a Queen of
sorts, if legend is the truth. Tis said she is
beautiful, and always keeps her youth.
Though she be very old, she looks as if she's
young and never have ye heard such notes as
the sweet ones she has sung. So we bring ye
to the Island and we see if ye can sing the note
that starts the magic, the most beautiful notes
ever heard.
Once the notes of her song begin, tis then the
rainbow appears, and sitting thar in golden
light is the pot, full of splendor, and full of
precious gold. The pot will be then visible to
all in her presence. Tis the legend told to all
young leprechaun lads and lassies, as wee
ones, told before an open hearth, while the fire
danced in our dear Father's eyes. We wish ye
no harm lassie. We wish this curse be done.
Our fields have lain untilled, our cloth
unspun, so much to do, so much undone. We
be consumed with only this pot of gold, cursed
to seek it forever. Even when we are at sleep
the curse it leaves us never. It's in our
dreams. We live on wildflowers that we pick,
nuts that we forage and a bit of fish that we
catch. Our homes are in ill-repair; our clothes
are shabby at best. Tis a terrible curse that
never lets go, not even for a minute, and
consumes the souls on Leprechaun Isle and
everything that's in it. So now me lassie we
go." He said.

 So Dylan McSwane then lifted up Geneva,
removed her bonds from her feet and hands
and gently placed her in the knapsack. "I trust
ye will remain, if I promise to let ye go as soon

as we see if ye are the rightful fairy. Ye can trust me word or I be not Dylan McSwane." He gently threw the knapsack over his shoulder as off they went hurriedly up and down hill, through the woods and across the pastures, on and on into the night.

The sun was coming up over the horizon when Dylan McSwane and his captive reached the mouth of the winding caverns. The sounds of birds singing filled the air and Geneva felt a strange liking for this peculiar leprechaun. For one thing he had been very gentle with her. He seemed to have a kindly face and he did untie her hands and feet and do away with the cloth covering her eyes. She felt a strange peace come over her in this new dawn. Perhaps Calliope has sent out a fairy search party by now. She didn't know exactly why she felt unthreatened but was rather content at the moment to be in the care of Dylan McSwane. He seemed like a reasonable sort, someone that her husband the King would find easy to take a liking to. Anyway he had promised on his birth name to release her as soon as they found out that she wasn't this rightful magical fairy with the magical voice. So she was quite sure, she would see her fairy family again, perhaps very soon.

As Dylan McSwane entered the cavern he began to whistle a merry little Irish tune. It echoed off the cavernous walls and seemed to travel for quite a distance before it disappeared. She could smell the damp cool air in the caverns. It had a pleasing sort of scent to it. Kind of like the smell of the air after an afternoon's rain. She also could hear something faint growing slightly louder with his steps. It was an odd roaring sound, something she couldn't remember ever hearing before. Yet she was not afraid. Somehow as ferocious as it sounded it brought no terror. This was no beastly sound but had rather a calming effect upon her. The smell grew stronger now and the air felt breezy and cool. She kept huddled in the corner of the knapsack, trying to imagine what it was she was smelling and hearing. Nothing from her memory came to mind. Then a thought occurred to her. Could this be the smell of an ocean breeze? The salty air that she had heard of that lay far from Horkland? Could it be that soon she would see this great wonderful thing, this mighty raging sea?

Dylan Mcswane's pace began to slow as he took a turn to the right and then she felt a very strong breeze that chilled her through the knapsack. His steps ended and he stopped and slowly lifted the knapsack from his shoulder. Holding it carefully he opened the cinched top, and for awhile Geneva was blinded by the bright light. Then he spoke to her, "Well Lassie here we be at the shore. Ye alright?" Geneva nodded her head and smiled. "Aye, good then, we be off to me ship, she sets a ways down this trail beneath this craggy cliff," he said. He once again cinched up the knapsack, put it over his shoulder and began the descent to the shore. There at the bottom was moored a fine Knorr sailing ship. She bore the name Muirin. Her white square rigged sail was glowing in the morning sun. Irish- built ships were "clinker built". Called knorrs, they were long and slender and had a large square sail. They were shallow and rather like a large canoe with two bows (pointy front ends). They were steered with a single oar from the side. They were swift and capable of long voyages. Before he reached the gangplank; he saw the heads of his dear brothers as they watched from the bow of the ship. "Ahoy, me dear brothers, he shouted." They carefully lowered the gangplank and waited for Dylan McSwane and his captive to board.

Geneva heard his boots as he walked across the creaking boards of the gangplank and stepped onto the deck. Then a certain lonely longing for the Fairy Meadow came to her heart as she soon realized that they were setting sail for Leprechaun Isle.

CHAPTER FIVE

THE ENDLESS SEA

Mighty McGillicudy began to assemble the crew and hand off orders. Including his brothers the crew was seven men strong. Dylan called out to his younger brother Patrick. "Patrick, me brother, lad, I am putting ye in charge of this wee fairy's care. Guard her day and night. Keep her safe always. Never let this knapsack out of thy sight." He clapped the leprechaun on his back and gently handed him the knapsack. "Hoist the anchor men," McGillicudy growled, "and hoist the sail, boys, there is a fine breeze today, men, a good day for sailing. The sea she waits for no one, can change in a snap, we need to make haste while the weather be good. For ye never can tell when the sea may turn into a raging fury and swallow us up, or spit us out, or even she may dash us on the rocks. But tis calm now and we can make good time."

He wet his finger and held it up against the breeze. Then he began to strut to and fro barking out orders as he proudly walked the deck. He took out his spyglass leaned against the side of the ship and peered into it tentatively. "Aye he said scratching the beard on his chin, it looks mighty fine, no signs of bad weather, tis good ,tis good. Oar boys! keep the bow steady, in front of the wind. Keep a steady eye on the sea lads. At the first sign of a squall get the bail buckets ready."

The leprechaun ship slowly picked up speed as it sailed before the wind. It was becoming smaller and smaller until from shore it disappeared over the horizon. The leprechauns were heading back across the seven seas to Leprechaun Isle, (a four day voyage).
Dylan McSwane was hoping this fairy had enough magic to keep their sailing smooth. He also hoped they had found the rightful one, (the one who would end the McGillicudy curse.)

Back on shore, an evil man was setting sail himself. He had carefully tracked the leprechauns back to their ship. He had untied the Ægileif, (what he assumed was an unmanned Vashing vessel) and hoisted its anchor. He had set the large sail and soon in front of the wind, he took the same course as the leprechauns had charted. This evil man was none other but One –Eyed Jack ,(the scoundrel pirate.) Staring out at the vast sea he began a pirate chantey. "For tis a pirate's life that suits me. I've sailed the seven seas in every kind of weather, from east to west, from north to south in search of buried treasure. Silver, gold, trinkets and pearls, and gems of every color. I'd gladly sell for any of these me own dear mother."

As the ship was leaving the shore he heard a clatter, and turning he found six young waifs, in filthy ragged garments, with dirty smudged faces standing near the bow. They trembled and clutched one another as One-Eyed Jack hoisted his musket and pointed it in their direction. "Well shiver me timbers," he said with a deep laugh, "It looks like I have me a crew. Man the deck men, watch the bow, keep her steady, boys, or I'll have ye keel hauled. Keep ye oars on the ready, and fetch the bail buckets. We want them handy if there be a storm. Don't worry lads, if ye do well, when we reach shore, I'll set ye free."

Then One-Eyed Jack began to stroll the length of the deck occasionally looking out to sea through his spy glass. He muttered to himself as he carefully searched for the Leprechaun ship and its precious captive fairy. The ocean waves were slowly rolling, and the sun shone brightly in the sky. The deep blue sky was filled with gently floating cottony clouds that slowly traveled in the upper winds. Magically some clouds took upon them the forms of man and beasts. It had an almost hypnotic effect upon him, and he began to feel his eyelids growing heavier.

On board the Muirin, the crew was busy gathering the bailing buckets. Patrick McSwane stood watch over the knapsack which he had carefully set down. He now stooped down to uncinch the top, just to get a

tiny peek inside. There in the corner lay
Geneva. Her tiny fairy wings fluttered a bit
with her every breath. She was such a
beautiful sight to Patrick. He hoped she was
the rightful fairy to end their search. Although
he knew he would miss sailing the seas in
search of fairies.

 The weather was pleasant enough, a nice stiff
breeze and the fine smell of salt in the air. The
sun felt warm upon him as he decided to rest
a bit himself. Me dear brother Dylan warned
me to not let her out of me sight, he thought.
So if I just sit down here next to her for a bit
I'm sure he won't mind. He soon found a
comfortable spot to rest and it wasn't long
before he himself fell fast asleep. The ship
sailed on through the day and at dusk as the
sun was setting the sky turned a brilliant
shade of red. Mighty McGillicudy strode the
deck and announced to the crew, "Well lads it
looks as if tomorrow be a good day too." Then
he pulled out his long stemmed pipe and lit it.
Pointing towards the sky with it he said "If the
weather holds we'll make good time lads,
better than expected." Little did he know that
just beyond the horizon to the south of him
there was another ship sailing, making good
time, with a strange crew headed by One-Eyed
Jack. The ocean had a very peaceful look to it
now as the light of the moon began to catch
its frothy waves. There was a calming sound of
the waves slapping up against the sides of the
ship. It grew darker and as he gazed up he
could see many brilliant stars now filled the
skies.

Dylan McSwane was busy trying to entertain
the crew with tales from voyages past. As the
evening wore on each man took a turn at
getting a bit of rest as the others remained

alert. The crew began to eat smoked fish from the barrels on board. There were also barrels filled with drinking water. All in all there were enough provisions to last four days at sea but no more as there was very little cargo capacity. Into the night they sailed, and from the deck was heard the sounds of talking and laughter. They were eager to return to Leprechaun Island. The night became a bit chilly as the wind picked up. There were blankets stowed on board and soon they were put to very good use.

The hours past quickly and then just over the horizon they could see the first signs of day breaking. The sun gave off a glorious pinkish hue as it began its ascent. It appeared to be very large and its beauty was captivating. They could see the rolling and pitching of the oceans waves. The sky was now becoming a kaleidoscope of colors. Today there was nary a cloud in the sky. The crew was refreshed from the calm night at sea. The day wore on and just before the sun was about to set, Dylan noticed dark clouds in the sky and the wind beginning to pick up. It was soon apparent that a storm was on the way. He quickly reported this to Mighty McGillicudy who then called the crew together. "Well lads we may be in for a bit of stormy weather, prepare for the worst. Grab a quick bite, for it may be a while before ye eat again." The crew took his advice and soon had eaten there fill. The sky was now turning even darker and the wind stronger when the first rain drops fell. Looking out upon the sea the swells had grown larger now and they were lashing up against the ship. The crew stood on the deck watching and waiting. The visibility grew lesser and lesser by the minute and then the terrible drenching rain began. The ship was now being rocked violently and the deck began to fill with water. Patrick grabbed hold of the knapsack now, and fearing he would lose it, he opened it, reached in, gently picked up Geneva and placed her inside his breast pocket where she would be safe and dry. Then he joined the others and began the long process of bailing.

The storm raged on for many hours as through the rain and fog a small island came into view, and Mighty McGillicudy, setting his eyes upon it, yelled "Grab the oars now boys and guide her into shore." He proceeded to turn the rudder a bit aiming toward the small island. "We will wait out the storm here," he bellowed over the noise of the wind and sheeting rain. It took a while due to the weather and the stiff wind to get the Muirin heading in the right direction, but before the night turned pitch black, they found themselves up against the island's banks. "Set anchor!" McGillicudy cried. "Bail the water the best ye can, and lower the sail." The crew scrambled about the deck, quickly obeying his orders. They soon had the mighty sail thrown over the deck and tacked to the starboard side. The crew then exhausted and wet, grabbed hold of their wool blankets pulled them up under their chins and settled in for a night's sleep. Patrick opened his breast pocket, and said "Ye be safe now me fairy, a good night to ye." Then he too clutching his blanket to himself closed his eyes to rest.

On board the Ægileif, the crew and One-Eyed Jack were in the midst of the terrible storm. They were much further away from the island, and the visibility had dropped to zero. It was pouring down rain as they struggled to bail out the ship. The size of the ocean swells had grown immense. They now came crashing down over the deck. The wind was sharply whipping at the large sail. One-Eyed Jack bellowed, "Matey's lower the sail, this wind is about to sink the ship!" He hollered at the crew as the ship began to pitch, ordering them to run to portside, then to run to starboard. The ship was being tossed and heaved upon the large waves, and their attempts to bail the deck and lower the sail were futile. There were not enough men on board. They tried as they may, but to no avail. Then they heard the terrible snap, as the huge mast, sail and all gave way and fell overboard. The ship kept getting tossed from side to side and their efforts to keep her steady were of no use. Then the largest swell just off the portside came crashing onto the deck and with a mighty splash, capsized her.

There was yelling and thrashing in the water as the entire crew of urchins and One-Eyed Jack now struggled to keep afloat. They grabbed onto the floating contents of the ship, the barrels, and such. The ship was now beginning to sink. The stern began first. Then quite quickly it was followed by the bow. Now the keel of the ship was all that could be seen, barnacles and all. Then in a matter of a few minutes she was gone. There were only a few large ripples upon the water where she once had been. Then the relentless rain slowed and the moon began to peek out from behind a dark cloud.

One-Eyed Jack looked around at all of them, as they lay sprawled upon barrels and planks. He looked across the vast sea, for any signs of land or a passing vessel. To his dismay there was nothing, not for as far as the eye could see. It was quite dark out here he thought. He was sure they would be rescued or find dry land by morning. He shivered and thought, I won't be joining me pirate kin in Davy Jones Locker anytime soon. I can't be further than a few hours away from landfall. I know these waters and there be many an island out here. It won't be the first time I be marooned at sea. That thought gave him comfort as he settled in for a cold wet night at sea. It was not his first time ship wrecked either. So feeling confident, he smiled smugly to himself. Then he thought, with no ship to sail, I have no need for these matey's. So he began to plan how to be rid of them. The barrels they floated upon he could use, so he would have to wait until they reached land. I'll use them just long enough to get all the barrels to shore and then I will have to be done with them. Hmm?? Musket or dagger? He mused.

Meanwhile the crew was fast asleep now onboard the Muirin. Geneva herself was resting quite peacefully. It was indeed strange how she felt so content with these strange leprechauns. She wondered about her kinfolk back home in the Fairy Meadow. The raging storm was over now and there was a quiet lull as the only sounds were of the waves as they came crashing down upon each other before reaching the shore. The ship gently rocked in their wake until the first signs of day break. Unknown to its crew members was the strange floating cargo that was slowly making its way to shore. In just a few short hours it would reach this tiny island.

The ruffians and One-Eyed Jack had been drifting in the sea now for quite some time. They were weary from clutching onto the barrels all night, and welcomed the sun's first rays as it peeked over the horizon. Squinting to focus their eyes they were all looking around now in search of land. Their throats felt parched and their bellies were grumbling. The smell of the salty air was now putrid in their nostrils. They longed to set their feet upon dry ground. They continued to search for other ships also, but they found to their dismay that there were none to be found. This ocean was a well traveled one that led to many different islands, and many ships sailed here during the warmer months of the year. Although today they appeared to be alone in this vast ocean.

As the morning wore on , when they had begun to lose all hope of rescue, just over One-Eyed Jack's shoulder there began to be visible the familiar sight of something looming above the ocean's waves. He wiped the sea spray from his eyes to have a better look and then slowly began to smile. "Well me boys I see thar be an island. I knew we be finding one, and it looks to me that we're floating right towards her." Sure enough there in the distance was the form of an island which was beginning to grow larger. They were being carried there by the waves now, and soon, yes, soon they would set their feet on solid ground. Then smiles broke out and laughter all around as they waited for the ocean's currents to bring them onto shore.

The crew on the Muirin had been woken by the change in temperature, it being quite warm now beneath the sail. Mighty McGillicudy gave orders at once to hoist the large sail. The sun was shining brightly as they prepared to ready the ship for travel. They had finished bailing out the rest of the water and the deck was drying quickly in the sun when McGillicudy said, "Eat a bite now me lads, for we be sailing soon. We have lost some time now, but it tis fair weather today." Then the leprechaun crew began to eat their breakfast of smoked meat and fresh barrel water. They were unaware that just around the southern tip of the small island there was a secluded cove where the ocean waves would soon carry the ruffians and One-Eyed Jack ashore.

CHAPTER SIX

ENCOUNTER WITH ONE EYED JACK

One-Eyed Jack was patiently waiting for the tide to bring him and his party of ruffians to shore. He was very thirsty now and hoped that the barrels that survived carried a bit of water or perhaps yes even ale. He felt quite sure now that he got closer to shore, that the island would provide shelter and materials to build a raft. He could see there was plenty of tropical plants and trees growing. He had no idea that just around the edge of the shore lay the Muirin and her crew. It was a pleasant enough day. The sun was shining brightly and a stiff breeze was blowing. The shore loomed large ahead now as the waves began to pitch and roll toward the beach. He was still clinging to his barrel and felt the cramping and stiffness in his fingers. It would feel very good to let loose of this barrel, he thought. Looking to the sides and behind him he could see the other members of the Ægileif as they too were floating in the surf. It appeared they had all survived their time at sea. They were quite frazzled looking, a bit of a sight for sore eyes. He remembered his thoughts of doing away with them and then quickly dismissed it. I need them to build me a raft, he thought. So, he set about to planning out his island escape. Then again he thought, no hurry, I may do nothing today at all. Then sooner than he was ready the surf rode him into shore, and he was thrown from his barrel as the next wave came crashing over him.

He stood up shook himself off and strode ashore. The barrel was already on the beach so all he had to do was roll it a bit further from the water and turn it upright. He was so thirsty, so tired, he just wanted to open it and have a drink. He looked around for something to pry it open with, and finally decided to use the butt of his dagger to pry up on the rim. With a mighty heave he popped it open and without even looking reached his hand inside. "Plunder," he said, as he drew his hand out which now held a bit of smoked fish. He quickly turned around and began to help the ruffians as each of them struggled with their barrels. All were desperately looking for water. He had almost given up, when they pried open the last one and by the smell he knew right away. "Tis ale mateys!" he exclaimed. Looking around he found a coconut and cracked it open upon a rock, then he scooped out the insides and dipped it in the barrel, to use as a cup. Soon he had his fill of the cool frothy ale. He was feeling pretty good now as he began to sing an old pirate chantey.

Then he looked around and noticed the ruffians who had also drunk from the barrel were all fast asleep. "Drunken fools," he muttered and he staggered off to explore the island. He noticed an awful lot of coconut trees up near the northern edge of the island and continued stumbling down the beach in their direction. It seemed closer than he thought and soon he realized he had been walking for quite awhile. They were very near now so he decided to continue on. By the time he reached them his ale stupor had wore off a bit and he soon scrambled up the steep embankment to reach the top. He was peering at the leaves, imagining how he could use the leaves perhaps for a sail if he wound them together, when just through an opening in the brush, he saw it. He rubbed his salty eyelids and stared," Me me now, isn't this a bit of a puzzle, how me crew and I ends up finding the very thing we went out sailing for. Aye it's right beneath me feet." There she was anchored close to shore, The Muirin. Now he said to himsclf," I won't be needing these trees, not when I have a fine sailing ship, ripe for me picking, setting right thar." But, wait, what did he see? Were they getting ready to set sail again? He saw the crew was about the deck, preparing to hoist the anchor, and Mighty McGillicudy was standing guard at the helm. Then One-Eyed Jack had a wickedly evil thought. Why I'll capture the crew and the ship and its precious fairy will be mine. So he slithered down the embankment through the brush as fast as he could, careful not to make a lot of noise. They were just pulling up the anchor when he reached the stern of the ship and ever so quickly he scrambled up its side and leaped onto the deck.

Patrick McGillicudy was the first to see him. He quickly produced an oar as a weapon and announced "Men we have a stow-away pirate, arm yer selves laddies." The rest of his brothers and crew soon took up posts beside him each clutching an oar or plank as a weapon. Mighty McGillicudy hollered as he stood near the bow. "Take him men, throw him overboard!" One-Eyed Jack had never seen anything like it before. The leprechauns jumped him and grabbed a hold of him. One held each leg and one held each arm. Then they proceeded to swing him back and forth building momentum. Then with a mighty "Heave ho laddies", they threw him over the starboard side just short of the rudder. It was followed by One-Eyed Jack's splash in the ebbing tide. Then they manned their oars to aim the bow in front of the wind, for they had hoisted the sail and now were slowly picking up their speed.

Dylan McSwane looked over his shoulder as he eased on the oar, and watched as the island grew smaller in the distance, until he could no longer see its swaying palm trees. The weather was perfect for sailing today. A nice gentle breeze was blowing and the skies were filled with fluffy white clouds. It was then that he noticed, the limp knapsack lying near Patrick. I wonder how the fairy is doing. "Patrick," he said, "Is the wee fairy alright?" Then Patrick nodded yes and pointed to his breast pocket. "Aye Dylan I put her near for safe keeping during the storm. It seems I've forgotten she was thar." Then he felt inside his pocket and gently lifted her out.

Geneva blinked tearfully trying to get use to the bright light after so many days in the knapsack and then his breast pocket. Then she gently smoothed her wings beside her. She couldn't help but smile at them. They were a silly looking bunch, these leprechauns. "Good day to ye then," they said as they gave a slight curtsy.

"Well Patrick, I believe she is well enough," he said with a wink of his eye. There is no need for pocket or knapsacks now, let's find us a proper place for our small cargo."

He then produced a small satin box from his pocket, carefully removed the lucky charm that lay inside, and placed Geneva upon the satin lining. "Sure and begorrah, it suits the wee lass." Geneva hearing this looked up and smiled. Then Dylan looked around for a safe location to put the box. He opened a chest that had only a few parchments inside with maps and such drawn upon them. They were carefully rolled and tied with string. He placed the box inside and closed the lid; almost shut all of the way, leaving a bit of a gap for light and air. "She'll be safe in there," he said to Patrick. "One more day, me lad and we'll be sighting the shores of Leprechaun Isle. Just one more day." Then he strode off down the deck.

Patrick glanced down at the chest and smiled, Dylan was a kind-hearted sort he thought. Yet it did surprise him how he gave up the box that carried his treasured lucky charm so easily. He looked around the deck now and noticed the crew busy, setting the oars and bail buckets out. They wanted them at arm's length just in case they were needed. Although today the weather looked fair enough and the sea calm, with a good steady breeze to carry them. Yes, he thought Dylan is right just one more day. As much as he loved the sea, he also looked forward to stepping off the ship onto Leprechaun Isle. All of his kin folks would be there, fair lassies, ale, song, laughter and dance. The good time they would have when they were welcomed home. The delicious home-cooked meals he missed the most. After days at sea the salted and smoked meat and fish became quite boring. He soon found himself in the middle of a daydream.

Meanwhile, One-Eyed Jack found himself washing up the beach head for the second time. This time he had nothing to show for it. "Arrr..." he said to himself as he stood up and shook off the water. He was not amused that his clear path to the gold had slipped right through his fingers. He even was angrier that he had failed at capturing the Muirin and her crew. Now it would be days before he had a raft built and the Muirin would have sailed quite a distance, with no chance of catching up to her. He was so angry that he growled as he scaled the embankment in search of the urchins. I best be making these urchins work hard for their share of the rations, he mused, scratching his scraggly beard. Then as he reached the top, he ran off in the direction he had left them, suddenly realizing how hungry he had become. Then finally in the near distance he heard them talking, they were all awake now and had opened up the food barrels. They were discussing how they hoped One-Eyed Jack had met a terrible fate and disappeared for good. It was just as they were laughing about this when he rustled the brush and with one leap, was standing right in front of them. "Ahhhhh", they cried and turned white as ghosts as they all retreated back from him.

One-Eyed Jack said "Arrr what's the matter mateys? Aren't ye glad to see me?" Then he busted out in a deep throaty laugh. "Well, well now," he said as he grabbed his dagger and pointed it to the direction of the trees. "Over there mateys tis trees fer makin a raft. They'll be no more of this," he said as he slammed shut the barrel lids. "Thar be no more food, nor drink until ye work be done."

They spent the rest of the day using sharp stones to break off small branches from the trees. They would use the leaves intertwined around the branches to make the platform for the raft. A few of them had wandered off to find larger stones for fashioning chopping tools. It was apparent to them all that this was going to take more than a few days to accomplish. One-Eyed Jack himself strode back and forth giving orders and waving his dagger. He held a coconut shell filled with ale to his lips from time to time.

As the day wore on, the ruffian crew kept a watchful eye on him, noticing that his pace was more of a stagger, they waited for him to be taken over by the drink. They wanted to quit for a spell, and perhaps get a bite of food. They knew that was impossible under the pirate's watchful eye. Eventually One-Eyed Jack stopped pacing, sat down and leaned up against a barrel. His pirate hat slipped down over his good eye and when he was no longer moving, the ruffian crew sent a lad to investigate. When the lad came up upon him, he leaned down ever so quietly and carefully to get a better look. He then could hear the deep breathing and smell the stinky ale breath. Ah yes, One-Eyed Jack was fast asleep. He raced over to the others and announced, "Meal time lads." They all hastily, yet silently laid their tools down and carefully crept over to the barrels. They then proceeded to eat and drink until the sun had sunken from view, leaving the sky a brilliant red. They could see the moon as it began to appear over the horizon, and soon the sky became very dark. There were stars all around, and the waves on the water bore white crests from the light of the moon. The waves were making a peaceful sound now as the ruffians gathered a bit of twigs to start a fire. One-Eyed Jack was fast asleep and had begun to snore. The ruffians huddled together around the fire, and soon they too became much too weary, and began to stretch out around it. Before long each and every one of them were fast asleep. The fire danced on until the last coals went out and the camp grew dark.

Onboard the Muirin, Mighty McGillicuddy was telling tall tales of his trips at sea as they sailed on through the night. Tomorrow they would reach the lagoons of Leprechaun Isle. His crew was very intent on his every word. Patrick was sitting near the wooden chest where Geneva was placed. Dylan was keeping a watchful eye on the ocean and the stars, to guide their course. He was reminiscing himself about home. He missed the lasses aye, and he missed the good green ale. There was nothing as peaceful as a nap on a lazy afternoon lying in a field of clover. He missed the cozy comforts of his tree home and his sitting room with its raging fire in the stone hearth. He missed his bookshelf that held all of his favorite tales that told of places far and wide. He missed his hay-stuffed bed and the warm hand stitched quilt that had kept him warm on many a damp cold Irish night. His own dear Mother had stitched him that quilt, and given it to him as a house warming present. Soon now he would be back in his dear ole home. He found himself a comfortable spot to sit down and leaned up against the food barrels. He dared not to sleep, for it was his turn to keep watch.

One-Eyed Jack stirred a bit as the first rays of the sun fell upon his skin. He sat up and tipped his hat back and looked about. He could see that some of the ruffians had begun to awaken. He could also see that they had done quite a bit of work on the raft. He stood up and walked over to the water barrel to get himself a drink. It was then that he noticed, the lid was still ajar. It be very odd it tis he thought. I shut the lid me self. Hmmm. Then he scratched his chin and a look of alarm came upon his face. Then with a stern shout he said, "Up ye blazed fools, I see ye been feeding yerselfs while I twas sleepin. No, food for ye now, not one bite. Ye may only have a bit of water and off ye go. I need her ready to sail tonight." Then he pulled out his dagger and pointed towards the raft. "The sooner ye finish her the sooner ye eats." He made a sly grin and reached into a barrel and pulled out some meat. "I be eating me self than I be watching ye, no ale for me today mateys." The ruffians each took a turn at the water barrel than grumbling to themselves went off to work on the raft. The mean ol pirate just sat in the shade of a palm tree leaning against its trunk and kept a watchful eye, his one good eye on them. As mid day approached and the ruffians pace had slowed, he allowed them one more bit of water. Then off to work they went again. The raft was taking form now; quite a few branches had been lashed together. They were now making a mast out of a small thin palm tree trunk. They were foraging for large palm leaves to fashion into a sail. The construction of the raft was indeed coming along quite well. They were tired, hungry, angry, thirsty, and determined to finish so they could have a bit of food.

The Muirin had been sailing along peacefully all night and it was as the sun was just rising over the ocean that Patrick McSwane cried out "Land ahoy!" Ahhh There she was their sweet homeland Leprechaun Isle. She rose prestigiously out of the ocean and sat there like a green emerald amongst the blue sea. The rolling hillsides of clover, the forests, and the white sandy shoreline began to come into view. There were small fishing boats moored, and the crews were busy hauling nets. They could hear their voices which were carried on the salty wind. There was laughter and old Irish chanteys being sung. The sun shone brightly as the powder blue sky was void of clouds. Getting even closer they could now hear the ocean waves and the sounds of many land and sea birds. "Aye laddies, tis good to be home," Mighty McGillicuddy said. "Men man the oars, keep her straight now, head straight into shore near that little cove and we can anchor her over there." He skillfully manned the rudder and guided the Muirin into her resting place tucked safely inside the cove.

"Drop the anchor now men. Hoist the gear and lower it over the deck, place it onshore and then lower the sail and tack her to starboard." Then he jumped from the ship with his knapsack onto dry land.

Patrick reached inside the wooden chest, grabbed the golden box, peeked inside, and after seeing Geneva there he carefully placed it in his knapsack and jumped out on the shore. The rest of the crew were busy following McGillicuddy's orders as the McSwane's strode off up the embankment, heading toward their familiar forest path which led toward home. Dylan had joined Patrick , Michael and Daniel. "I can't wait to see dear Mother, and taste her leprechaun stew," Michael said. "Well Michael, what if Mother hasn't any leprechaun stew? said Daniel. "I be glad just to lay me eyes on me Mother than, stew or not," Michael chuckled. "I be glad to lay me eyes on me dear Hannah," said Dylan with a laugh. (Dylan being the only son of the McSwane's which had a wife.) Walking through the lush green forest, Daniel looked up at the canopy of trees above him. It was so peaceful and the shade was very welcome. He could hear the birds as they flew from limb to limb, and the tree squirrels with their busy chatter. Something was rustling the carpet of leaves that lay upon the forest floor. Then just ahead in some thick brush he heard a commotion, and as he grew nearer to it he could see faintly through the growth the outline of a fawn. Yes a small deer was standing ever so still watching them. Such beautiful creatures he thought. They were now coming upon a well worn forest trail that led up a small moss covered hill. The rays of the sun were like light beams that were being filtered out by the overgrowth of trees. In places on the ground and the hill there were bright beams that illuminated the area. The foliage was less dense near the trail and as they climbed the path up over the hill and started coming down the other side, careful not to get cut on the sharp stones that littered the path, a clearing came into view.

There stood a group of thick oak tree trunks in a circle, each one had been hewn and carved into a perfect leprechaun cottage. These cottages were camouflaged to the naked eye. The tops of the trunks were thatched roofs from the deadfall and leaves of the forest. These were held in place by a thick clay mud mixture. They all looked identical with the exception of the tiny name plate above each door. From their hidden chimneys rose a dense smoke that created somewhat of a foggy atmosphere. They could faintly smell the evening meal cooking. There was the scent of roasted nuts and smoked fish. There also was the aroma of fresh baked wildflower pudding. This tis a little bit of heaven thought Dylan as he strode up to his door and gently rapped upon it with his knuckles. Then he slipped back and hid around the side of a mulberry bush waiting to spring upon his beautiful wife Hannah. He heard the wooden door creak a bit as it was swung open and quickly leapt out from his hiding place. There stood Hannah her red hair neatly wound in a braid that fell gently down her right shoulder onto her breast. "Ahh Dylan," she cried, as she hugged him tightly, "I've missed ye so much." She planted a large kiss upon his ruddy cheek. "Come inside me dearest, I have a pot of

leprechaun stew upon the hearth." Dylan
followed Hannah through the door, gently
closing it behind him.

Meanwhile Patrick was getting ready to knock
upon his Mother's door. He realized then that
he was still carrying the knapsack with
Geneva inside. His father Conor McSwane and
his mother Megan McSwane had thought
these travels in search of the "rightful" fairy
were pure foolishness. They had long ago
written off the "Curse" as a yarn of yore,
handed down from generation to generation
and told to wee lads and lassies around the
family hearth. Even as wee lads though
Patrick and his brothers Michael , Daniel and
Dylan knew that this curse was a very real
thing, and they each felt the burden lain upon
their shoulders to put an end to it. They had
always shared a thirst for adventure and were
ready to embark on a new voyage at a
moment's notice. During the quieter times
they enjoyed fishing and mending their nets,
foraging for nuts and wildflowers in the
woods, and hiking through the mossy trails of
Leprechaun Isle. As young lads they often
spent the night sleeping in her lush forest and
embracing the ghost tales told around the
campfire. They felt very much at home in
nature and favored sleeping beneath a star
filled sky to any of the comforts of home. So
when the time came for the young lads to
venture beyond her shores they were eager
and willing. The first time they traveled abroad
as hired hands on a fishing vessel, and from
there they gained access to many more
opportunities as they met sea going men from
other ports of call. When Mighty McGillicudy
posted his flyer for able ready hands in the

town square at the local Shamrock Pub it was Patrick McSwane who signed up first. His brothers were soon to follow. It wasn't until the next day when McGillicudy called a meeting that they learned the purpose of this venture. This voyage was to find the "rightful" fairy that would break the leprechaun's curse. McGillicudy had been persuaded shall we say by the large bulging coin purse that Altaire McFarlaine had lain on the bar at the Shamrock Pub a fortnight ago. Altaire McFairlane the eldest of the wealthiest clan on Leprechaun Isle could be very persuasive. After weeks of preparation they had set sale in the Muirin and well.. now here Patrick was standing at Dylan McSwane's door, knapsack in hand and wondering what to do with it.

So he turned and strode off into the night in pursuit of Mighty McGillicudy. Since we were hired by McGillicudy than this knapsack should be in his possession, Patrick mused. Mighty McGillicudy was a man of honor and he would see to it that McFarlaine was given the treasure he had paid so well for.

Patrick was nearing the town square, which too was camouflaged from the naked eye. He could see the tiny wafts of smoke coming up from the chimney of the Shamrock Pub which was carved from the base of a large oak tree and the firelight dancing in its windows. Leprechauns senses were very keen, more so than fairies, (Although the fairy wives were taught how to expand theirs from their leprechaun husbands.) The laughter from within spilled out into the evening air as Patrick threw open its door and strode inside.

CHAPTER 7

IN SEARCH OF SYNCORE

Bjork awoke to the sound of rapping upon his door. He had slept very deeply in this Vashing Castle and it took a few moments for him to realize where he was. He called out, "Come in," as he sat upright in his bed. The large wooden door swung open and there stood Nimrod accompanied by his fairy men. "Bjork the Vashing King has summoned us to breakfast". It was very early and Bjork could make the serious expressions on their faces out by the dim light of the torch which Nimrod held. "We must hurry Bjork, his servant informed us that his Highness does not like to be kept waiting."

Within a few moments Bjork who had hurriedly dressed was now following the group through the winding halls into the Castle dining room.

As he entered the well lit room, he could see the well-laden table through the flickering torchlight, and the beginning of daybreak through the high windows. Last night's feast had been very elaborate and Bjork was pleasantly surprised to see the breakfast fare was equally abundant. His stomach began to growl then as he and his companions were ushered into their rightful seats.

King Lore sat at the head of the large table with a serious look upon his face. He clasped his hands together and placed them out in front of him on the table top. Then looking up he spoke in a slow and sober manor. "Good morning me friends, I have slept upon this problematic situation and have come to this conclusion. This morning I have given strict orders to me Vashing fleet. Me personal vessel Naglfar will set sell midday, with the finest of me seafaring men, and her captain Sigmarr, the finest of all me captains. I have given them orders to allow ye and thy fairy men to accompany them in their pursuit of Syncore the Sailor and his vessel the Drakkar, and recovering our stolen ship the Ægileif. I have also decreed that if they are unable to locate Syncore or the Ægileif they are instructed to continue on until they reach Leprechaun Isle. They have been warned that a battle may ensue. They are prepared to fight for the return of our vessel. They will assist ye anyway they can to accomplish thy goal of finding Nimrod's mother Geneva. Once they reach Leprechaun Isle they are instructed to stay upon her shores until they have thoroughly exhausted efforts of finding Geneva, although they will send a small crew back with the Ægileif if they are successful in retrieving her. I believe gentlemen that this will accomplish both of our goals while expending less time and manpower." King Lore smiled than as he saw the look of relief upon the faces of Bjork and the fairy men.

This King is a wise one indeed Bjork thought. He has accomplished a difficult task of how to solve two puzzles with little expense to his men and his fleet.
The platters of steaming food were passed around as the pitchers of steaming hot grog were soon emptied. Bjork sighed deeply as he pushed away his plate and rose. "I propose a toast to his Highness King Lore," he said as he thrust his mug to the center of the table, "Long live King Lore"! "Aye Aye," said the fairy

men as they clashed their mugs together.
Then they all offered their thanks, politely
bowed and scurried off to grab their
belongings and make preparations for the
voyage aboard the Naglfar.

The Naglfar and Syncore's vessel were both
built in the same fashion. Syncore's was larger
due to the size of the Vashing people which
only stood five feet at the tallest. These were
fine vessels ornately decorated with carved
bows and bearing each owner's Family Crest.
They were long ships, intended for warfare
and exploration, they were designed for speed
and agility, and were equipped with oars to
complement the sail as well as making them
able to navigate independently of the wind.
The long ship had a long and narrow hull, as
well as a shallow draft, in order to facilitate
landings and troop deployments in shallow
water. They were quite an impressive sight.

The sun was shining brightly on the carved
stone path that led down from the cliff from
the Vashing Castle as Bjork, Nimrod and the
fairy men made their way to the shore.
They could hear the voices of the Vashing
crew as Captain Sigmar strolled about giving
out orders while barrels of provisions were
being loaded onto the Naglfar's deck. He was a
short stout man, with blazing blue eyes and
golden hair. His face was covered with a
blonde bristled beard and rather unruly
mustache. His eyebrows were knitted together
in a tight somber furrow, and weathered
creases were around his eyes. Together these
gave him the appearance of a well-seasoned
seafarer. The Captain's wardrobe consisted of

a dark brown woolen tunic reaching somewhere
between mid-thigh and the knee, a pair of black woolen trousers, a pair of dark brown leather
turn shoes were on his feet. He wore a leather waist belt, which held a leather pouch, and a knife.
His head was covered by a lined woolen hood and a rectangular cloak was pinned at his shoulder. (Over the weapon arm).

The Vashing crew which numbered roughly forty were armed with a spear, iron cap and shield for each member,
There was one mail shirt per man, and one bow and arrows. These were stowed away in the event of a battle. All in all the entourage was very impressive. Bjork and Nimrod as well as the other fairy men were quite taken aback by all of the attention to detail as each item was marked into the inventory logs. They tried their best to stay out of the way and let the crew work diligently on making preparation to set sail. Yet more than once they had offered an embarrassed "Excuse me, pardon me", as they backed away from the crew loading its cargo.

The sun was now high above head and by its position Bjork assumed it was midday or high noon. As the final provisions made their way on deck and were meticulously strapped down for the voyage, the Captain ordered, "Set the sail men, hoist the anchor and man the oars!" Long ships were fitted with oars along almost the entire length of the boat itself. The average speed of a Vashing long ship under favorable conditions was around fifteen knots.

The sky was a deep blue with endless billowy white clouds that moved quickly in the stiff breeze, as the Ngalfar set sail, her large sail heralding the King's royal colors of purple and gold. Bjork stood at the bow looking at the shoreline as the Vashing Castle upon the cliff grew smaller and smaller and finally disappeared. Now as far as he could see in any direction was the endless sea and her foamy frothy waves. A few lone seagulls cried out above his head as the Vashing crew began a Nordic sea chantey in rhythm with the strokes of the large wooden oars. Nimrod stood beside his friend Bjork and great hope filled his heart as he thought of rescuing his mother. He felt blessed to have King Lore's finest crew, heavily armed as his allies. He knew that no matter what may lie ahead that his mission was well protected by professional warriors. So he sat down and rested along with his friends as he readied himself for the long voyage.

The good weather held up for most of the day until the sun was setting and dark clouds began to roll in. The air had taken a chill to it now, and Bjork gathered his cloak tightly around himself. The ocean waves seemed to be cresting higher now too, along with the intensity of the wind which had went from a gentle breeze to a gusting northerly wind. He could smell the scent of rain in the salty air as he snuggled close to the provisions out of the direct wind. There were canvas sheets onboard that could be tacked over the cargo and above the men to keep them out of the elements.

The crew had ceased oaring as the sail was billowing and there was a stiff north wind. They were busy placing the canvas, providing shelter and lashing their corners down to the deck. It was apparent that seas were rising and as the large ship rode each wave the sea foam spilled over onto the deck. "We're in for a rough night crew," the Captain bellowed over the sounds of the wind and sea. Just then above his head a clap of thunder and the sky was illuminated by the bright flash of a lightning bolt that stretched from the clouds to the ocean. It was so loud it startled Bjork and his companions. Then one after another more thunder and flashes of lightning and blinding sheets of rain. They hunkered down under the canvas as the brave crew lowered the sail to prevent damage to the ship and its crew. The long ship was now at drift and the Captain stood precariously in the storm looking through an eyepiece searching for safe harbor to anchor and wait out the storm.

This continued for some time and the nervous tension of the crew fell thick upon the travelers. It was then when Bjork tried to swallow the lump that had formed in his throat. He had heard tales of seafarers lost at sea, capsized vessels and the like, all the horrors told in the pubs by experienced sailors and salty captains. Was this to be their fate? Oh alas woe to this vessel and her crew he thought, was he destined to never return to Horkland? To never see his beautiful Naomi? To never reach Leprechaun Isle? He was deep in these dark thoughts when out of the raging storm came the cry, "Land Ho mates! man the oars bring her carefully around men. There look! See the rocky cliffs of the island and at their feet a shallow cove, which sits the leeward side. Point her towards there men, let her rest in the cove. It is here we shall wait out the storm."

It seemed to Bjork a long while before the Ngalfar drifted on the tide into the shelter of the rocky island's cove. The captain had masterfully kept her on the right course with the aid of his skilled oarsmen.
It was then that the Captain ordered the men to drop anchor for the night. They were anchored a few yards from shore.
Their distance was far enough away to keep her from being grounded in shallower water and close enough for a good swimmer to easily traverse. The island was dark and the storm raged on as the men hunkered down beneath the canvas covered in thick wool blankets, waiting for the dawn. The crew was given orders to sleep except for four men who held watch at each side of the ship, alert to the dangers of piracy on the seas. They were prepared at a moment's notice to battle if anyone dared to try to overtake the Ngalfar. Their daggers were lashed to their thighs and were easily retrieved within seconds.

Bjork had witnessed contests at the Pub in Horkland where the men tried to out throw each other. They were highly trained in this art. Knowing this Bjork was totally at peace and did not fear his safety, nor his companions. So within a few moments he had found a comfortable spot against some of the provisions and wrapped securely in the woolen blanket the crew had provided he found himself drifting off. His last senses were the sounds of the waves gently rolling into shore, and the rocking motion of the Ngalfar, along with a few distant claps of thunder, and the drip drip of raindrops on the canvas above his head. Nimrod looked over at his friend, as Bjork took a deep breath and fell into a deep sleep. Soon he was snoring peacefully. Nimrod smiled and thought, it's too bad fairies can't sleep, it looks rather enjoyable.

Bjork awoke to a feeling of discomfort, it was very hot beneath this blanket. He removed it, peeked under the canvas and noticed the sun was rising out of the east. The crew members were stirring now as the Captain's bellowing voice was heard on deck. "Get busy men, remove the canvases, stow them away and settle down for a quick bite. We set sail soon." The sky was a brilliant hue of colors as the sun continued to rise. Bjork looked about and noted there were few clouds in this sky. The clouds that were there were fluffy and white. Ahh good he thought, no storm in sight. He had seen enough of rough weather at sea.

Ryob was talking to Nimrod about the provisions, of course he was a little annoyed with the fact that there was no ale drinking aboard the Ngalfar. Nimrod was explaining how dangerous it is to have drunken crew members aboard a vessel. Jacor was admiring the fine weaponry that the Vashings had stowed aboard. He would love to try his hand at using one of their bow and arrow. Not to mention perhaps learning the art of knife throwing. Jeziah was thinking of a strategic plan for locating Geneva on Leprechaun Isle and Mahew was busy sketching a seascape. It was a very peaceful morning as they all enjoyed the bread and smoked meats. Ahh but too soon it passed and the orders were given to hoist the anchor and man the oars to chart a course to Leprechaun Isle. It was a calm day with not much of a breeze. The decision was made to not hoist the sail until the wind picked up. Today they would travel on oar power alone. So the oarsmen took their place and began to row the Ngalfar back out into deeper waters. It was beautiful weather and the sounds of the oars slapping the water in unison and the waves of the ocean, set Bjork's mind off to daydreaming of home and Naomi.

The hours quickly passed. Bjork was startled by a crew member's cry, "Captain, look, look, it's a vessel just peeking over the horizon!" The Captain grabbed his eyepiece to get a better look. "Men, I believe we are not alone on our quest, it appears to be The Cursed Crusader (One-Eyed Jack's vessel. It is common knowledge that one of the pirate's own men (Evil Gunnarr), organized mutiny on board one dark night and seized her as his own. One-Eyed Jack was forced to walk the plank. As Jack fell overboard his ally the witch Hagatha who was aboard, threw an empty crate over the side for Jack to grab hold of. She then vanished into the darkness, and hasn't been seen or heard of since. I've heard tale of Jack being sighted here and there but never have I laid me own eyes upon him. Nevertheless men make haste for Leprechaun Isle it appears the Cursed Crusader is far enough away that if we gather speed we can outrun her. Be on guard men. If Evil Gunnarr or his crew has spied us, their course will change direction. A pirate's crew would love to pillage a long ship such as the Ngalfar."

Then out of nowhere a stiff steady wind came up. The Captain kept watch upon the horizon and the Cursed Crusader. "Men hoist the sail!" He bellowed above the sounds of the sea and the wind. Soon the large sail was up and conforming to the wind and the men abandoned their posts at the oars. "All men stand guard over the Ngalfar, keep eyes and ears open, for we sail until the wind gives out. No rest tonight, we must keep on our course and outrun the pirate ship. If we keep our speed we should reach Leprechaun Isle tomorrow," he shouted as he ruffled his beard with his hand.

Throughout the morning, the Ngalfar continued to travel at a comfortable speed with the aid of the wind. The seas were relatively calm, and the sun shone brightly on the crew and the passengers as well. They had approached mid-day and were now ravenous. The Captain gave orders to break for noon meal. Bjork had to admit as hungry as he was that the mere rations of bread and smoked meat were more appetizing. He felt an enormous thirst. Soon the entire crew and passengers were enjoying the provisions. He felt energized after eating and began to stroll the huge deck, taking in the scenery. He noticed the pelicans diving for their feast of raw fish, and the occasional ripples caused by a large fish or perhaps even a shark that caused dark shadows beneath the surface of the waters. He could hear the seagulls as they fought in mid air over one of the flock's catch that was clenched tightly in it's the bill. The wind upon his face and the smell of the salty air was invigorating. He felt that all was well.

Nimrod and the fairy men kept busy, each with his own thoughts as how to pursue overtaking the leprechauns and rescuing Geneva. They knew that it was never wise to rush into anything without having a plan. They also knew that it was wise to think of an alternative just in case the first plan failed. Nimrod would gather with them and they would lay out their ideas, and Jeziah would carefully calculate the risks involved. They knew time was running out and soon they would be reaching their destination. They had very little time today to dream as Bjork was doing. So as Bjork continued to stroll and day dream, the fairy men plotted Geneva's rescue. The sun was now much lower and the air had taken a bit of a chill. The wind kept steady at fifteen knots as the Ngalfar's crew kept watchful eyes upon the course of the Cursed Crusader. She now appeared to be traveling away from the Ngalfar on a different course. Nevertheless the crew would not let their guard down. Bjork turned around and noticed the faint glow of the moon in the sky as the sun was beginning to set. The skies above were still clear with no sign of inclement weather. The color had changed from a soft blue to a brilliant orange hue. "Ah red sky at night, a sign of good weather," Captain Sigmar said. "It's time for the last meal break of the day men. Eat up for the night is long," he said.

Bjork tried as he may to keep awake, but as the night wore on he found himself drifting off to the sounds of the waves. The crew meanwhile kept watch on the sail and the seas, looking for any signs of the Cursed Crusader. They were used to sleepless nights at sea. So they found themselves swapping tales of previous voyages. The fairy men and Nimrod were finding these tales extremely interesting as they were somewhat novices at sailing. The night was brightly lit up by the full moon which cast its rays upon the water. The sky was void of clouds and because of this the stars seemed endless. The men were pointing out the different constellations, such as the Big Dipper and such. It was a very peaceful time aboard the Ngalfar. Nimrod was anxiously awaiting a glimpse of Leprechaun Isle. He had heard the Captain say that they should reach it by early morn as long as the stiff wind continued to propel the Ngalfar across the seas. She was keeping a fairly stable speed around fifteen knots. As far as they could see, which of course was diminished by nightfall, there were no signs of the Cursed Crusader. She must have plotted a different course. This gave the crew and the fairy men a sense of well-being. So they had let their guard down and a few of the crew proceeded to play "King's Table" a well-known board game, aided by the light of torch lashed to the bow of the great ship. The game itself played on a wooden or textile board was as unique as it is asymmetric. The chieftain with his soldiers is outnumbered but defends himself against attackers and tries to escape. The chieftain in his castle in the center of the board may save himself from the attackers by fleeing into one of the corner castles without being taken prisoner during the flight. Although the rules of the game are rather simple, it requires tactical skill to take the enemy by surprise and win the game. The fairy men were mesmerized with the game. "I'll have to remember this game so we can introduce it to our kinsfolk," Nimrod said.

"Bjork too will surely like this, he loves a challenge."

Nimrod was aware of the fact that his dear friend Bjork loved to play games that required strategic thinking. Nimrod looked over his shoulder and noticed his friend Bjork was still snoring, sound asleep with his blanket pulled up to his chin. He had no idea how long he had been sleeping as fairy men don't sleep and there for they pay little attention to lapses of time. Although it did seem to him that quite some time had passed. He wondered how hard their task would be to locate his mother. Better than that he wondered how difficult and perilous it would be to rescue her from the leprechauns. He had never come into close proximity with a leprechaun, but he had heard many tales of their ability to cast curses upon their foes. Not knowing a leprechaun himself though, he didn't know whether this was a true fact or not. Still to be sure he knew it was best to be prepared for the worst. Having the Captains finest warriors at his disposal did help considerably. It felt as though this mission would be successful. There was one thought though which he always pushed aside, that being that perhaps his mother Geneva hadn't been captured by the leprechauns but had met with some other dire fate. This thought was dismissed as quickly as it came to his mind. It was too painful a thought for him to think that he may never see his mother again. So once again Nimrod pushed it aside and began to concentrate on the rules of the Vashing board game.

Time passed quickly and soon Nimrod noticed the moon had given way to the sun rising over the eastern horizon. The board game which had greatly intrigued him had been carefully stowed away for another time. The wind was still blowing suffiently to power the Ngalfar without the aid of the massive oars. The Captain had begun to look over the ocean now with his eyepiece as the dawn gave more light. "Good news men", he proclaimed "No signs of the Cursed Crusader. We should be catching our first glimpses of Leprechaun Island off the leeward bow."

Nimrod reached over and excitedly shook Bjork awake. "Bjork, my friend, soon we will be arriving at Leprechaun Isle." Bjork threw off his blanket and jumped to his feet. He felt refreshed from his night's sleep and was now anxiously awaiting the end of their voyage. He couldn't wait to place his feet upon solid ground. He also was apprehensive as to their meeting up with the leprechauns. He fondly patted his cloak and mused, I hope you have some magic that will be useful in this situation. Then he remembered he had brought the list of spells. It had been neatly folded and packed away in the inner pocket since he left home. He should carefully examine it before they hit shore. There wouldn't be any time for that if they were ambushed by leprechauns. So sitting down in a quiet corner of the deck out of the crew's view, he carefully pulled the list out of his inside breast pocket. There were quite a few on the list that may be of some help he noticed with relief. Some more dire than others, even some curses. Yes indeed, he knew he must not let the list nor his cloak fall into the leprechaun's hands. He reminded himself of his traveling companions and the skillful Vashing warriors that would aid in their search for Geneva. Should he disclose the facts that he possessed this list and wore a magic cloak? Or should he be wary even of the consideration that although the Vashings were sworn to the King's loyalty they were not sworn to Bjork's nor the fairy men's. He dared not risk the word leaking out and him succumbing to the thievery of a dishonest Vashing. So he was determined now not to let anyone know. He knew Nimrod and his fairy men were aware, but they were loyal to King Calliope and would not betray their friend Bjork. He was becoming rather nervous now as a sweat broke out upon his furrowed brow. He stroked his chin and wondered what the outcome would be. Then he smiled to himself as he remembered his envious desire for an adventure as he was back home reading The Tales of the Wimpet King. "Well Bjork," he said to himself "Adventure you want, adventure you shall have".

The Ngalfar sailed on and within no time the green hills of Leprechaun Isle appeared sitting high above the shimmering blue sea. The bright rays of the sun caught the trees on the hills which cast large shadows down the banks toward the beach. As they sailed closer to shore Bjork could distinguish that some of the trees on the hills appeared to be large oak trees. Bjork knew that the leprechauns lived in hollow logs and oak trees that could be found in densely wooded areas across the island. He also had heard that most leprechauns were said to enjoy the delicate and calming sound of a babbling brook. Hence he reasoned they would probably not live far from one. But because leprechauns are also shape shifters, and can change from their normal two feet in height to the miniscule size of an insect, a leprechaun can live in just about any habitat known to man or beast. Being able to change their shape and size also makes it easy for a leprechaun to keep his identity hidden. Strange how leprechauns avoided the fairy men who also were shape shifters and could change back and force quite easily. They both had a few other things in common as well. Living in forests was one and fairy dust was kin to the leprechauns magic. Such magic an Irish leprechaun would perform to escape capture would be to grant three wishes or to vanish into thin air! Leprechauns are also very keen musicians who play tin whistles and the fiddle. The leprechaun is fond of drinking potent moonshine and they often hold night concerts with drinking, dancing and musical instruments. They are shoemakers, as legend tells us they dance so much they always need new shoes.

The island was looming ever larger now as the Ngalfar was now being pulled into shore by the tides. Captain Sigmar had ordered the sail lowered as they came closer to their destination. The crew oarsmen were hard at work keeping a course toward the North side of the Island where a small cove lay. It was sheltered from wind and sea on two sides by large rocky cliffs. It would make a good place to lay anchor. Since it lay in a secluded area they were on the outlook for any signs of inhabitants. To their great relief it appeared to be quite void of leprechauns. There were no trees on this side of the island, and no grassy knolls. The cliffs were made of large jagged weather worn rocks. Near the water's edge these rocks took on a mossy appearance. There were small enclosed pools of water where sea life abounded. During low tide many a sea creature could be found nestled closely on a moss covered rock. Bjork wondered how they would possibly climb these rocky precipices to reach the top. Then he noticed a rather strange trail that was worn in the face of the cliff to the portside of the Ngalfar. It had been eroded away as if by water. Of course this had taken hundreds of years, as the water line was much lower now. Nevertheless they could manage the climb by staying on this trail and holding onto the rocks.

The sun was shining brightly when the Captain ordered the anchor dropped, and called the crew together. "Men we must send out a search party to accompany our friends Bjork and his fairy men friends. I would say this party should consist of no larger than a dozen of our finest warriors. The others will remain aboard ship, guarding her from pillage and plunder. This island is rather small in area; I would estimate ye should have completed a full search of her borders in two days. Take enough smoked meat to sustain ye and weapons that are light. There should be a fresh water source, but still fill gourds with water and cinch them tightly around thy waist. Travel light men, as ye will not tire so quickly and will be able to travel farther in one day's time. I will look for ye back on board the

Naglfar in two days. If ye don't return by the third, I will send out more men and weapons to ensure thy safe return. I know loyalty lies with the King, and Captain, fare well men." With his last word he turned and strolled down the deck, taking inventory on the provisions.

The Ngalfar had not sustained any damage during the storm and they had not lost anything overboard. So Captain Sigmar was confident that they had more than enough left to sustain the crew until their return to the Vashing Castle.

The search party had quickly gathered their weaponry and rations and had dis-embarked the ship with Bjork and the fairy men taking up the end. They had slowly begun their assent up the side of the cliff. They kept care to stay with the trail while gripping rocks on either side. It was a slow process but as the hour passed the last of the party had reached the summit. The land was still rocky but off to the left there was the beginning of green grasslands which gave way to hillsides. The trees were clustered together near the center and were of various types, hazel, willow, oak and birch. There were many stumps and quite a few regal oak trees.

Many folks were under the misconception that leprechauns were nocturnal. The fact is they like the fairy men never sleep. They are more active at night it is true, this is when most of their dancing, drinking, and fiddle playing occurs. During the day they are dressed in green and hidden from view as they forage for mushrooms, nuts and various wild flowers. These are the main sources of their diet. In the afternoon they love a good rich brew of dandelion tea. Leprechauns are tricksters, yes; they love to play practical jokes and can be very frustrating neighbors, to be sure. But at heart, leprechauns intend no harm, and in fact want nothing more than to live at peace with their neighbors, human or fairy. Leprechauns come from a rainy country known for its sparkling green forests, meadows, and hillsides. So of course leprechauns make sure their everyday clothing is green, to blend in with their surroundings and reduce the risk of being seen. But late at night, when they go to their evening festivities for the dancing and the merry-making and the eating and the drinking, they aren't as worried about being seen. Then, leprechauns will get dressed up in their brightest crimsons, golds, and violets, sport top hats, coats and tails, and get ready for many hours of fun. Therefore as Bjork, the

Vashing warriors and the fairy men began to travel across the flat rocky plain to reach the grasslands they kept a very careful eye out. It would be very difficult to find a green clothed leprechaun in the midst of all this green, Bjork thought. Yet he knew they were there, looking back at him. It was a rather eerie feeling indeed. He had never heard of a leprechaun warrior but he was aware of their pranks and their magic. Leprechauns can sense when they are being hunted, causing them to hide all the better. Nevertheless, they pushed on into the grasslands and onto the mossy hillsides. As they scaled the hillsides it was more apparent that there were a vast amount of trees on this island. Large stands of them reached towards the sky. There were deep forests of lush green. Getting nearer now they could distinguish the different sounds of animal life. There were many birds singing and squirrels chattering and the occasional rustle of the leaves upon the forest ground as they reached the forest edge. Bjork swallowed hard in anticipation as the last Vashing warrior entered its cool darkness. Then Bjork and the fairy men followed.

The air smelled of damp earth and moss in the forest. For a time it was very dark until Bjork's eyes were accustomed to the light. In some spots there were bright rays of sun that bled down between the massive trees onto the ground but for the most there were dark shadows that each tree cast that grew into each other until the path ahead held very dim light. The path was worn, he could see and it traveled in an upward slope, gradually reaching toward the sky. At the top of the path Bjork could see blue sky and what appeared to be green grass. There was a large clearing in the forest which took longer than he expected to reach. The path went up and up through the dark cool forest and the light which had been faint grew brighter and the foliage grew thinner as they reached the top. Looking around Bjork could see how high the trail had been and being afraid of heights he rather quickly turned his view away from the forest they had left behind. In front of him stood an immense clearing filled with grass and clover. On closer observation he noticed these were shamrocks. Then he noticed in the very middle of the clearing stood a rather odd grouping of oak tree stumps, (some larger than the others.) Further beyond he noticed another forest loomed. This forest was even denser, darker and much larger than the one they had just traveled through.

It was growing late in the afternoon as the head of the Vashing warrior spoke, "We shall rest a little bit here, have a bit to eat and then we will travel on into the night. This mission must not fail. We will be searching for Geneva, then for the whereabouts of Syncore and our pirated ship." Little did the Captain know that the few remains of the Ægileif were setting on the bottom of the ocean. Nor did he know that Syncore was on his way to Leprechaun Isle when his search for the Ægileif left him empty-handed.

CHAPTER 8

SYNCORE'S TRAVELS

The Drakkar, Syncore's vessel was far from any mainland and Syncore was determined to not come back without news of the Ægileif's fate. He had decided that he would travel two days to reach the Celtic Sea and meet up with his sea comrades near Skull Island. They often could be found there at the Buccaneer, (the local Pub), near port with their vessels moored at the docks.) Here Syncore could find information about the coming and goings of pirates and maybe one of these men would give him a clue as to the location of the Ægileif. Skull Island had originally belonged to the pirates but the King of England had sent his army across the seas to overtake the pirates and claim the Island for England. This island was to be used as a trading outpost. There were many vessels in port, laden with spices, cloth, tea and much more. They were laid up in port waiting to transfer their goods onto the British vessels that would then carry them back to the Motherland. Syncore had made many friends in this port,(British and foreign), he was sure if anyone had heard or seen anything about the Ægileif this would be the best place to find them.

Syncore was a large muscular man. He stood six and a half feet tall and was built more like a blacksmith with huge muscular arms. He had blonde hair tied at the back, tucked beneath his woolen cap. There was a stubbly growth of blonde hair upon his cheeks, above his lip and on his chin. He had a dark complexion from years at sea. His laughter was deep and contagious. He wore a woolen tunic belted at the waist and dark trousers tucked into knee high leather boots. These were laced up and tied. All he carried with him was a pouch which contained his pipe and tobacco, (this hung from his waist sash), a flask of some curious ale, (which he had inside his breast pocket of his tunic), and a compass and many rolled up maps, (these were kept in a locked trunk in his cabin). His crew consisted of twenty five ruddy men, some English some Swedes. They were all trained in skills of warfare. There were expert archers and knife throwers. They were trained to fight man to man without weapons also. They were highly respected by friend and foe. There for Syncore's fine vessel The Drakkar was never pillaged nor plundered. There wasn't a man, or pirate alive who dared to come against Syncore and his crew. They had all come to respect each other as well, so there was nary a fight on board, nor a harsh word spoken. There had been a time when the men had tested each other's strengths and many brawls had broken out. These never occurred while under Syncore's command. As time wore on the arguments ceased and the challengers and victors made peace. Now they spent their time in port, drinking and playing games of sport. Their competition became games of archery skills and knife throwing for speed and accuracy. They had been at sea a long time and looked forward to arriving at Skull Island. The wind had been favorable and they had not had to use the oarsmen as much as anticipated. All in all except for the lack of finding the Ægileif, it had been a good trip. As the sun began its descent in the west, Syncore strolled the deck and smoked his pipe of tobacco. The men kept watch for the Ægileif and waited for the evening food rations to be passed around. The sky was taking on a brilliant spectrum of reddish orange as the clouds gently passed over the face of the setting sun. "Eat hearty fellows; it will be a long time before dawn. Ah... red sky a good sign, we should make good time tomorrow if the wind keeps up, we might reach Skull Island by tomorrow night."

The Drakkar was quite an impressive vessel. There were ornate carvings on her broad sides and the bow and prow. She had once belonged to the Vashing King and had been bestowed upon Syncore in return for the loss of his vessel during a battle at sea. He had long been a friend of the Vashings and often fought beside them to defend King Lore's kingdom. Often it was fighting to protect the vessels that were laden with goods to trade to the King. There was high piracy on the seas and many vessels were pillaged and plundered and the crews jumped ship or swore a pledge to the victorious pirate captain. Often the Vashing Captain was slain as they were sworn to loyalty to the King and would not leave their vessel as long as she remained afloat. The only time they did abandon their vessels was when they had suffered great damages and she was no longer seaworthy. Then they commanded all the crew to take the row boats and lower them over the deck. They gave orders to abandon the vessel and the Captain remained onboard until the last man was safely lowered into a row boat. It was during one of these battles that Syncore's vessel was sunk and his crew was rescued by a Vashing long ship commanded by Captain Sigmar. He had deep admiration for this Captain, for he was a very courageous warrior, loyal to King Lore and a man of his word. He was also an excellent seaman, who had logged many hours at sea, during exploration, and battles. No other Vashing Captain came close to matching his ability, for that matter few foreign Captains did either. Syncore now wished he had Captain Sigmar aboard this vessel, perhaps he would have taken a different course in his search for the Ægileif. Perhaps he would have traveled to the east to Leprechaun Island and beyond in search for her. Syncore scratched his chin in deep thought, and then dismissed his undecidedness. "I'm sure I'm on the right course," he muttered to himself as he drew deeply on his pipe. He blew smoke rings as he looked about the Drakkar. The men had long finished eating and were now busy swapping tales. The sun had set and the clouds were bright by the reflection of the full moon. He could make out stars here and there behind the wispy clouds. The wind had picked up and he felt a bit of a chill now so he strolled down the deck to his cabin and opened the door.

This cabin had been constructed on the Drakkar for the sole purpose of providing a comfortable place for the King to sleep if he was on a dignitary mission. King Lore had traveled quite often in times of peace in his younger days. He loved to visit his allies in their Kingdoms, and rather enjoyed all of the indulgences and pampering bestowed upon him by his friend's servants. He had quite a few Kings that were allies with King Lore. They lived far and wide across the seven seas, so in order to visit them all King Lore had to set aside an itinerary. This allowed him to travel most of the year, returning to the Vashing Kingdome for the winter months.

Once inside the cabin Syncore shut the wooden door, lit the lantern on the wall and sat down upon the regal chair before his desk. He opened a drawer, which contained a hidden key, attached on the upper side way in the back by a bit of sticky tar pitch. This was the key that opened his chest. He then bent down and slid the chest out from beneath his desk and turned the lock with the key. He carefully lifted the lid and reached inside for his maps. It took him a while to reach the map of the continents. Once he had he shut the chest, locked it and slid it under the desk, he returned the key to its hidden place and carefully spread the map out upon the top of his desk. The corners kept curling up so he found two paperweights and set them on two corners, and two carved wooden long ships, (replicas of the Drakkar and the Ngalfar) and placed them on the others. He was calculating the distance from Skull Island to Leprechaun Isle. He would follow that course if no new information was revealed at The Buccaneer. He estimated the time it would take to reach Leprechaun Island from Skull Island would be four days, depending on the weather conditions. There for he decided he would not tarry long at the Buccaneer. One evening on Skull Island and then set sail early morn for Leprechaun Isle, (unless he gathered information about the whereabouts of the Ægileif which changed his course.) So as the night grew darker now he grew restless. He placed the paperweights and boats back on their shelf behind him. Then he rolled up the map, bent down, opened the drawer, retrieved the key, unlocked it, and carefully laid the map inside. He was meticulous with this; he never let the chest remain unlocked for any length of time. He knew the value of his maps and compass. Some of these maps were very rare. The compass was a gift given to him by King Lore. King Lore had acquired it in trade with a British dignitary. The Vashings did not use compasses, for they navigated by the position of the sun and stars. So he slid the locked chest under his desk, returned the key to its hiding place, pushed away from his desk and rose. Then he walked to the wooden door, opened it and stepped out on the deck. He closed the door behind him.

He looked up and took notice of the powerful sail; she was still conformed to the shape of the mighty wind. This wind had picked up considerably and the Drakkar was sailing now at top speed. The prow of the ship slapped down hard upon each cresting wave as she journeyed on throughout the night. At times the waves would reach heights that would send them crashing down upon the deck. The frothy seawater disappeared below through the drain holes, but left the deck slippery and wet. Syncore's crew held watch and didn't notice his presence at first. They were entertaining themselves with a bit of arm wrestling over an upturned barrel. The two men sat on upturned wooden crates facing each other, as their elbows touched the top of the barrel, their right hands were clasped tightly together in a struggle for power. Their faces were sober with teeth tightly clenched as they grunted and sweat as either man struggled to slam his opponents hand backside down upon the barrel. The contest would differ in endurance depending upon the two men involved. The longest crew members had grown wise to who were the strongest of the men and seldom challenged them. The new crew members were usually the ones who made this fatal mistake. Such was the case tonight, as Addison (the newest mate) took on Hans the undefeated winner. Hans had held this great notoriety for some years. Syncore's men all looked on with amusement, anticipating a quick victory for Hans. Addison was quite the build and match for Hans. In all respects they were almost identical in height and weight and both were extremely muscular specimens. The only differences were age, hair color, ethnicity and experience at sea. Hans was of Swede descent while Addison was of English ancestry. There was a proportionate amount of both in the crew members, yet they didn't disagree that Hans had the upper hand, so to speak in arm wrestling. The competition continued and the men were surprised how long the contest endured. There was considerable straining of muscles, and sweating by both opponents. Syncore found himself lost in the match. He crept closer to his men to get a better view. It was as he was getting nearer that with a large groan Hans was defeated as Addison successfully slammed Hans' back hand down upon the barrel. The crew roared with laughter by the puzzled expression on Hans' face. Addison was beaming proudly as the crew members one by one clapped him on the shoulder and declared him the victor. Hans himself shrugged grinning embarrassedly and soon joined the others in congratulating Addison. "Well mates I believe I have met me match," He said. It was then that the crew realized Syncore's presence and began to resume their watch.

Syncore took quick assessment of the wind speed, the weather, the hour, and came to the conclusion that soon, perhaps before daybreak they would reach Skull Island. He reached into his pouch for his tobacco and pipe and began to pace the deck in anticipation. The first glimpse of daylight would reveal better their position by observation. He could tell by the subtle change in the sky that dawn was approaching. Before he drew his last puff on his pipe, it had begun. The sun rising over the ocean never ceased to amaze Syncore. In all his days at sea he had seen so many different types of sunrise. He had seen red sky in the morning and he had seen the brilliant orange rays of a soon to be bright yellow sun. The cloud formations had differed as well, along with the fact that some days there were none present. All in all he didn't think he had seen a sunrise that was identical to another. This in itself proved to Syncore beyond a doubt that his Mother was right in believing in the Supreme Creator. His Mother was devout in her beliefs and had raised him to be the same. There for upon the sunrise Syncore offered up a prayer to his Creator for safe passage and for his voyage to be successful. He tapped his upside down pipe against the outer boards of the Drakkar and watched the contents as they blended in with the sea. Then he began to take in all points of view from portside, looking for the first glimpse of land.

The sun shone brightly now and way off in the distance, in front of the prow, beyond the glistening waves he caught glimpses of a mound rising out of the sea. It was rather wide and not very high. As he watched and listened, he could distinctly hear the cries of shore birds. The mound continued to grow in height and width and take a more clear definition. He could now make out what appeared to be palm trees. He blinked his eyes to clear the salt film and looked again. Yes it was Skull Island, now he could make out the images of vessels moored in port. He waited until they were within range and then ordered the men to prepare to row. It was crucial that they lowered the sail and brought her slowly into port. This was a large port with many merchant vessels leaving no room for error. Then he gave the order to change course, telling them to "Bear left men". At the right side of the ship near the back was a large paddle tied to the hull for steering. This was manned by an oarsman highly skilled in steering. The remaining oarsmen sat on storage chests and each man rowed in unison with the others. It was a splendid thing to watch, a sort of concert with the sea, as the men rowed in harmony with the waves. Syncore continued to bark out orders over the sounds of the waves. They would have to be very careful riding in on the tide. As high tide was now approaching. The men being excellent oarsmen took this into account and let the tide do most of the work. Then a turn bearing sharply to the left took them into the cove where the port lies. The tide was less evident here, and caused very little rocking of the vessels as the seawater rose. There were many vessels in port, as they discovered. Just as they were maneuvering the cove tides they noticed one empty slip. Gently the oarsman steered the Drakkar into position and the others pushed off with their oars letting her slowly ease into the tight spot. The remaining crew jumped from the vessel onto the dock and steadied her into position. Then they tied her off to the pilings with large coiled hemp rope and returned to the vessel.

It was early in the afternoon as Syncore stepped onto the dock turned and said, "Hans, you are in charge of the crew, take inventory of our provisions, I'll need an itemization when I return. We can replenish what we need from the local merchant. See to it the men eat their fair share, before taking stock of the inventory. I'll be taking my meal at the Barnacle, conversing with the patrons and hopefully I'll return with some helpful information." Then he turned and strode off down the dock, the sounds of his boots growing muffled as he got farther away.

Syncore could hear the sounds of chatter and laughter as he got closer to the Barnacle and the voices became clearer until he could identify a few. Then he strode up to the large wooden door with the huge swinging weather-beaten sign that hung above it attached by a length of chain and a hook on either side. The letters had faded a bit and were written in Runic, illegible to his eye, yet it was common knowledge to the patrons that it was referred to as The Barnacle. He rapped on the door with his knuckles and within an instant it was thrown open by the owner, one Benjamin Fry. He was a short stout man with a ruddy complexion, red nose and chubby red cheeks. He was mostly bald except for a few unruly shocks of hair that grew above his forehead and on the sides above his large ears. He wore a large smock apron cinched about his waist over his tunic which hung down to his knees and left his woolen trousers and his high pointy boots exposed. He carried a small pistol in a pouch strapped to his side. Being the proprietor of the pub, he had encountered many a fool taken to drink who had threatened the peaceful establishment. It was common knowledge that Benjamin Fry stood for no brawling, nor robbery on the Barnacle's property. He would often be heard telling the patrons to take their arguing outside. So it was that many different seafarers of violent reputation were told to leave their weapons upon the bar. This Pub was one of that distinction, where a Privateer and Merchant trader could sit side by side peacefully and enjoy a bit of ale, swapping tales. It was a very good place to glean information on the whereabouts of almost any vessel at sea, (friend or foe). Syncore noticed William the Bold, a fellow sea Captain and his first mate. He also noticed Leif Erikson the explorer of distant new lands, whom had traveled many seas. He was somewhat wizened in his old age but it hadn't affected his mind. He was still overflowing with knowledge and experience and could definitely entertain with tales from all of his wondrous adventures. He had survived warfare and tumultuous times and had reached the ripe age of fifty. Syncore, who was barely thirty, held deep respect and admiration for him. He had only once a long while ago had the opportunity to converse with him. Today he made his way to the empty chair at the table where he sat. Then peering into the explorer's eyes he said, "Excuse me sir, may I sit here awhile? I would like to ask advice on a very important matter." Leif smiled as he spoke, "Why young man, I would like that very much, Syncore is the name be it not? I never forget a name or face of a man that I've conversed with about the sea. If I remember right, I spoke with you last in this very same place, but on the docks it was and you were much greener as a seafaring man." Then he held out his hand in a friendly gesture and motioned for Syncore to take the seat. He no sooner sat down then a young lad appeared with two silver drinking bowls of ale. "Drink up and tell me what it is that is so worrisome a matter. I can see the seriousness upon your face."

Syncore proceeded to tell Leif about his predicament. They spoke for quite awhile as Syncore's story unfolded. He spoke of how he was commissioned by King Lore to search out the whereabouts of the Ægileif, overtake her crew and reclaim her as King Lore's vessel. He had been traveling at sea for quite some time with neither a sight nor sound of her fate. He had decided then that he would sail to Skull Island, the only place available for him to inquire of so many seafarers about her whereabouts. Here he could also eavesdrop on the privateers conversations, paying close attention for the mention of her name. Leif listened intently to each word as Syncore spoke with a heightened sense of coming to this man's aid.

He had traveled distance places and traveled these seas for many years, only stopping in ports along the way to replenish his provisions and make trade with the merchantpersons. He had acquired many friends from all ports of call and knew he could greatly help Syncore in finding the stolen vessel. Lief was acquainted with King Lore's allies and so it was he offered his help to Syncore. "I will be setting sail for the West Indies come dawn, I will keep an eye out along the way. If I hear tell of the Ægileif I will leave a message for you to be returned by sea merchants traveling near Leprechaun Isle. They will leave their message at any island ports along the way. I will also tell merchants traveling toward the Vashing Castle to do as well. If you have not heard or found anything by the time you reach Leprechaun Isle, then I recommend you stop at every possible port or harbor on the way back to the Vashing King. If this too is futile than my friend I would say she is lying somewhere at the bottom of the sea." Then with that he vigorously shook Syncore's hand, stood up, tossed a shiny silver coin upon the table and hailing his goodbyes walked out the door.

Syncore had been very surprised at the strength in his hand. He saw the tall figure of a seafarer man with slightly stooped shoulders dressed in woolen tunic, trousers and pointed boots. He noticed the pack that he stooped to pick up at the door and threw over his shoulder as he opened it and stepped outside. Syncore felt a deep sense of accomplishment;

this great Viking explorer was now part of his trusted comrades. He knew Leif as a man of his word, who had this distinct reputation, so he felt secure in the fact that if Leif found no word, it would be as he had spoken that the Ægileif was lost at sea and had taken up residence somewhere on her vast bottom. He tarried only a brief while longer, listening to the privateer talk of their great success in acquiring much ill-gotten goods. There was no mention of the Ægileif, so when the last privateer had left the Barnacle, Syncore tossed a coin upon the table, pushed his empty drinking bowl to the middle and stood up. He called out farewell to Benjamin Fry and William the Bold, as he knew none of the other stragglers. Then he walked to the door, threw it open and stepped out into the night.

The sun had long set and as he looked toward the Drakkar he noticed the beams of the full moon dancing upon the ocean waves behind her. He looked up and as he looked around he could see the brilliance of the universe. All the stars and constellations were shining bright. The sky was void of clouds and Syncore thought finding the Ægileif, in these vast Oceans, which all ran into each other was much like looking for one tiny star in the midst of all of these. He felt small and insignificant in comparison as he stepped out upon the Drakkar's deck. His crew was awaiting him eagerly. He strode out near the bow and proclaimed, "We sail at morn men, get some rest, will be setting a course for Leprechaun Isle. Addison it's your turn for night watch," he said with a smirk, then he turned and walked toward his cabin. The crew began to get their blankets out and were soon huddled near cargo in different areas on the deck.

CHAPTER NINE

LEPRECHAUN ISLE

Once Patrick's eyes had been accustomed to the dim fire light, he noticed the Shamrock Pub was filled to capacity with the locals. His eyes continued to scan over the crowd of men, scouring every inch of the area. He was about to retreat when he heard a very familiar voice coming from a table far in the dark corner. There was no doubt in his mind that the voice belonged to none other but Mighty McGillicuddy. Patrick continued to work his way to the back, careful to avoid bumping into the other patrons and the barkeep. He managed to narrowly escape being flooded with wooden cups of ale being carefully carried on a wooden tray by the barkeep's partner Cadan. He could now clearly see McGillicuddy, he was sitting at a table alone with a mug of ale. He looked up when he heard the commotion and grinned, "Patrick me lad, ale is for drinking not bathing. Have a seat and join me for a bit of Leprechaun Isle's finest brew," he said. Patrick sat down and carefully placed his bundle upon the table top. Then he leaned forward in a hushed voice and spoke, "I am here to give ye possession of the wee captured fairy. I'm afraid that in our haste to see our families, it seems me brothers and I had forgotten this detail. The responsibility of bringing her to Altaire McFairlane, should fall on ye, as ye were the one directly hired for this purpose." McGillicuddy listened intently and then said, "I was going to collect her later tonight, but I am glad ye have saved me the trouble. I will see to it she is put in Altaire McFairlane's hands by no later than tomorrow morning. I may be enjoying me ale for a few more hours and I won't be waking the likes of Altaire McFairlane. She'll be in me care and I'll keep her safe until morn. Thank ye Patrick me lad." Then with that said Patrick finished his ale and stood up. "Well a goodnight to ye then, I'll be off to me home," he said. Then Patrick carefully made his way through the crowded pub to the door, threw it open and stepped outside. It would be quite awhile yet until St Paddy's Day, and the first full moon after that, the great gathering would take place. The leprechauns would all meet by the light of the moon in the secret garden to see if this was the fairy with the musical voice that sang the enchanted notes that would end their long dreaded curse. Until then he knew Altaire

McFairlane a highly respected and feared resident would keep Geneva safe in his tree estate, under watchful eye. She was now Leprechaun Isle's most prized possession. So Patrick walked home humming a tune, feeling content and very happy to be home.

After Patrick had left, Mighty McGillicuddy could not resist peeking into the bundle. So he placed it carefully upon his lap, out of other's view, and very gently opened it. The light was quite dim in the pub so he had to squint a bit to focus on its contents. Then he saw her, staring up at him from a crouched position, trembling with fear. Her fairy wings which were tucked behind her back were also shaking. Poor creature, he thought as he closed the bag. Then he continued to drink until the wee hours of the morning. The Shamrock Pub had thinned out considerably by the time he decided to leave. Then McGillicuddy stood up put a gold coin on the table, grabbed the bundle and headed toward the door. He waved goodbye to the barkeep and stepped out into the night. It was quite late so he hurried down the beaten path into the forest to his humble abode. Once inside he didn't bother lighting a candle. He carefully latched his door and made his way to his bed. He opened the bundle and spoke softly, "Ye have nothing to fear, ye are in safe hands." Then he cinched it up and gently slid it beneath his bed. Then he removed his outer garments, crawled into bed and fell deep asleep.

It was late morning when McGillicuddy was awakened by the sounds of knuckles rapping on his door. Oh me who would that be, he thought as he hurriedly got dressed, ran his fingers through his hair, and then went to the wash basin to splash cold water upon his face. By the time he reached the door, the visitor was turning to leave. He recognized his profile instantly. "Wait Altaire," McGillicuddy cried. Sure enough it was he. Altaire spun around quickly and asked in a most serious tone, "Where be the fairy I sent ye to retrieve? I paid ye well and I don't expect to find ye empty-handed. Word came to me late last night that ye had been seen conversing with Patrick McSwane at the Shamrock Pub."

He was quite the site when his dander was up. His ruddy colored wrinkled face was clean shaven with the exception of two long red sideburns and a neatly trimmed red goatee. His unruly bushy eyebrows were arched while his mouth had a deep scowl. He was dressed in the finest suit of clover green with a matching top hat and short brown boots. Shocks of his red hair bulged out from beneath his hat. He carried an ornately carved cane with a golden curved handle hooked over his arm. His feet were impatiently tapping on the wooden porch in anticipation of McGillicuddy's answer. "Well... don't be wasting me time lad," he said gruffly.

McGillicuddy couldn't help from smiling at this silly old man. "Altaire hold onto thy senses, I was on my way to deliver thy prize. Ye caught me for I left, that's all. Come inside and I'll fetch her." Then Altaire and McGillicuddy went inside and closed the door behind them. "I'll be right back, Altaire have a sit by the hearth." McGillicuddy said. "Oh well alright then," Altaire muttered.

McGillicuddy went to his bed and crawled down to reach underneath and soon retrieved the bundle. He opened it to check on the contents. Geneva was there staring up at him from a seated position, so small and fragile, he thought. "Well me lady, ye be off now to ye new home. Come the first full moon after St Paddy's Day we'll be meeting again, to see if ye are the fairy to break the leprechaun curse. Ye shall be in Altaire's possession now. Don't worry he's very careful with his prize possessions, ye shall come to no harm." Then he winked at her, cinched up the bag and walked back into the sitting room.

Altaire turned and saw the bag in McGillicuddy's hand and rose from the stool. Then he hurriedly walked to Mcgillicuddy and said, "Hand it to me lad, me time is precious." He grabbed it out of McGillicuddy's hand and carefully opened the top. "Let me have a look see to make sure it's not empty. Not that I don't trust ye, but I has to be sure." Then he looked inside and upon seeing Geneva, he looked as though his heart had melted. His scowl vanished and was replaced with a gentle look of compassion."What be its name?" "Geneva", McGillicuddy said. "Well well Geneva I be taking ye home, I'll see to it ye have anything ye require, ye are with friend here not foe," Altaire said. Then he cinched up the bag turned toward the door and with a hasty, "Good day to ye then", he was gone.

I must look a mess McGillicuddy thought as he turned towards the sitting room. Well I'm glad that Altaire came after all, now I can clean me self up a bit and start a warm fire. Then I must gather me some berries for a quick meal. He felt very hungry all of the sudden. Patrick had risen early and feeling quite refreshed he soon was dressed and went into the sitting room to light a fire in his hearth. There was still am ample supply of wood left stacked near the grate. So in no time he had a nice fire going. Then he went into his kitchen and opened the door to the pantry. There on the shelf were dandelion tea leaves in an apothecary jar. He also noticed a bit of lavender tea leaves in a wooden box. He decided on these. He was quite hungry this morning so he hung his kettle high upon the rod above the hearth, grabbed a wooden basket and decided to forage for wild mushrooms and berries. There were a few wild geese down near the area where he was most apt to find the most succulent mushrooms.

The path wore down the hillside to a small running creek. He watched his footing as the path was strewn with small rocks and mossy areas. In no time he had reached the bottom, and began to search the ground for large mushrooms. He filled his basket a quarter of the way and then started looking for wild strawberries. He found a few of these as well. Then he turned his attention to the ground beneath the oak trees, searching for acorns. He found surprisingly few, but as he got closer to the creek on the ground he noticed a nest of goose eggs. These were indeed a rare find. He had to be careful as mother geese are very protective of their eggs. So he carefully bent down and grabbed the eggs. There were four of them. He took a bit of grass and lay it inside the wooden box, to make a bed for them, to prevent them from breaking on the way home.

Just as he was standing up he heard an awful cackle. He spun around abruptly to find the mother geese running on the water crossing the creek and madly flapping her wings. He was in for it now he thought as he scampered up the path. She was hot on his trail, and not a bit happy with the discovery of her empty nest. Patrick kept a steady gait, near running, but still cautious of the stones in the path. He was quite out of breath as he came to his door, threw it open and ran inside. He peered out the front window and could see the goose had given up her chase. There was no sign of her now. He had deep respect for a mad goose and had been pecked by one a few times in his life. Given the ability to fly some have been known to catch their victim, and peck them in mid-air.

He laughed to himself and went to check on the kettle. It had come to a boil, and was sputtering over onto the hot fire. So grabbing it by the handle he set it down on the brick flooring before the hearth. Then he went into the kitchen. Soon he was back with a roasting pan for the acorns and a frying pan for the eggs. He reached over and placed the grate over the fire and set the pans upon it. Then he shelled the acorns and tossed them along with a bit of tallow into the pan. He took another bit of tallow and placed it in the frying pan. He watched it melt and then grabbed two of the eggs cracked them and stirred them in the frying pan. He placed a few lavender tea leaves in a wooden mug and slowly poured the hot water from the kettle over them. He was even hungrier than before after working so hard for his breakfast. He usually kept his pantry well-stocked, but let it dwindle down to much of nothing before leaving for a sea voyage. He went into the kitchen and retrieved a few jars to place his berries and mushrooms and left over acorns in. The eggs he kept in his wooden box. He placed these on the pantry shelves and returned to the hearth, plate and fork in hand. Soon he had eaten and drank his fill.

He was beginning to clean up after himself when there was a knuckle rapping at his door. He walked to the door and swung it open. There Dylan stood clean shaven, bathed and wearing fine woolen clothes. "Patrick, I've come for the fairy, I was so glad to be home with me wife, I had forgotten about it until much too late. Ye look well-rested me brother." "Dylan there is no need I met up with McGillicuddy last night at the Shamrock Pub, he be taking her to Altaire McFairlane this morning." Dylan looked relieved as he smiled and said, "How about some friendly fishin with ye brother? I'll run home and fetch me rods and meet ye near Potter's Pond. I'll bring a bit of green ale with me. We deserve a day of rest. Besides I'll be telling the wife I am catchin our supper." Then he winked his eye and hurried off down the trail to his home.

Soon the two brothers were sitting upon stone slabs overlooking Potter's Pond. He held the end of a fishing pole with the other end cast in the water. There was a fine basket of food and ale which Dylan's wife had provided, along with a kiss for luck. Patrick could smell the scent of Irish stew which made him hungry even though he had eaten such a hardy breakfast. The sun was brightly shining upon the water, which rippled now and then when a fish swam close to the bait. They had dug up a few worms and placed them on their hooks.

The afternoon wore on, and Dylan growing hungrier by the minute opened the lunch basket. Soon he and Patrick were feasting on a delicious meal of Irish stew. When they had finished they sat back and poured a bit of green ale.

"It won't be long now til St. Paddy's Day." Dylan said. "Hannah is quite excited about it and busy stitching up a new green dress. She loves to dance, and this is one of the rare occasions when I can show off me talents with an Irish Jig." Dylan laughed. "I wonder how long after will be the first full moon, I'm looking forward to hearing Geneva sing," Patrick said. "Altaire McFairlane has a wizard in his employ, he can tell the next full moon by his maps and charts of the stars. I believe his name is Pennar. I suspect there will be an announcement made, perhaps on St Paddy's Day," Dylan said.

"He has a wizard in his employ? Well that explains a few things," Patrick said. "I knew he had a few foreigners employed,(him being a very wealthy leprechaun.) I dare say I didn't quite know how he always knew when the full moon would occur, although it has been a spell since the last captured fairy sang. She married into the O'Brien clan of Emerald Bay I believe."

The brothers enjoyed their green ale and conversation long into the day. There were few bites on their lines, but by sunset they had managed to catch enough for a smoked fish dinner. They gathered up their fishing gear, and Dylan grabbed the basket of leftovers and Patrick the pail of fresh caught trout.

"Well Patrick, we have quite a good catch for Hannah, to clean and fry. There is plenty to share, stop by after ye clean up, it should be a mighty tasty supper.
Michael and Daniel are dropping in tonight, so bring ye fiddle. It's been awhile since the McSwane brothers have played together."
"Indeed it has Dylan," Patrick said. Then Patrick walked off down the path to his home whistling a leprechaun tune.

When Altaire McFairlane returned home, he was met at the door by Pennar. "I have great news Pennar", he said, "I have a new fairy candidate for the first full moon after St. Paddy's. She's quite a fine specimen. Take her to thy chambers and mind ye don't touch a hair on her head. Place her in the gilded cage and keep her comfortable. Don't let her out of thy sight. I have paid quite a handsome price for the likes of her." Then he handed the old wizened Pennar the cinched bundle. Pennar bowed in respect and turned toward the great hall which led to his basement chambers.

When Pennar reached the door leading to the basement, he opened it and began his descent down the wooden stair way. His chambers were well lit in the daylight by the sun's streaming rays that came in through the large windows. It was a simple abode. There was a hearth, with a large cauldron and stacks of firewood. There was a wooden bench that sat in front of it. There were shelves on the walls on the sides of the hearth which contained small bottles of different potions and herbs. Off to the right was a large wooden bed, and off to the left a wooden chest of drawers. On the top of this chest was the gilded cage. The gilded cage had simple comforts along with a miniature bed (although fairies never sleep, they do rest.) He carefully opened the cinched bundle and gently held out his large hand to open the door of the cage. He then gestured with the other hand for Geneva to enter. "Come along dear this cage is much nicer than that dark dingy bundle." Then he sat down on the bench and placed a log onto the fire.

After Pennar had left the room Altaire strode off into the dining area where his large wooden table and chairs stood. He was rarely visited by guests. So today as well as most others the table was set for just one. He could smell the delicious scent of corned beef as he got nearer the table. There was a glass of mulberry wine already poured. Soon his cook appeared a short stout little dwarf. His name was Lipkin. He had been a stow-away aboard a ship heading to Leprechaun Isle, he was a misfit in his own land, and had been in his fair share of troubles. His culinary skills were superb, and he had gotten into many a spat over a stolen recipe. He was content to be in Altaire's employ, as he had the finest kitchen in all of Leprechaun Isle. The kitchen was furnished with everything and more than he would ever need. He had free rein on what to prepare and cost was not an object with Altaire. So every morning Lipkin would leave for the marketplace and return with exotic plants, herbs, the catch of the day and more. Altaire did not have a finicky appetite so he lavished compliments upon the cook. This pleased Lipkin very much. He liked his quarters, which were off to the kitchen. The room was large and the view of Leprechaun Isle was spectacular. He had a cheery little hearth and a very comfortable bed. He also had a large bookcase that was stocked with great novels from Altaire's massive library. He felt quite content here, and being the only dwarf on Leprechaun Isle gave him a bit of notoriety. Altaire had been in such a great mood today after obtaining the fairy, that Lipkin was inspired to prepare a lavish supper. He had made corned beef and fresh roasted turnips, with huckleberry tarts and dandelion tea for dessert. Altaire was very pleased with the choices Lipkin had made. He loved corned beef and the dessert was ambrosia. He was very full and content when he pushed his chair back and wiped his face with his napkin. Then placing the napkin on his empty plate, he said, "Well done Lipkin me lad, I never tasted such a delicious meal. I'll be taking me tea in the library. I have a bit of reading to do." The he rose and walked off across the dining room out into the large foyer and up the stairs to his library.

Geneva had been a bit timid about leaving the bundle, but after seeing the cheery little cage, and the bright sunlight filtering through the large windows, she gladly followed his orders. She didn't feel really afraid, knowing she was a valuable possession of the owner of the mansion. She did feel a bit apprehensive toward Pennar. After all he was a sorry sight to look at. A thin frail old wizard with wild grey hair that flowed from his head to his shoulders. He had a large grey pointy beard and a grey pencil moustache that drooped at each corner of his mouth. He was a very drab character except for his steel blue eyes. His face was wrinkled and there were deep creases at the corners of his eyes, and furrows in his brow. His cheeks were a ruddy color as well as his nose. Probably from drinking too much leprechaun brew, she mused.

She knew the leprechauns had been well-known for their fermented berry and wildflower wine. None the less he didn't frighten her, he fascinated her. She had never been so close to a wizard as this. She planned to watch him very carefully. Perhaps she could learn a few things from this wise old man. The she settled down upon the comfortable little bed, and began to dream about the future. What if she was the fairy who could sing the magical note? Or what if she was not? How long would it be until they let her go, if she wasn't the fairy with the magical voice? She wondered what her family at home was doing. How were her dear Calliope, Nimrod and Naomi? Had they been searching for her? All these thoughts were rushing into her mind as she gazed out from the cage to the large windows, the green mossy hills and beyond in the distance the deep blue sea. My heart lies across that deep blue sea she thought and a large tear slid down her cheek and landed upon her bosom.

CHAPER 10

ST. PADDY'S DAY PREPARATIONS

Leprechaun Isle was a hub of activity as St. Paddy's Day approached. There were so many careful plans that had been made. Thus soon the decorating of the Great Hall began. The town square was filled of activity into the late hours of the night. They were hurrying and scurrying about measuring banner materials, and taking inventory of leprechaun ale in stock. There was a great bit of detail and planning that went into the food faire also. The menu was carefully and meticulously planned down to the last detail. The linens were checked for need of mending or cleaning. They paid especial detail to the tablecloths and napkins and the wonderful centerpieces that would be placed on the grand table in the Great Hall. Leprechauns were busy in the Great Hall until the wee hours of the night led into the first rays of dawn. They were stringing green banners and suspending beautiful shamrocks from the ceiling. The great table as well as the long benches were being treated with tree oil until a gleaming finish appeared. The Leprechaun Isle brewers were busy as well each trying to out-brew the other with their distinct ales. Each one was a different blend of wildflowers and berries, fermented to perfection. This process had begun quite awhile back, and they took careful measure of the fermentation processes. There would be an ale tasting and the winner of the event would be given the Golden Medal of Achievement as a reward. So much was going on that Patrick and his brothers could not help but be pulled into the frenzy. Trying to avoid the confusion was impossible and invariably they were pulled into taking measurements, steadying ladders, and offering their opinions on the menu choices and decorations. All the population of Leprechaun Isle was focused solely on planning the best St Paddy's Day celebration that Leprechaun Isle ever had. The leprechaun orchestra was practicing their tunes under the direction of the Royal conductor. Their gay fiddles played long into the night. Each year they had higher goals, and their achievements were immeasurable. They had a special committee that spent the entire year planning for next St. Paddy's Day. They would review the past year and make note of the mistakes that were made, and offer suggestions for improvements. The committee was made up of the eldest leprechauns who held a high place in Leprechaun Isle society. Most of them were local merchants and business owners. They were allowed to choose one prominent female fairy as a consultant for the decorations and food faire. The committee remained the same for five years. After five years had past they were given the opportunity to resign, and if need be elect new members. This being this particular committees fifth year, they were dedicated to making St Paddy's Day better than ever. They burned the midnight oil many a night, pondering on how to achieve this. Now their great laid plans were being put to the test. An immense amount of pressure was put upon them, as they were very meticulous in seeing that all went exactly as they had planned. They had but two short weeks to pull it all together, and as the time grew closer they were less tolerant to mistakes.

Patrick was always glad to do his part in helping, and even more so he looked forward to going home and retiring for the evening with a spot of dandelion tea and a good book before the hearth. Tonight he was particularly looking forward to this as he found himself in the middle of a squabble between the committee and the cooks. The cooks wanted Patrick's opinion as to the preparation of a certain entrée for the St Paddy's Dinner and asked him to sample a bit of the main dish.

Patrick obliged while the head cook Timothy and the members of the committee looked on. "Very delicious," Patrick said not wanting to offend the prideful cook. Then the head of the committee William McGill a very old and wise leprechaun, the owner of the Commercial Trading Company was offered his try at tasting the sample. Within moments he spat it out and with a stern voice cried,"Ye gads what are ye feeding me, this food isn't fit for me goats.!" At once Timothy's face grew red with rage as he shouted back waving his large wooden ladle as a weapon, "How would ye know what is good? Ye taste buds are too old to taste anything. Ye wouldn't know good from bad any day." This gave Patrick the escape he needed as he bowed out and said, "I best be leaving ye two to discuss the finer matters. I'm a poor Leprechaun of simple pallet. I am not a man of impeccable taste to measure this gourmet feast. So I bid ye a good eve." Then without further ado Patrick turned on his heels and strode out the door into the black night and down the moonlit path to his home.

Meanwhile Mighty McGillicuddy was busy doing his part for the St Paddy's Day events. He was known as a leprechaun with impeccable taste for his ales. He participated in each year's ale tasting as one of the head judges. Every night for months leading up to the celebration he would be seen at the Shamrock Pub with the local brewers. Each night the brewers brought him samples to taste. He took this very seriously and would smell the bouquet before drinking from the cup. Then he would pause for a while and finally he would offer his critique. He would say, rather bitter, too sweet, too flat, and the brewers would take note and retreat to their cellars to work on improving the taste. Tonight he had his fair share of sampling and finally he refused the last cup, stood up with a slight stumble, and said "I have tasted so much, I can't taste anymore, me tongue is numb and so is me mind. I believe I shall go home now and try to clear me foggy head. I suggest we keep the sampling to no more than five brews per night." Then he hiccupped, turned on his heels and left the Pub. As they looked out the window the brewers could see him stumbling down his path, teetering from side to side. "Oh me, said Bradan, the owner of the Pub, I've never known McGillicuddy to show his drink , he does make a sorry sight," and then they all laughed and bid good evening.

Dylan McSwane's wife Hannah was busy planning her husband's attire for the St Paddy event. She had busied herself for months with her elaborate embroidered green gown, trimmed with fine lace, cinched at the waist with a satin sash of emerald green. She had finished the last touches the evening before and now realized she must turn her attention to seeing that Dylan was dressed as handsomely. She had a few short days now to get this accomplished, so she was busy choosing from his wardrobe. She found a pair of green dress trousers which he had outgrown, and decided she would let out the waist a bit and add a colorful pair of sparkling emerald green suspenders. She had made the suspenders for him a few years back and they would be the perfect accompaniment to these trousers. She found a lime green dress shirt with laced bodice, and a dark green vest and matching top hat. She decided to do some fancy embroidery stitches upon his vest and hat. Now for the feet she thought as she dove deeper into his wardrobe closet, and there way in the back she found a pair of fine leather boots. Now if she could just get her dear Dylan to model them for her, she could get a better idea of the full effect. He so hated to do this, and often found a way to escape from this task. Tonight, though she found him easily, resting near the warm hearth with a thick book open in his lap. As she carefully snuck closer to take a look over his shoulder, she noticed it was a book of songs. He was deeply engrossed in selecting his music for the St Paddy event.

Every year the men folks gathered together from each family and played three of their favorite melodies to the St Paddy committee. This was done a week before St Paddy's Day. At the end of the evening the winning family was selected from all contenders. This family was given the high honors of playing for the St Paddy's Day events.

He must have had this in mind when he invited his brothers here for dinner and music a while back, Hannah thought with a smile. She remembered the evening well, Patrick and Dylan had been fishing all day and the dinner's main course was pan seared trout. She had paid special detail to the food preparations and tried to serve favorites of the McSwane brothers. She even remembered the fermented dandelion ale. The brothers had played well together that night, and their fiddles had brought much cheer to the hearth. Hannah found herself lost in the Irish jigs and laughing with the boys as they took turns dancing with her. It had been a wonderful evening. So she stepped back from behind Dylan and began to walk away, when she accidently stubbed her foot and cried out. Dylan sprang to his feet and spun around, "Hannah, ye gave me a fright, are ye alright." "Yes Dylan, Hannah laughed, "I'm just a wee bit clumsy. I see ye are deciding what song ye will play for the St Paddy committee. I'm sure ye will choose well. I won't be bothering ye then, maybe a bit later we can talk."

"Me dear Hannah, I have days before the contest, what is it ye wanted? Dylan said with gentleness about his eyes. "Ummm," Hannah cleared her throat, "Well dear I know ye hates this, but I need to see ye in thy St Paddy's attire. I need to make some alterations and I always get inspired when I have ye to model, but.....of course dear if ye don't want to do this now, I will understand," she said as she looked toward her feet.

Dylan gave her a gruff scowl and then spoke, " Hannah I do hate this modeling, but I dare say ye always make me proud of the fine work ye do with a needle and thread." Then he set the book down and stood up. "Well off we go then, I know I won't get any rest until I do this, besides I'm in a good mood tonight," and he stooped and kissed her on her brow.

Meanwhile Geneva was busy trying to figure out why there was such a heightened sense of urgency in Altaire's estate. She kept noticing servants hurrying and scurrying about and secret meetings between Altaire and Pennar. It seems as if all had forgotten about her very existence. No one paid her any mind at all. She had grown quite bored with the gilded cage, and looking out the large windows only made her realize how imprisoned she was. She ached to use her wings and found that most times they hung limply at her sides. There was no need for opening them as she had no room to fly. She felt sad and very alone, and was beginning to think she would never see her homeland again. She even missed the leprechauns, (Dylan and Patrick). She was so isolated and had no contact with anyone except for Pennar, who now was too occupied to pay her any mind. She had no way of knowing neither the time nor the date, and there for did not know how close it was getting to St Paddy's Day.

It was on one particularly lonely boring late afternoon that Pennar entered the room and rushed to a large bookshelf on the wall opposite the windows. There were many books on this shelf and their titles were illegible to Geneva. He perused the covers and taking a long boney finger he traced the titles on the spines, until his finger came to rest upon a large volume in the middle. Then he carefully pulled it out from between the others and placed it on his large wooden bench. He opened the hard cover and tracing the index with his large index finger he stopped half way down the page. Then he meticulously leafed through the pages until he found the one he was looking for. He sat down on a wooden stool, his large frame bent over the bench, reading and mumbling something to himself. Geneva could not make out what he was saying at all, try as she may. Then he turned and looked out the large window gazing upward toward the sky. The sun at this time was making its slow descent in the West as the sky took on a reddish appearance over the water. Geneva knew in a short while it would be nightfall. She had no idea why this meant so much to Pennar. This was a common occurrence which happened every day. How could this sunset mean more than the others? It was a short while later that she would find out the answer to this puzzling question.

 As it always did, night fell and it was then that Pennar rose and went to a far corner and returned with a quadrant which he set before the window. A quadrant was an instrument for measuring the altitude of celestial bodies. It seemed like hours until he was satisfied with their position. Then after looking at the quadrant which was aimed at the heavens, he walked briskly to his table, dipped his pen in the ink well and began to write on parchment paper. His face was so serious that Geneva couldn't help but wonder what it was all about. Pennar continued to move from the window to the table each time moving the quandrant's position a bit and writing down more on the parchment. Finally after what seemed like many hours he arose and went out the door walking toward the foyer. Geneva could barely make out Altaire's and Pennar's conversation as their voices echoed off the walls. "Altaire, I have calculated the next full moon will fall on March twenty first, exactly four days after the St Paddy's Day celebration. Ye may begin preparations for this evening. Notices may be posted in the Great Hall."
"Ahh very well Pennar, I am well pleased, I will see to it ye are rewarded for ye time and labor. Preparations will begin tomorrow." Then Pennar bowed out graciously and retreated to his chambers for the night. Geneva's heart

raced when she heard the good news. Soon she would be given her opportunity to sing, and the decision would be made when she would be set free. Free!! She thought. Now only if she knew how long it was until this March twenty first. Oh well, she thought maybe I will find out more when these preparations begin. Then she settled down upon her bed, shut her eyes and let herself dream of her family and homeland.

Time flew by with so many tasks consuming it. Each day was a continuation of working on the leftover tasks from the day before. The evenings were consumed also with fiddle practice and sewing. The leprechauns were also busy re-soling and dying shoes. It seemed as if the work would never come to an end. Then as suddenly as with the change in the weather, each day grew a bit longer. The hills had now taken on the appearance of Spring. Flowers were in bloom everywhere. The trees branches were becoming fuller with leaves and the air had a warm fresh scent of dandelions and wildflowers. The competition for the high honor of playing at the St Paddy's Day event had been completed and the winner was announced. The McSwane's had run a close competition with the McGills, but by one swaying vote had managed to win. Now Dylan, Patrick, Michael and Daniel were busy practicing their tunes into the wee hours of the night. The fairy wives had completed their long hours of embroidery and sewing, all the attire had been cleaned, altered, and made ready. The cooks had all came to agreement as to the menu for the day, after much arguing, and much sampling. The last finishing touches of the pain-staking preparations came to a close as The Great Hall stood in wait of the last setting and rising of the sun before the long awaited St. Paddy's Day had arrived.

The excitement in Leprechaun Isle was felt from every corner as all now waited in anticipation for the Festivities to begin. The McSwane's had risen early, donned their attire and headed out to the Great Hall for the traditional St Paddy's Day morning feast. Upon arrival they found the Hall was filling up with cooks and servers as they hurried to spread the feast upon the great tables. The peoples of Leprechaun Isle were steadily pouring into the Hall, each clan dressed in grand attire. The musician's stage in the foreground was set up with fiddles and other instruments leaning against their stools. Streamers filled with green shamrocks dangled from the ceiling above and around the edge of the stage flooring. There were booths set up for the audience and the large dance floor was gleaming, waiting for the first dancers to begin. The Great Hall was full of laughter and chatter and the wonderful scents of Traditional Irish cuisine.
The leprechauns had made a perimeter around the town square and the Great Hall, which they had sprinkled carefully with magic dust. This magic dust would keep their festivities hidden from the naked eye; the magic dust also camouflaged the sounds, making them inaudible. This would prevent anyone from stumbling upon their secret Hall as the leprechauns were very careful to never be caught by anyone, and only seen by their fellowmen and allies such as the fairies and dwarves. Now as the last leprechaun clan signed in on the great guest list, the great door

was closed. Then the feasting began. Everyone ate until they had their fill, then the McSwane's went up on the stage, picked up their instruments and began to play. Soon the Great Hall dance floor was filled with leprechauns and their fairy wives dancing in rhythm to the music from the fiddlers. The booths were filled with spectators too, and the green ale was flowing from the vats.

As the day wore on, more food was brought out for the mid day meal. The dance floor now was being used by couples and singles alike. When the dancing competition began the first contestant was none other than Altaire McFairlane. Each male leprechaun did his share in trying to out best the other. The winner was none other than Mighty McGillicuddy dancing a traditional Irish jig. Then the ale tasting began, the judges all sat at the long table, while cups of each brew were placed before them. They took their time in tasting and then each judge pushed the cups away waiting for all of the judges to finish. Then they drew their heads together and in hushed whispers they concurred. Ira McGill stood up and said, "The winner of this year's ale contest is Brian McGill," and the winner strode to the table to receive his award, The Golden Medal of Achievement. As the day progressed the leprechauns grew merrier and the ale vats grew low in their supply. The last meal had been served, which was prepared to perfection, and every last morsel had been devoured. The sun had long ago set and the moon was now casting its light through the Great Hall windows. All of the festivities had concluded and the awards had been handed out. Then the head of the St Paddy's committee made an announcement. "This year's festivities are coming to a close. As ye all well know it is time to vote for a new committee. Our five year term has expired. We graciously thank ye for the privilege of being able to serve ye. The voting ballots will be passed out tomorrow afternoon. May the next committee enjoy their service as much as we have." Then he gave a little bow and a swoop of his hat and walked off in the direction of the kitchen. The leprechaun clans bid each other a farewell as they gathered their belongings and exited the Hall. Soon there were only the sounds of the McSwane's gathering together their instruments and the cooks and servers clearing away the plates. The brewers collected their empty vats and made their exit also.

 Another St Paddy's Day had come and gone, Patrick thought with a sigh. Tomorrow volunteers would return to clear away all the remnants of the gala affair. Then he remembered with a smile, the next full moon we shall see if Geneva is the rightful fairy, the one with the magical voice to sing the special note that would free them forever from their endless searching for the pot of gold at the end of the rainbow. If she was, Leprechaun Isle would not be the same, the curse would be gone and all leprechauns could return to their shoemaking and tilling of the fields, and the casting of their fishing nets. They would no longer need to hide in the daylight for along with the curse would be gone the greed of foreigners who wanted the pot of gold for themselves. All memory of the curse would be erased from time. It would be as though it had never happened. It would be as though there never was a pot of gold at the end of a rainbow. He tried to imagine being free to pursue his own dreams, with no fear of any foreigner that came to Leprechaun Isle. The world would learn much about the gentle side of the leprechaun people. He was still dreaming of this when he found himself standing outside his door with his fiddle in hand. It was the wee hours of the morning now and he shivered in the cold air as he opened his door and went inside. Then he latched the door behind him and went straight in to his bed. There he set his fiddle down, removed his outer attire and crawled into his comfortable bed. Ah, too soon the sun would raise he thought; I must get a bit of rest now. Within minutes he was fast asleep, dreaming of brighter days.

CHAPTER 11

THE FULL MOON ARRIVES

Leprechaun Isle had cleared away all evidence of the St Paddy day festivities and had returned to its natural slow pace. Altaire McFairlane was busy planning the Full Moon Event. It was customary that a speech was given telling the significance of the magical fairy. The tale had been told many times over, by each leprechaun who had provided a new candidate. It had been handed down from generation to generation as all waited in anticipation of the end of the evil Hagatha's Curse. The song that the fairy contender must sing had been carefully preserved on an emerald green scroll of satin. This scroll was kept under lock and key, only to be brought out for these occasions. It was held in the Great Hall office in a locked wooden chest. Altaire McFarlane had requested possession of the scroll from the leprechaun sage, (the oldest and wisest leprechaun alive, Ira McBaine.) He now had it in his possession and was carefully unrolling it onto his large desk in his home library. It was inscribed beautifully and each beginning word of each stanza was italicized. The song read as follows,

I am proud to be of service to the grandest folk of lore,
The ancient tales have fooled us; we know not who ye are,
We call ye magical leprechaun, as we seek to find ye out,
Not really understanding what our quest is all about.
For a leprechaun has magic, as all the world does know,
Yet his magic does not lead him to the rainbow's pot of gold.

It was during the singing of the last stanza that the rightful fairy would hit the special high note. So unfortunately in the past they had endured some really bad songstresses. It was never allowed to stop them until the last note had been sung. He clutched it tightly in his hand and went out seeking Pennar. "Pennar! Pennar!, he cried. Within moments Pennar appeared and stood in front of him. "Pennar, make haste, prepare the fairy for her performance. Teach her the lyrics and notes well and summon a fiddler to accompany her." Then he thrust the scroll into Pennar's hands. "Take special care of this scroll, it cannot be destroyed or even slightly damaged." Pennar appeared to be rather indifferent to Altaire's tone as he casually spoke, with a gesture of his hands, "Master McFairlane, it is but a few hours we need to prepare for this event. The fairy has been well kept and the announcement has been posted. Word has spread through hill and dale, not one leprechaun soul has been forgotten, we will have a large audience tomorrow night. I will see to it that the fairy arrives safely and will be just as careful with the scroll in me possession. All will go as planned, as it has for many generations on Leprechaun Isle." Altaire made a "Hmmf"...sound and then turned abruptly toward his library. He was careful not to directly scoff at Pennar, for he was no fool, and was wise to the spells that a wizard could cast. He sat down in front of his large desk and turning glanced over his shoulder at the large window. The sun was still high in the sky, he estimated it to be mid day. This day will never end he thought as he rose and shuffled down the hall to his foyer. "Lipkin!, prepare the midday meal, I suddenly feel ravenous," he said. At once the cook appeared apron donned with a steaming bowl in his hand. "Boiled beef and cabbage sir, just the way ye likes it." Then he placed it at the head of the table gave a little bow and returned to the kitchen. He felt rather awkward now for yelling at the man, who had indeed already cooked the midday meal. Oh well he thought I am a bit tense, I'll be better come sunset. Then he proceeded to slowly eat from the steaming bowl, savoring every bite. Lipkin returned with a spot of dandelion tea, and cleared away his dishes. Then he sat gazing out the doorway into the foyer and beyond to the large window. Time seemed to stand still as he sat there sipping his tea. He rose to go into his chambers to change into his evening attire just as the sun began to set. "Pennar!, do tell the chamber maid to draw me a hot bath," he called with his head sticking out of his doorway into the hall. Then he strode to his large wardrobe and swung it open. "So many choices, what shall I wear," he said to himself. In no time his chambermaid had arrived with hot water to pour into his ivory footed bath tub. She had assembled the kitchen cleaning crew, who each took turns pouring hot water into the tub. Soon it was filled and the chambermaid and her helpers retreated, pulling the large wooden door closed behind them. Then Altair closed his window curtains, stripped off his clothes and slowly sank into the steaming bath water. A clean towel had been placed thoughtfully within arm's reach. He sank back and closed his eyes, relaxing and dreaming of tomorrow's events. After awhile he rose grabbed the towel and stepped out upon his floor. He dried carefully and then began to dress, setting aside the attire he had carefully chosen for tomorrow eve. He then retreated to his library to read.

As always time passed and soon Lipkin was knocking upon his door. Altaire called "Come in". "Master McFairlane supper is served," Lipkin said as Altaire rose to face him. "Very well Lipkin, I'll be along shortly," Altaire said as he placed a bookmark in his book and set it upon the top of his large desk. As usual Lipkin had outdone himself with a very fine feast. Altaire finished every bite and after drinking his dandelion tea he rose and walked out across the hall leading to his library. The

evening passed very quickly as Altaire
returned to his library to take up his reading
again. He felt a slight draft, so he went to the
large hearth and threw a few logs on the hot
coals. He then sat down to read in his
comfortable overstuffed chair which was
positioned before the fire. As the hours wore
on the fire grew dim and went out and Altaire
fell asleep. His book had fallen into his lap
and his glasses had slid down the bridge of his
nose. It was as this that Pennar found him.
Not wanting to wake him Pennar left and soon
returned with a warm blanket to throw across
him. Then he carefully backed out of the door
and closed it silently behind him.

It had arrived just as Pennar had predicted.
Exactly four days had passed since St Paddy's
Day. It was March twenty first the day when
all the leprechauns would meet in the Sacred
Hollow to finally hear Geneva sing.
Oddly the day passed rather quickly and soon
Altaire was getting dressed for the occasion he
had waited so long for. He had carefully
picked out a green velvet suit with a matching
top hat, and an ivory tipped cane. He
complimented this with his high brown leather
boots which tied below the knee. Then he
carefully groomed his moustache and ran a
hand through his grey hair, placed the top hat
upon his head and started toward the library.
"Pennar!, meet me in the foyer with the fairy,
we must be on our way to the Sacred Hollow."
Pennar appeared in the foyer with the gilded
cage and its occupant soon after. He had
dressed appropriately in his finest wizard
gown of shimmering green, with his pointed
hat upon his wizened head. Then the large
wooden door was thrown open and the two of

them stepped out into the moonlight and began their walk down the trail to the Sacred Hollow.

It was an event that always had a large turnout, leprechauns came from far and wide and every side of Leprechaun Isle. The Sacred Hollow was full of them tonight as they exchanged their names and shook hands. The Hollow was well lit by the light of the full moon and the air had a scent of spring flowers. In the midst of the Hollow was a large oak tree, the oldest oak on Leprechaun Isle. It stood proudly with its branches covering the entire expanse of the sacred area where a small tree stump came rising from the midst of the great oaks roots. The top had been carefully leveled off and was used as a platform for the fairy contestant. A flat boulder was conveniently at the base and made a nice seat for the owner of the selected fairy to sit and tell the ancient tale of the Wicked Witch Hagatha's curse, and the significance of the full moon event. This tale even though heard so many times in the past, renewed the anticipation of each leprechaun as he intently listened. The youngest lads were deeply engrossed and the oldest reminisced of full moon events of the past. Tonight Altaire McFairlane sat upon the flat boulder, casting his yarn upon the audience, with deep resonance in his voice and emotion he told of the hardships suffered by the leprechaun people as they searched for the end of their long wretched curse.

Geneva had been placed carefully upon the flat tree stump in her gilded cage. She was intently listening to every word and by the time Altaire had cleared his throat and finished she had come to feel a deep sorrow for the leprechauns and how desperately they were seeking the fairy that would sing the special notes and end this ancient curse. In her heart she hoped that she could be the one to finally set them free. They had after all been very kind and gentle to her, not at all like what she had been told by her fellow fairy men. As long as she could remember they had been teaching that all leprechauns were wicked and evil and that a fairy must never venture outside of their kingdom alone. This she had found was far from the leprechauns she had come to know. They were family oriented, hard working, and jovial, never brutish or harsh, but a quiet people who held a deep respect for all nature. They shied away from most foreigners and led very simple lives. She had come to be fond of these people and now within moments they would know if she, (Geneva), could set them free. This felt suddenly like a very large burden to her, and she silently prayed that this would be so. Then before she could open her eyes Altaire spoke, " Now me dear fairy sing the song Pennar has been teaching ye, and regardless of the results when ye are finished ye shall be set free." Then he rose and stepped back a few feet closer to the crowd, waiting for Geneva to sing.

Looking out onto the large crowd, Geneva swallowed hard and with her eyes closed she began to sing the song that she had memorized from Pennar's scroll. "I am proud to be of service to the grandest folk of lore, The ancient tales have fooled us; we know not who ye are,

We call ye magical leprechaun, as we seek to find ye out,
Not really understanding what our quest is all about.
For a leprechaun has magic, as all the world does know,
Yet his magic does not lead him to the rainbow's pot of gold." Her voice was beautiful and filled the leprechaun's with amazement, but even so more amazing was the pitch of the last note when she sang "gold....." It was at this very instant that the night turned into broad daylight and a huge rainbow of many colors appeared. The rainbow had stair steps of every color that led along its bow to the end of the rainbow where sat a huge pot of shimmering golden nuggets. Without haste the eldest sage of the leprechauns began his climb as he stepped out onto the stairway each step he took disappeared until he came to rest at the foot of the rainbow right in front of the huge gleaming pot. Then he reached out and took a hold of it and with a big poof it blew up into falling sparkles, that filled the air and ground.

Geneva looked upon the faces of the leprechauns who all seemed puzzled as to why they had gathered in the Sacred Hollow. She as well as the fairy wives wondered the very same. How did she get here she thought, where am I, where are my fairy men? Her mind was flooded with thoughts and fears. Who are these strange little people? Then she slowly flew away from the wee people down to the seashore. She felt a need to be alone and to gather her thoughts. She tried to remember what had happened. Then slowly it began to return to her. She remembered the festive day at home in the meadow, she remembered leaving to gather a bouquet of wildflowers.

She stood in the swirling sea mist looking out to sea remembering another time. All she knew was she missed home, and her family and her dear beloved Calliope. Her heart felt pangs of sorrow as a tear flowed down her cheek and fell upon her breast. Even if I can't remember why I am here, I know I need to get home, she thought. But how? She stood there for a long long time and then feeling a chill she retreated to a sheltered cove and curled up against the rock to rest.

CHAPTER 12

SYNCORE'S SURPRISE

One-Eyed Jack had succeeded in getting his ruffian crew to finish the arduous task of constructing a raft. It had taken the whole of two long days to complete, but now it was drying out in the sun. They had gotten it wet, and were drying it out to tighten the straps of hemp. It would be ready to sail by morning he thought. They had quite a few provisions left from the sunken Ægileif. They would have to choose from them carefully. One-Eyed Jack had decided he would keep two on to help steady the raft and steer its course. The others would be left behind. He would bring this up to them tonight. He was in better spirits than usual so decided not to kill them, they would have an even chance of being rescued or dying alone on the island. His crew and he would also have an even chance of making it to the nearest island, or being lost at sea in a storm.

There for he reasoned they wouldn't be fighting over either position.

They had caught a few fresh fish and there was wood for a fire, so the ruffians began to prepare the evening meal. One-Eyed Jack found himself content in drinking a bit of ale and resting beneath the shade of a large palm tree. When the meal was prepared, he rose and strode across the sand to the crew. "Men, I shall set sail tomorrow, I will choose two of ye to go, to help steer the raft. The rest will stay behind. We all have an even chance of survival. I will take only the provisions me crew needs. If we make it safely to land I will send a rescue party. Ye may meet up with another ship, as this island is clearly in view. Ye have a broad beach to light signal fires upon and much wild berries, coconuts and fresh fish. I think me crew and I have lesser chances of survival. Never the less we leave first light." Then he tipped his cup of ale and walked back toward the palm tree to once again rest against its trunk.

In the morning, true to his word, One-Eyed Jack and two of the bigger ruffians loaded the raft with supplies, attached the mast and sail, and pushed off into the water. Each using long bamboo poles for steering purposes. The sail was billowing quite freely and the raft was moving quickly out to sea. The ruffians on the island stood at the shoreline and watched until the raft was no longer visible, then they turned and headed back to camp.

Aboard the Drakkar Syncore was busy assessing the course. He knew he would reach Leprechaun isle in about one day if the wind held up. The Drakkar had been sailing right along keeping good speed, so the crew members and oarsmen were busy playing games and telling tales. The sky was a deep blue with white fluffy clouds that raced across it in the wind. The ocean was relatively calm and by all standards it looked like they would reach their destination without any interference from the weather. The day wore on and as the sun was setting Syncore noticed the sky was not red, but rather a dark purple. The wind had picked up a bit also, and the temperature had dropped, so he clutched his tunic around him. Then he reached in his pocket and pulled out his pipe. Soon he was walking the deck blowing circles of smoke from his mouth. He was deep in thought now, apprehensive of the weather.

 Sure as begorrah as Syncore had feared the day began with a red dawn. The wind had picked up considerably during the night and the sea was filled with white caps. He could smell the scent of rain in the salt air and knew from past experience that today's weather would bring with it a squall, (perhaps one of great fury.) The Drakkar was slicing through the waves now as each one seemed to grow a bit larger, sending flotsam and jetsam over the forward bow. It was difficult to keep one's balance as Syncore made his way toward the bow. What were these items that were now floating out upon the deck? Getting a bit closer now, he reached down and retrieved a Vashing tunic. Upon closer inspection he noticed the shield of arms belonging to the Vashing long ship the Ægileif.

The seas had become so turbulent and the wind so strong that he had commanded his men to lower the huge sail. They were moving with the tides now and drifting. The sky had become very dark and rain was now imminent. Syncore stood on the open deck near the portside of the bow looking intently out to sea. He called to his oarsmen, "Man the oars and keep her on a steady course due east, if memory serves me right there is a small island up ahead, with a large sheltered cove. If we are lucky we'll get there before the heavens open up. We are in for a bad storm men."

The visibility now was reduced greatly as the ocean became an eerie foggy place. Syncore kept careful watch for any signs of land. It was pouring down rain with thunder off in the distance when he finally spotted the beach head of the tiny island. "Keep her steady men, heave ho, put her in near the east side of the island. The sheltered cove is around the bend, just below that jagged cliff," he cried as he pointed his finger in its direction.

The Drakkar crew was hungry and wet when they finally came to rest in the waters of the sheltered cove. The sea became very shallow here as it got closer to the shore so they dropped anchor about twenty feet out from the beach. "Tack the sail down men, we are in for a long wet afternoon," Syncore said. Soon the crew and Syncore were sitting on the deck beneath the shelter of the Drakkar's huge sail, eating and drinking from their provisions. "Well men, this will cause us to lose a bit of time, but after the storm passes, we can take a spell to stretch our legs and explore this little island. We will set sail for Leprechaun Isle from here tomorrow," he said. "Perhaps we are in need of a bit of relaxation," he said. "I believe all things happen for a reason. As a wise man once said, "Mine is not to question why, mine is but to do or die." Then he got himself in a comfortable position and tipped his hat over his eyes and drifted off to sleep.

His afternoon nap was interrupted by the frantic shouting. He sat up and listened and realized the rain had stopped. The men had begun to remove the sail and as he looked out he could see people standing on shore. There were only a handful of them. They were yelling and jumping up and down and waving their hands. Then he realized that his ship the Drakkar was being mistaken for a rescue party.

Syncore ordered his crew to lower the skiff and taking two of his trusty seamen with him he began rowing towards the shoreline. Within a few minutes they were beached and standing upon the shore. The castaways were a ragged looking group. It appeared they had been here for some time. Upon closer examination Syncore found more remnants of the Ægileif's. Then he spoke slowly not knowing if they would understand his language. "What fate met with the Ægileif? Are you her crew? If so where is the scoundrel who stole her away from the Vashings?" They stood looking about at each other hesitant to reply, when suddenly one short stout fellow with a ruddy complexion and shaggy red hair stepped forward. "We were only aboard the Ægileif as stowaways seeking a better life in another port. When she was stolen we were forced by the evil pirate One-Eyed Jack to be a part of her crew. He be the one ye are seeking. He lost the Ægileif at sea in a wretched storm.

She quickly capsized and sank to the bottom, with only a few provisions left floating. We rode these barrels in to this very island. For days we slaved away under the scrutiny of One-Eyed Jack, building him a raft. He sailed away only a couple of days ago with two of our men and left the rest of us to fend for ourselves. Oh he's an evil pirate that one, I believe we were given the better deal than the poor mates he took with him."

Syncore took a deep sigh, "I was expecting the worst as my travels had brought no news of her whereabouts. We will be glad to bring you back with us to the Vashing King. He will make it well worth your trouble if you relay this information to him. We have time to rest and gather up any provisions; we shall set sail tomorrow at dawn. With Leprechaun Isle so near, (only a few hours away), we shall visit there briefly before returning to the Vashings. I am confident you will find the Vashing kingdom a very nice place to visit. Many ships travel there to do trading with the King. Perhaps you will find work onboard some of them. At any rate you will fare far better than being left here." The ruffians nodded in agreement and began to show Syncore's men, where the remainder of the Ægileif's provisions were kept.

It was a peaceful evening, under the stars as the last of the men and provisions were placed aboard the Drakkar. The skiff was raised and locked in place upon its deck. The men were enjoying swapping tales and sampling the new provisions. Tomorrow would be a good day Syncore thought. He hadn't been to Leprechaun Isle in a long time. He didn't realize how good it would be and what he would discover there.

The new day dawned bright with no signs of bad weather. There was a steady wind blowing when Syncore gave orders for the sail to be set. Then he hollered to his crew to raise the anchor. He stood by the bow giving careful instructions to the rudder man to steer the Drakkar on a set course for Leprechaun Isle. In just a few short hours he would be within her shoreline. He felt a strange anticipation, and shaking it off, he pulled out his pipe and began to smoke walking the deck, waiting for.... He didn't really know what he was waiting for.. but the feeling was strong none the less.

It was high noon when Syncore saw the first glimpse of Leprechaun Isle. The day was a warm and breezy one with blue skies and not even the trace of a cloud. He could hear the sounds of wild birds as the Drakkar sailed closer to shore. The sea gulls began their frenzied flight around the deck, in anticipation of food. He could see the mossy green rolling hills and the large majestic oak trees that outlined the island. There was a scent of clover in the salty air as the Drakkar sail was lowered and the oarsmen began to maneuver her into shore. Syncore noticed another long ship which was moored in the cove. On closer examination he found the name on her side "Muirin". She was quite an impressive vessel and he found himself entranced by her. Soon the Drakkar was moored beside her and Syncore stepped out upon the dock. The vessel looked somehow familiar to him, but for the life of him he couldn't remember his last encounter with her. He made sure that his crew had secured the Drakkar and then he gave the order to disembark, save for three of his men that would stand guard while they were in port. The island wasn't very large so Syncore estimated they could hike her trails and be back before sun down.

Syncore and his men strode up the embankment and down the forest path. They were amazed by the size of the forest, the large trees reaching towards the sky. There was moss on the large roots that crossed the trail, and in the clearings there were wildflowers and fields of clover. It was a very serene peaceful island. After walking for a while they came upon the leprechaun village. There were busy leprechauns tilling their fields and shoemakers at work in their shops. A few had gathered together to mend their fishing nets and swap tales of the grand catch that got away. Syncore noticed a small Pub, too small for his stature and that of his men. He bent down to shake the hand of the barkeep that had opened his door. "Well hello foreigner the barkeep said, I would offer ye a bit of me ale inside, but I see that is not possible, so if ye shall please find a seat out here, I'll bring ye a mug." Then he motioned to some large flat rocks, which the leprechauns had used for a wall or partition in the middle of their town. Syncore laughed and said, "Why thank you kind sir, bring a round for all my mates," as he tossed the barkeep a fistful of coins in a burlap pouch. "Take what you need and bring me the change." The barkeep quickly disappeared and returned with his help to serve the crew and Syncore. The cool refreshing leprechaun ale was a welcome taste to Syncore and his men. When they had finished they bid their farewells and continued their exploration.

They had found themselves in a different type of forest now, the trees were short and wide, and the trails were many going off in different directions. They spotted what appeared to be a wild rabbit and began to give chase, when they stepped out from the foliage into a large meadow and beyond a cliff. Syncore walked carefully to the edge and looked straight down. His face took on a strange puzzled expression and then a broad grin as he exclaimed, "Why I'll be if it isn't the Ngalfar herself anchored in a secret cove." Well men we aren't alone there are others here sent by King Lore." Then he began to look for a way down the cliff.

 The first trail was very steep and very rocky, but he did manage to find a wider one just a few yards further. Soon Syncore and his men were shouting, "Ahoy!" The watchmen of the Ngalfar were standing on deck. Syncore strode down the rocky path and stepped out upon the shore. Looking up he asked the men, "Where be your Captain?"
"He took a search party with him, they are looking for …. Isn't that odd he said as the man scratched his chin, I can't remember what they are looking for. Come to think of it I don't know why we are here… We should be looking for the Ægileif."
"Ah the Ægileif, Syncore said, "She is lost at sea, I have a few of her provisions and the stowaway crew that One-Eyed-Jack held hostage after he stole her."

"The Ægileif was lost at sea? said the man with a scowl. "Captain Sigmar will be sorry to hear this news. He'll be returning soon I would imagine. He has been gone for quite a few hours."

Little did they know that Bjork and the fairy men along with Captain Sigmar were now entering the Leprechaun Isle township. The leprechauns were busy at work when they came upon them. Bjork felt an odd feeling as if he had forgotten something very important at home. Why were they here? He couldn't for the life of himself figure it out, when he questioned his friend Nimrod, he too was puzzled. "I don't remember why we came here either, perhaps Captain Sigmar will know," Nimrod said. They had the very peculiar feeling that they had been on the island for much longer than one afternoon. "Captain Sigmar, Nimrod called, "Why is it we are on this strange island?" The Captain stopped and turned slowly toward Nimrod, he scratched his chin whiskers and mumbled, "I don't know." Then he stopped walking and said, "I do remember we were given orders by King Lore to find the Ægileif, and to take her thieving Captain prisoner. We were to search for Syncore the Sailor as you Bjork and your fellow men were inquiring to his whereabouts. How or why we came to this place I strangely don't remember. Perhaps we have all been victims of a curse or cabin fever has set upon us. I can only hope it is the later. At any rate we shall return to the Ngalfar before sunset." Then they continued to walk through the township bidding hello to the friendly leprechauns.

Suddenly Nimrod felt a very strong impulse to follow another trail leading away from the village. He wandered off in that direction, not paying any mind to his traveling companions. The trail led him through a dense forest of oak trees and then out to an embankment which led down toward the sea. There to his amazement he saw a very familiar shape standing by the water's edge, looking out to sea. He almost stumbled down the embankment in his excitement. He now realized why he must be here, he hadn't seen her for a long time, yet there she was in front of him, her back to him. She may be able to shed some light on this predicament. He recognized her flowing hair and his heart leapt from his chest.

"Mother? Dear Queen Mother? It is I Nimrod, he called." She turned and instantly began to run towards him, "Nimrod? My son? How did you find me?," she cried. Her heart felt it would explode from joy. Now it didn't matter that nothing made any sense, it only mattered that her son was there and he would bring her home. Tears of joy streamed down her face as she reached out and grabbed hold of him, clutching him tightly, she wiped her tears upon his tunic with her face pressed tightly against his chest. "Nimrod, I have missed you and Naomi and your dear Father. I never thought I would see you again," she cried. "Well Mother, I don't know how I came to be here myself, but I do know why. I have come to bring you back home to our meadow. Careful now Mother we must hurry and catch the others. We shall return to our ship now. Tomorrow we set sail." He held her hand and gently guided her up the embankment and back down the trail leading to Bjork and the fairy men.

The sun was low in the sky when they finally caught up with them. Bjork called out in surprise upon seeing Geneva and clutched his breast. "My dear Queen Geneva, I am so happy to see you. King Calliope has been so lonely without you." Then Bjork thought strange, how did I know this, that she was gone? Perhaps this is why we came to Leprechaun Isle. Being a Hork he wasn't affected as greatly by the Leprechaun's Curse, so when it was removed he didn't lose all of his memory, it was returning now in bits and pieces.

 They were carefully descending from the top of the high trail downward toward the Ngalfar. The forest gave way to a wider path now and as they got closer there lie the Ngalfar and on her deck stood none other but Syncore himself. "Who is that strange tall seaman," Nimrod asked. "I recognized him right away, its Syncore himself," Bjork replied.
This would be a very interesting evening Bjork thought.

Soon they were all aboard the Ngalfar's deck swapping tales of their voyages and encounters with One-Eyed Jack. Syncore was eager to meet up with him and bring him back to King Lore in shackles. The moon was high and full and gave a splendid light as the men enjoyed their last night in Leprechaun Isle. Tomorrow they would set sail for home. Syncore bid his farewells and tipped his hat to Queen Geneva as he disembarked. Soon he was seen going up the trail that would lead him back to his great ship the Drakkar. Little did he know that before he reached her, there would be an even greater surprise.

He was smoking his pipe and enjoying the evening solitude when he took the turn in the path that brought him to his discovery. He had somehow turned the wrong way and reaching a clearing that looked out upon a steep rocky cliff, he could clearly see in the moon's beams floating upon the water, a raft. It was a very strange looking handmade raft. It had wedged itself between two rocks, and aboard there was a scuffle going on as it appeared that one of the passengers was trying to throw the other overboard. Then he crept closer to listen and watch. He noticed a few yards out from the raft there was another figure, someone swimming, and calling out. This strange bit of events puzzled Syncore for a spell. At that moment the moon light shone brightly upon a metal object on the raft and for a split second Syncore saw the outline of a face, with a prominent nose and an eye patch. Where have I seen that face before?, he thought. Then he remembered wanted posters for piracy at sea. He listened as he heard the pirate cry, "Off with ye, I be done with the likes of ye, into the salty sea ye goes. Ye have served me well, now I find no further need for ye service." With that he kicked the man overboard. Then he took a cup and dipped it in a barrel and sat down upon the raft, his musket at his side. Now Syncore was sure this must be One_Eyed_Jack. He began to think of how he could sneak up upon him and capture this evil pirate. He noticed the tide was coming in now and the water was rising near the rocks where the raft had been wedged. If he waited patiently the tide might rise enough to release the raft. Then once it landed on the beach he would be able to ambush the pirate. He estimated he had about an hour to reach the Drakkar and co-ordinate a plan with the use of a few of his crew members and some shackles, he would be able to finally capture the man who was guilty of piracy of the Ægileif. He tore off a piece of his shirt cuff and tied it carefully to a branch to mark the path. Then he quietly slipped away down the trails leading to the Drakkar. He was careful not to follow the wrong path as he had done before. In short time he was out of breath and standing upon her deck. "Men I need a few of the strongest of this crew, I have come to find the whereabouts of the man responsible for the theft and capsizing of the Ægileif. We have very little time to prepare for an ambush, arm yourselves and bring along the shackles. I shant leave this island without this pirate. I have sworn my loyalty to King Lore and given my word of honor to not return without the Ægileif or the man who stole her. I can't bring her back from the depths of the sea, but I shall see that this man receives his just punishment for the crime of piracy against King Lore."

  Soon the men had been chosen who would participate in the ambush and they disembarked the Drakkar, each armed with dagger and Syncore possessing the shackles that would bind the pirate until he met his fate with King Lore. The moon was full and their paths were lit so they easily found the branch that Syncore had marked. When they reached the clearing they could see that the raft was now free of the rocks and being slowly brought into shore on the crest of the waves. The tide was high and there was a possibility that the raft would capsize before it reached the beach. So they scanned around the clearing and found a trail that was fairly wide and not too steep that lead down to the beach. There was a large area of foliage where the captors could hide in anticipation of the arrival of One_Eyed-Jack's raft. Quickly and stealthily with silence the men and Syncore descended the path and soon they were huddled behind the foliage, hearts thudding, adrenaline surging, in wait of the moment when they would spring forth and ambush the pirate. "Wait for my signal men," Syncore said with a whisper, "When I raise my hand we attack."

They lay in wait and watched the make-shift raft and its passenger as it slammed into the waves and spun around more than once almost capsizing. Then it somehow straightened itself out and gracefully rode into shore. With a large splash a wave crashed overboard and the pirate was soaked by the salty foam. He stumbled off the raft and it was apparent he had been imbibing in the ale for quite some time. He shook off his body and his braided hair and then seeing his hat floating in the surf he waded out to retrieve it. Soon he was back on shore.

Syncore waited as One-Eyed-Jack walked up the beach and then he raised his hand. At full speed his men attacked. The pirate had time only to spin around to see what the commotion was and then he was body slammed and being held down by two very strong men. A third stood over him with his dagger drawn, and then he saw Syncore coming closer with shackles in his hands. "I am taking you prisoner to face charges for the piracy of King Lore's vessel the Ægileif. As King Lore's spokesman I have been giving authority by him to hold you captive aboard the Drakkar until we reach the Vashing Kingdom. It is by his authority you will be held as prisoner. You will be treated fairly. No punishment will fall upon you until the King has passed his decree."

In a flash One-Eyed_jack was shackled and searched for hidden weapons. They found a dagger which was now in Syncore's possession. Then he ordered the men to bring the shackled wet pirate to his feet. "Bring him along men, careful now we don't want to harm the prisoner." One-Eyed-Jack still in a bit of a drunken stupor obligingly went along, he didn't attempt to struggle he only mumbled under his breath. When asked what he was saying, he just flashed a silver toothed smile and shook his head. His hat was crooked upon his head, and his gait was wobbly from ale and from the weight of the shackles. He looked rather pathetic and for what reason Syncore did not know, he somehow took pity upon this wretched soul. Then he reasoned, King Lore was a fair and good king, he would only decree the punishment he felt that would be fair for the loss of such a fine vessel. Perhaps he would be forced to work it off in servitude. King Lore was not a hard man and would not decree death or long years of imprisonment unless absolutely warranted. In fact One-Eyed-Jack was very fortunate that he chose to steal a vessel that belonged to this

King, others would not be so kind and some would pass a decree of death in this situation.

The men trudged on with the drunken pirate in tow and soon there appeared the sight of the familiar trail which would lead them back to the Drakkar. The full moon lit up the night sky and it was much easier to travel the paths, staying clear of the dark forest. Syncore was in lead as they came to the embankment and began their descent. On board he could see the night lamps were lit and there were the shapes of his men as they busied themselves aboard the Drakkar. They were eagerly making preparations for their dawn departure. It had been quite some time now since they had seen the familiar shore of the Vashing Kingdom. They reminisced of the many pleasurable events that they had partaken of in the King's Castle. King Lore threw marvelous parties, and the feasts of such were eloquently lavish with rare delicacies. The maids were attentive servants and watchful that their guests had no lack of nectars to imbibe. The musicians played magical music as the magicians and the dancers entertained the guests. They were sure that King Lore would order a party beyond their dreams to honor their return and to show his gratitude to them for the pirate's capture. They were indeed in for a rare treat. So anxious were they to return that taking inventory of their provisions and such was accomplished in a very short amount of time.

They noticed the shadows of men descending the embankment and on closer observation; they saw they held one as captive. As they grew closer to the bottom of the trail, they could now see it was indeed their brave Captain Syncore and his men. They also could see that the one in shackles was dressed in the attire of a pirate. None of them knew just how notorious this pirate was until he was brought onboard and on their deck under the moonlight they saw the patch which covered his left eye.

Syncore strode to the middle of the Drakkar's deck and announced, "Men this is the pirate responsible for the theft and capsizing of our King's vessel the Ægileif. He is to be kept under lock and key until we reach the Vashing Kingdom. He will eat where we eat and sleep where we sleep. We shant let him out of our sight. He is to be treated fairly according to the Vashing Code for prisoners. Do not trust him, for a pirate never is trustworthy. Be wary of him always, and be on guard. He shall try anything to escape, but don't allow him a chance. From this day until he is locked in the dungeon of the Vashing Castle two men will guard him. This guard will be done in rotations, so each man will have his twelve hour watch. We set sail tomorrow at dawn, so be prepared." Then Syncore strode down the long deck to his cabin went inside and closed the door. Once inside he reached into his tunic pocket and pulled out his pipe. Then he sat down behind his desk and leaned back, with a deep look of satisfaction upon his face. There had been a wonderful turn of events and he looked forward now to the look upon his friend King Lore's face when he returned with this prisoner. Tomorrow he would be a bit closer to the Vashing Kingdom and then he could take a much needed rest from his travels. King Lore would reward him and his men handsomely and he looked forward to spending some time with his friends in nearby Horkland as well.

CHAPTER 13.

THE NGALFAR SETS SAIL

After Syncore disembarked the Ngalfar Captain Sigmar gave orders to his crew to prepare to set sail at dawn. The hour was late so the men quickly set to making the necessary preparations. Bjork and his fairy men friends along with the Queen Geneva found a quiet spot on the deck near the bow to sit and wait for dawn. The fairy men were quite excited by the realization that soon they would be back in their meadow with their family. Nimrod was busy bringing his mother up to speed on the situation at home. Ryob was anxious to return himself and looking forward to the grand welcoming feast and party that King Calliope would host. Jacor was admiring the skills of the Ngalfars warriors as they began to practice a bit of combat skills, in preparation for guarding the Queen. Jeziah was busy thinking of the calculated risks that the Ngalfar was taking with Queen Geneva on board. He was highly aware of the acts of piracy at sea and was no stranger to the dangers. He must protect the Queen at all costs. Mahew was thinking of doing a portrait of the Queen, perhaps during the return voyage he mused. Bjork was suddenly overwhelmed with a deep exhaustion. His eyelids were growing very heavy as he leaned back against a wooden crate. He pulled his coat around him closer and within moments was sound asleep. His snores were a welcome sound to his traveling companions, who had grown very fond of this dear old Hork.

Come dawn Captain Sigmar would call out his orders as the crew scurried about the deck. Nimrod looked out upon the shores of Leprechaun Isle and bid her a farewell. The crew had all found areas upon the deck to lie in wait for the first glimpse of the dawn. Some were ordered to keep a night watch from each side of the large vessel. The others were told to catch a few winks. The Captain himself had retired for the evening and as the hour passed the snores of the men were mixed in with those of Bjork.

The new day dawned with a brilliant splendor unlike any other Bjork could remember. The sky was colorful hues of orange and red as the huge sun began its rise above the tides of the ocean. It was a warm day as well with a bit of a North wind. The crew of the Ngalfar was busy untying mooring lines and lifting her anchor. The oarsmen had taken their posts, and were now gently rowing out to sea. Captain Sigmar stood on deck calling out orders for his men to set a course due East for the Vashing Kingdom. He also gave orders that once the breeze picked up they were to hoist the sail and abandon the oars. Then he strode down the deck toward Queen Geneva and her entourage. "Good day my Queen, I hope the crude living accommodations, are bearable at the very least. If the weather holds we should make good time today. I have inadequate provisions aboard that are not suitable for royal digestion, but if you so desire feel free to partake of anything the Ngalfar can provide." "Why thank you Captain,

I assure you I am not offended in the least. Your crew has been kind and provisions are more than adequate. I have not partaken of a royal diet in quite some time. I am sure the provisions you carry will be acceptable fare for all. I believe Ryob and perhaps a few others have already partaken of the ale," she said with a wink and a smile casting her eyes upon the reddened face of Ryob. "I do feel a bit of a twinge in my stomach," Bjork said, "I believe I'll sample a bit of this repast." With that he began his walk down the deck heading towards the barrels and crates. "Anyone care to join me? he said over his shoulder. Within moments the fairy men and Geneva were enjoying their morning meal. Spirits were very high as they all were so glad to be returning back to their homeland. Bjork couldn't wait to see the look upon his dear Naomi's face when she saw her mother. Her father Calliope would be filled with great joy and gratitude. The celebration would be heard from far and wide throughout the land. Perhaps King Calliope would send out royal invitations to the other kingdoms. Nothing as wonderful as this celebration had taken place in the Lands of Nod for as long as Bjork could remember. The safe return of the missing Queen would be spoken of and passed down from generation to generation. The royal scribes would be busy writing on the silken scrolls with the woven golden threads. Their impeccable calligraphy would tell this story in a gracious and artful masterpiece to be treasured in the Royal vault. It stirred excitement in Bjork's soul to think of how blessed he was to have partaken in this memorable voyage. He had ached for an adventure, but this had more than met his expectations. He truly could think of none that held a candle to it.

He looked out upon the deep blue sea with its gentle rolling waves. The crisp smell of salt air stung his nostrils a bit. He took a deep breath and held it. Looking up into the sky he could see the cottony clouds that billowed high aloft in the breeze. The wind had picked up a bit now and the oarsmen were now abandoning their posts. The large sail was being hoisted as a member of the crew scaled the mast to unfurl it. Soon the Ngalfar was picking up speed, racing along the waves, plowing into them with her prow. The Captain kept constant watch giving the rudder man instructions to keep her on course. The crew kept constant watch for pirate ships. They were traveling dangerous waters. These waters were highly traveled by cargo vessels, and were well-known to pirates. Although the Ngalfar was not a cargo vessel, she carried the colors of the Vashing Kingdom and may be mistaken for having wealthy royalty onboard. They did not dare to let their guard down. It would be a three day voyage back, if the weather held out. If they made good time they would visit Skull Island for an afternoon to restock. The Captain knew they had barely enough provisions for three days at sea. If bad weather fell upon them, they would have to be rationed. He shrugged off the thought of this. This time of the year, (spring), the weather should hold, he thought. Although he knew very well that rogue waves and other unexpected weather could fall upon his vessel at anytime. He would not rest until he had anchored in port at the Vashing Kingdom. Having much experience as a Captain, he was wary of his travels on every voyage. He enjoyed the danger and the challenge of the open sea. He had made the mistake for awhile of going into retirement. It was good at first until the weeks passed and he grew bored with the peace and quiet of the landlubber lifestyle. It was then he knew he must return to the sea. He swore on as chief Captain and advisor to King Lore and had captained many of his vessels. He also served as a tutor to young seamen, earning their Captain's title. He knew in his heart he would always love the sea and never feel at home unless his feet were standing on an open deck with the waves pitching to and fro. The motion was a comforting feeling to him, not so to the new seamen who had difficulties holding their food down. He often smiled when he saw the green look upon their face, and told them, "Come lad, toughen up, the sea will be home for many days, she pitches and rolls, but in time you will learn how to walk with her upon these planks."

The Ngalfar was the finest vessel Captain Sigmar had been placed in command of; her crew was the finest of the Vashing Kingdom. The Ngalfar being King Lore's chief transportation to allies kingdoms across the ocean. Her Captain's quarters were furnished with impeccable royal taste. Deep plush burgundy tapestries and upholstery, and walls of the finest timber, which were polished to a gleaming finish. The large wooden desk itself was covered with ornate carvings upon the drawers and legs. There was a small elegant table for dining and a well-stuffed bed covered with a hand stitched burgundy quilt. It was indeed suitable for royalty. Captain Sigmar rarely took his meals in the cabin area; he was a very simple man of simple taste and found it rather stuffy. He preferred the company of the crew and passengers and enjoyed listening to their conversation while he dined. Today he felt a sense of anxiousness which put his senses on high alert. He had come to respect his intuition and now was strangely aware of the feeling that all was not what it seemed. Although the weather was calm and the brisk wind was easily propelling the Ngalfar through the frothy waves. Her sail was billowing and the sun was shining brightly upon the deck. He stood at the railing looking out in all directions, awaiting the impending doom. He told no one of his thoughts for fear they would think he was daft. The crew sensed his somber mood and went about their business paying him no mind.

Bjork and the Nimbus fairies also noticed the Captain's odd behavior. He had been talkative and jovial the night before. Bjork wondered to himself if there were a reason to worry, but not knowing this man very well, he did not know if his moods were easily swayed. He said nothing to his comrades. Little did he know that Jeziah was busy trying to read the Captain's body language. He was the brain-stormer of the group and often was quiet, deep in concentration. He had a very serious nature, and seldom laughed at any of the comical aspects of their journey. Nimrod was busy talking with his mother, apparently neither of them sensed anything peculiar. Mahew was carving an ornate drawing into the side of a provision barrel. Ryob was partaking of the last bites of smoked fish and enjoying the view.

The afternoon passed calmly enough and by the end of day as the sun was setting, Bjork began to shrug off his earlier feelings. The Captain had given his orders to his men for the evening watch and had quietly slipped away to his cabin. Bjork began to watch the crew as they started a round of "King's Table". The watchmen were posted all around, and one had shimmied up to the crow's nest.

The evening seemed peaceful enough and as the hours wore on Bjork succumbed to the tossing of the waves which lulled him into a deep dream. The Nimbus fairies, whom never slept kept watch over their Queen. As the hours passed Nimrod noticed a strange steam rising up from the waters. It soon engulfed the Ngalfar and all the sea around her. It was then he smelled the scent of rain and realized it was a dense fog that had rolled in. He could not see either end of the vessel now and could only make out persons and objects close to him. He heard the Captain's voice call out , "Lower the sail men, we have to ride this foggy spell out slowly and cautiously. Man oars and prepare to change course rudder man!" There was such an eerie feeling as being adrift in this fog, the sounds of the waves hitting the prow sounded unfamiliar. The men stood close to the railing looking for shallow water and signs of rock, not knowing how far in either direction that the Ngalfar had drifted. It seemed the fog would never lift. Then out of the dampness and darkness of the sea, they could hear the sound of voices. These voices were not from aboard the Ngalfar. "Quiet men, the Captain whispered, we have company in these waters. I know not whether friend nor foe."

Bjork felt a huge lump raise in his throat as his heart was racing out of his chest. He swallowed and grabbed hold of his cloak. His cloak, oh yes, he remembered as he gently tapped on the list of spells in the inside pocket. There was silence aboard the Ngalfar as the voices grew closer. The crew and Captain feared a ramming, as they knew not the course of this vessel. The oarsmen stood guard ready to push off from the vessel if she approached them slowly. They feared the vessel may be moving too fast and might slam into the Ngalfar causing severe damage. Still the fog wore on deeper and thicker by the minute.

Bjork's hair felt damp, as well as his face. Time passed at a snail's pace, the voices getting clearer all the time. Then in a flash there she was headed parallel with portside, a pirate ship. They now could distinguish the pirates chatter on board as they prepared to ambush the Ngalfar. There was no time for weapon armament. Bjork hastily pulled the list from his pocket and holding it closely to his face, he saw the spell leap out from it. The cloaking spell, he would make the Ngalfar invisible to the naked eye. He touched his cloak and said , "Fiddle dee daddle gum diddity boo, make all comrades hidden from view."

Within seconds the Cursed Crusader passed by the portside, the oarsmen could have reached out and touched her, yet the pirates saw nothing. They strode the deck of the Cursed Crusader puzzled and the largest crewman of the group, scratched his bearded face saying "She was right beside us, the wretched sea has played a trick upon our Captain." "Perhaps she was a ghost ship, and she'll be coming for our very souls tonight, shuddered the small toothless portly one." Evil Gunnar appeared, "Well mateys , when this fog lifts we be changing course. I believe we'll test our luck near Skull island. Keep ye heads and watch for rocks, I don't aim to lose me vessel." Then he strode off down the deck to watch from his Captain quarters.

As always the new dawn brought the sun's rays which began burning off the fog. Soon the sun was shining brightly and Evil Gunnar could see they had drifted far off course. He could tell his bearing by the position of the sun, and gave orders to his rudder man to change course heading due east for Skull Island.

On board the Ngalfar the sail had been hoisted and she was moving along at top speed. The oarsmen had abandoned their oars and were now on high alert for signs of pirate vessels. Last night's scare had made all the crew uneasy. They were unaware of Bjork's spell and assumed the fog had hidden the Ngalfar from the pirate ship as she passed by. Bjork would keep it a secret until they reached the Vashing Kingdom. His cloak was a high-end commodity, it would fetch a fare price and he didn't want any dishonest seaman trying to steal it away. He knew the invisibility spell would only last for twenty-four hours, which was long enough to allow one to escape and get a good league ahead of the enemy.

Captain Sigmar seemed to be in good spirits today and was enjoying smoking his pipe. He waited until mid afternoon and then called his crew together. "Men we have lost precious time due to that heavy fog, which caused the Ngalfar to be adrift for some time. As you well know we were off course and now must proceed directly to the Vashing Kingdom. There is no time for stopping off at Skull Island. I believe it would be in our best interests to get the Queen back to her homeland as soon as possible. That being said we must ration our provisions and take only two meals a day." There were hushed murmurs and groans of discontent from the crew.

Bjork knew in his heart that the Captain was right in doing this. That pirate vessel was still out there and they needed to make it back without running into her or any other for that matter. It made him uneasy to have the shared responsibility of protecting the Queen.

The weather held out and before the last rays of the sun cast a red glow upon the sky and the clouds around it, the crew and the passengers finished their evening meal. The Captain gave orders to his crew for the evening and then retired once more to his cabin. Bjork knew that if the weather held and the red sky had been a very good indication that it would, they should reach the Vashing port by late tomorrow. Just one more day and he would be back on solid ground.

He sat down upon the deck, and feeling a sudden draft from the stiff sea breeze he pulled his cloak around him. He began to imagine the fabulous feast the King would have prepared for their return. He had grown tired of the smoked meats and longed for a slice of warm huckleberry pie and perhaps a cup of spiced cider. He leaned back against a tall wooden chest and closed his eyes. As he was drifting off he heard the sound of the wind and the waves, and felt the steady rocking of the Ngalfar.

He woke to laughter and the hot sun on his face. It seemed as if he had only slept for a few hours. He looked about and noticed the crew and the Nimbus fairies were chatting away and enjoying their breakfast. The wind had picked up and the Ngalfar was effortlessly plowing through the crests of the waves. Sea spray was flowing over the bow, drenching the deck, and disappearing through the drain holes. The sky was a deep blue and there were only white cottony clouds that floated high aloft. The water was a spectacular hue of turquoise and every once in a while Bjork would spy a flying fish, or the fin of dolphin. This would be a glorious day, the day of their victorious return. The Captain was speaking now, he had a smile upon his deep wrinkled face, as he said, "We have made good time during the night, God speed us to our home port. If I calculate our position I would estimate we shall be sitting at dock before this sun sets. I know you will miss these tasty provisions, and will miss sleeping upon a damp hard deck." Then he laughed and walked down the deck looking out to sea.

Bjork kept his attention on the sea around him, and was glad to see that the Ngalfar was sailing alone. Every now and then he would look at Geneva and smile knowing how much his Naomi had missed her. There would be two grand celebrations upon their return, one from the Vashings and another from the Nimbus fairies. This would indeed be a very happy time in the Lands of Nod. He hadn't thought about his own homeland for awhile, but now he wondered if he had been missed. He longed for his own comfortable bed and his unfinished reading of "The Tales of the Wimpet King." He had desired an adventure and this had been a grand one, of epic proportion, yet he now felt like a tired old Hork, longing for home and longing to see his dear Naomi again. Even upon their return to the Vashing Kingdom, their travels back through The Land of the Cyclops to the Eastern side of Horkland awaited them. It would still be a few days before he reached his home. Dangerous travels? With Queen Geneva and his Nimbus friends. They would have to take every precaution to see that the Queen safely reached the Fairy Meadow. He shook this off and thought, I won't let this worry spoil the grand celebration by King Lore. Then he began to watch and wait for the first signs of the long-ships.

 The Vashing Kingdom had a large port and many vessels traveled there to do trade with king Lore. The king had quite a large fleet of his own so Bjork knew that soon they would be greeted by allies at sea. It was customary to blow one long note on the Ram's horn to acknowledge the ally vessel. He felt anxious as he waited for the first horn blow. Captain Sigmar had his horn blower standing in wait on the forward deck. The large horn hung from a leather strap around the burly man's neck. The man had unruly red hair and green eyes and by the size of his arms, he was not to be taken lightly. He looked much more like a warrior than a horn blower, Bjork thought.

A few minutes passed by and then he heard the faint sound of a horn, growing louder in the distance. The horn blower looked in the direction where the noise had come and could now see out over the water a large long-ship off the stern. She bore the colors of the Vashing Kingdom. Then as the horn blower blew a long note back, there came more horns resounding over the open waters, and as they passed by a small remote island and the port came into view, they saw many vessels were in port. They looked behind them and could see more heading toward them, off portside and off leeward side too. There were perhaps ten vessels or more all headed for the Vashing port. The sun was setting now as the rudder man and oarsmen carefully and skillfully brought the Ngalfar into dock side. The sail had been lowered at quite a distance from shore and was now being carefully tacked down. The Vashing Castle stood in its splendor high above the port. Bjork could see the tiny specks of travelers moving across the bridge to and from the Castle. The evening torches would soon be lit.

The Captain called a meeting with the crew and the men were chosen who would keep watch over the Ngalfar that night. "Come on then," he said to the rest of his crew. "Men stand guard in front and at the rear of the line. Nimbus fairies and Queen Geneva are to be in the center of the line, (of course Bjork the Hork shall also accompany them). I will be in the lead as I have my walking papers to show the guards of the bridge. Make haste I want to be safely within the Castle's walls before nightfall."

Quickly they disembarked doing just as the Captain had ordered. The stronger more intimidating warriors taking the lead and the rear and the fairy clan and Bjork wedged in between. The stone path that climbed up to the Castle seemed to be shorter than he remembered, but also when he first trod it, he was not in such a hurry to get to the top. He had been wary of this strange new Kingdom and its peoples. Knowing that his fears were ill found, he now was in a hurry to reach the Castle door. As the Captain reached the top first, he reached into his tunic and presented a set of papers to the guard. The guard then handed the papers back, blew on his horn across the moat, and hearing a returned note blown back from the other side he waved him on.

The group continued to climb until Bjork himself was passing the guard, he noticed with amusement that it was indeed the very same one he had encountered on his first trip here. "Hello Bjork isn't it?," Darryl the guard said with a sheepish smile." "Why yes it is, I'm a bit surprised that you remember me, though," said Bjork.
"Ah it's easy to remember ye, the Vashing don see many Hork here," he said with a deep belly laugh. Bjork stepped out upon the bridge eager to greet the other guard,(Jarrel), upon the other side. "Hello there me friend,"Jarrel said. "It's good to see ye fared well on ye voyage. Word has been sent ahead to King Lore, he shall be awaiting ye and the Nimbus fairy Queen. There be a grand celebration

tonight, in ye honor." Then he waved his hand toward the castle door which was open.

The Nimbus fairies and the Captain's crew were standing in the hall. As the last of the group filed into the hallway Bjork heard the familiar sound of the creaking of the ropes and the gears as the huge door was lowered. This gave Bjork a great sense of security. The entrance hall seemed grander than he remembered, and the guards on either side seemed less intimidating. Once again they were greeted by the King's guards who escorted them off into the acceptance room. "Wait here, one of the guards said, "I will announce thy arrival to the King." Then he scuffled away and began the long ascent up the stairs leading to the upper chamber.

The Captain and his men and the nimbus fairies were admiring all of the fine statues and treasures of the Castle. Geneva was entranced by it all, it being her first visit to the Vashing Kingdom. Bjork was also noticing how quiet everyone was, all seeming to be preoccupied with their thoughts. In the distance he could hear voices, then coming closer they became recognizable. He stood looking at the end of the acceptance area where the guard had vanished, waiting, patiently. Then he heard the distinct sound of boots upon the well polished castle floor, one set moving slower than the other. In time they rounded the corner and stood in front of the Ngalfar's entourage. Bjork was amused and pleased to see it was none other but Prince Lars and King Lore himself.
The young prince was assisting his father by allowing the King to lean on him as they

walked. Prince Lars extended their welcome with a large flashing smile and a sparkle in his blue eyes. "Welcome back to our home, Father and I would like to commend ye on thy successful mission. We will be holding a celebration in the grand ballroom tonight in honor of the Nimbus fairy Queen Geneva. Please do follow our servants to thy guest quarters, where ye may take rest and freshen up a bit for tonight's event."

He was a stunning young lad dressed in spun silk of golden yellow and a burgundy sash. His blonde long braid was draped across one shoulder. His father King Lore was also dressed in spun silk. His robe was a deep burgundy with a golden sash. His long grey braid was draped across his back. Upon his head was his gold crown bearing his name "Lore" and encased with rows of rubies and pearls. He looked old and frail in comparison to his young son. Yet there was a strong resemblance to each other. It was evident that his son was now blossoming into a robust young man, the muscles were more defined. Soon he would be King, Bjork thought. What a fine King he would make; the lad had all the good qualities of a child destined to be great.

The King's servants appeared and soon all of the guests were being shuttled off in different directions to their assigned guest rooms. Bjork was looking forward to the evening festivities; he was very pleased with his accommodations. He also was pleased to see that the servant was drawing him a nice warm bath. Upon the bed was a new tunic and trousers, provided by the King. The servant woman spoke, "I hope the temperature of ye bath is suitable and if the clothing provided does not fit ye properly I can have the King's tailor make some adjustments," she said with a smile. She was an older woman with a portly figure and a warm smile, her hair of grey neatly wound and placed upon her head. She was dressed in the servant attire of a drab grey dress and a white apron. "I'm sure it will be just fine, thank you, "Bork said. She left the room and Bjork went to the door and closed it, latching it behind her.

In no time he was up to his neck in warm sudsy water. It never felt so good as this he thought. He enjoyed a rather long bath and then drying off he decided to try on the clothing provided. First the tunic, which fit perfectly, then the trousers, once again a perfect fit. He groomed his beard in front of the large mirror upon the wall and ran a comb that he found lying on the dresser through his fine grey hair. Then admiring his new look, he stepped out of his room and headed toward the grand ballroom. His stomach had begun to grumble as he realized it had been a long time since his last meal. He could hear his footsteps upon the highly polished tile floors. It sounded so strange and hollow in these halls. Where were the others?

The Castle was immense and Bjork not being familiar with its winding passages, soon found himself to be disoriented. He didn't know which path to take as he came to hallways that crossed each other. Which way? which way? he pondered, as he held his ear toward the halls direction, waiting for the sounds of his companions, or the Vashings. Finally he decided to take the path to his left which seemed to go on for many steps before ending at the junction of another hallway. There were doors on either sound of the immense hallway that ran its length. He stopped at them and put his ear to the wood. Eerily quiet, no sounds from within or without. Still he continued on when he reached about half way down the hallway he began to hear the faint sound of music. Getting closer the notes grew louder and seemed to be coming from the end of the hall near the junction.

He walked quickly now, as this hallway seemed to be void of all people, and he felt yet the presence of someone or something watching him. He could not shake the feeling, which made him very uncomfortable. At last he was at the end of the hall and looking toward the left of the adjoining hallway, he noticed an open door, with laughter from within. He moved to the doorway and looking inside he noticed a very large kitchen area.

There were many servants busy stirring pots and chopping vegetables. He could smell the scent of fresh baked pies and breads. A rather large and stout fellow wearing an apron, pointed his large wooden spoon in his direction and exclaimed, "Out of me kitchen, there be no guests in here, me recipes are me own. Scoot now, out the door and turn to ye right through the archway, this will take ye to the Grand Ballroom. Dinner be served in one hour." Bjork felt himself blush as he backed out of the doorway and followed the cook's orders. As he turned toward the right he saw the large arched doorway with two of the King's guards at each side. They wore the royal Vashing colors of gold and burgundy and stood perfectly still with arms crossed. They both smiled when they saw Bjork and then waved him inside the arch in unison. Bjork returned their friendly smile and continued inside. He was now in a huge reception area decorated with fine statues and oil paintings. The walls and furnishings were draped with fine linens and silks from around the world. Looking up there was a huge raised domed ceiling, with a large oil painted mural upon it. The mural was a seascape with Vashing long ships. He could hear loud music now coming from another large archway located directly across the room. As he began to walk towards it, he heard a loud voice and then suddenly from out of the archway stepped Nimrod. "Bjork, I see you have found the dining room, come inside and sit with me and Mother. She wishes your company this evening." Nimrod pulled gently on Bjork's arm as he led him into the Grand Dining Room.

The room was filled with tables lined with tablecloths, and off to the side was a group of musicians. There were many servants hustling and bustling about placing flower arrangements as centerpieces on the tables. The tables were being set with the finest china dishes and crystal goblets. Fine linen napkins were placed at each setting along with fine silver utensils. The kitchen servants were seen entering from another small doorway carrying in platters of steaming food. Some of the other tables were being set up as buffet tables, laden with every sort of delicacy known to man, and some Bjork had never heard of. There were many women dressed in their native attire, ready to perform their dances at the King's command. In the far right corner there was a special table reserved for "royalty" only. It was here that King Lore and his son would sit. The boy's mother had passed on during childbirth, and he had been raised by the King's private nanny. He was born when King Lore was getting on in age and was the sole heir to the throne. The King had taken his other wives only recently as he needed full time care in his old age, and he also deeply missed the Prince's mother. Most days he spent reading, and napping. He had grown far too old, and soon the Prince would assume his position as King of the Vashings. The Prince was learning his skills at combat and foreign diplomacy. King lore would retire his reign within the year, upon his son Lars sixteenth birthday. Syncore had divulged this information to the Nimbus fairies and Bjork and they had sworn themselves to secrecy. Once that a Nimbus fairy or a Hork took a vow of secrecy, it was to be trusted that they would die to keep the secret from being divulged. Syncore himself had not taken a vow, but had heard of this while eavesdropping during a visit at the Vashing Castle. He had overheard the nanny talking to King Lore. All of these thoughts now came rushing into Bjork's head as he prepared for the evening feast and festivities. It would indeed be a grand event.

He let Nimrod lead him to the table where his mother sat. Geneva looked very beautiful and content Bjork thought, he could see the fine resemblance that her daughter Naomi bore. He imagined many years from now Naomi would look like Geneva, (Long, long years from now, when Bjork himself would no longer be among the living in The Lands of Nod.) Being a Hork his life span was not anywhere close to that of the Nimbus fairies. The thought made him swallow hard, as he pushed it away. This is time for rejoicing and celebration, I won't think of such sad circumstances he thought.

"Hello my dear friend, Bjork," Geneva said as she extended her hand and gestured toward the empty seat next to her.
It was at this time that the chatter of the ballroom guests came to an abrupt stop. A messenger boy stood in the hall excitedly talking to the Vashing guards, "He has just now arrived, and his prisoner has been taken to the Castle Dungeon," the lad proclaimed. "I have been given orders by the Captain to personally relay this message to the King."
"Wait here lad, His Majesty will be attending the evening ceremony, he shall be along shortly," the tallest guard said. "Ye may wait in the dining room near his table," he said while he pointed inside the room toward the King's table. The young messenger was dressed in the attire of a Captain's steward. His unkempt brown hair hung across his forehead and in front of his eyes, which he kept brushing away in a futile attempt to groom it. He looked rather awkward standing there avoiding the stares of all the dining room occupants. Bjork felt sorry for him and decided he would keep the lad company. "Excuse me dear Geneva this poor lad looks lonely over there, I believe I'll introduce myself to him," he said as he rose from his seat and strode across the dining room floor.

The boy looked up as he saw Bjork approaching; he had a look of apprehension upon his face. "Hello lad, I be Bjork the Hork, and whom may you be?" Bjork said as he extended his hand. Grasping Bjork's hand and giving it a firm shake, the grinning lad answered, "I'm Benjamin Winkle, chief steward to Captain Syncore, very glad to make your acquaintance." Soon they were both chatting away as the lad told Bjork that the Drakkar had just arrived back in port. Syncore and his mates were guests as well of the celebration and they were in their guest rooms preparing for the evening festivities. What a grand party this would be. King lore would be very well pleased to see his Captain's return and to find that they had succeeded in capturing the rogue pirate thief of the Ægileif.

The announcement of the King's arrival came with the sounding of trumpets. Bjork stepped back and said, "I best be returning to my seat, it was very nice speaking with you Benjamin." He hurriedly found his way back as the sounds of feet crossing the outer hall came closer to the ballroom archway. Then slowly on the arm of his son Lars the King entered into the dining room and took his place at his table. His son Lars sat down beside him as the messenger approached them both. "King Lore I have been ordered by my Captain Syncore to relay to you the message that the Ægileif has been lost at sea. The thief responsible for her demise has been captured and is none other than the evil pirate One Eyed Jack, who now lies shackled and bound in your castle's dungeon." Then he bowed and presented the King with Syncore's sworn statement written on a scroll and neatly bound with ribbon.

King Lore slowly rose from his seat to announce, "Me friends and fellowmen, it is with much gladness that I announce the return of me Captains and their crews. Sadly the Ægileif is lost at the bottom of the sea but because of Syncore's loyalty the pirate responsible for this act of piracy is now held in me dungeon awaiting me decree. I also would like to add that we have a much honored guest present tonight as well. The Nimbus fairy Queen Geneva is with us, along with her son Nimrod and his comrades. Let there be music, dancing and feasting in the Vashing Kingdom ! All is well, all is well! I also wish to announce that in a fortnight it will be Prince Lars sixteenth birthday. Ye are all welcome to stay on for the new King's Coronation, I will be relinquishing me crown. It has been a long reign, but a joyous one and now me age and health fails me, so it is time for a fresh young King to lead our people. The Vashings will have a King with compassion and honesty, a King with a deep loyalty to the Vashing people. This King will be none other than me son Lars. Now please enjoy the festivities and the fine delicacies prepared by me finest chefs. Let the music begin."

Then the aged King sat down upon his seat waiting for his servants to begin the serving of the feast. The musicians began to play gaily as the women began to dance and twirl in unison with the beat. Prince Lars was a charming host and led the festivities with his command of the musicians and his requests for different songs and dances performed. The food was absolutely delicious, and the variety was immense. There were so many different foods from far off cultures and delicacies that Bjork had never heard of before. The ale was a special blend of old secret Vashing recipes. Queen Geneva and the Nimbus fairies were enjoying the evening listening to old seaman's tales.

Syncore had arrived dressed in fine Vashing attire and was content to entertain the curiosity of the Nimbus Queen. There were so many tales of far off lands that Syncore could tell, and as the evening wore on he had drawn quite an audience. He was seated at a table behind Queen Geneva, and eventually she turned her chair around to better hear his tales. The other crew members as well as Captain Sigmar were seated near Syncore and they too turned their chairs in toward his table. Bjork was absolutely entranced with Syncore's tales of adventure. The way he described the scenery made Bjork feel as if he had been there before.

Syncore had experienced so much in a very little amount of time. He was a young man, yet his experience at sea could easily match that of a much more seasoned seaman. The voyages he had been on were requisitioned by the King and were full of mystery and danger. He had traveled to faraway lands, where vessels had never dared to sail before in pursuit of knowledge and exotic goods. King Lore was a man of impeccable taste and had quite an impressive collection of foreign art and crafts. His collection was like no other in the world. He was always in pursuit of something rare to add to his accumulation. The guests were held captive to Syncore's every word.

The evening wore on and when the last of the feast had been consumed along with the Vashing ale, Prince Lars returned to his father's table. The Prince had been spending a bit of time at each table socializing with the guests. The King had fallen asleep, his chin upon his chest. Prince Lars motioned to the King's royal servants to assist him in escorting the King to his chambers. "I will bid ye farewell for the evening, me Father wishes to thank ye for thy attendance. Feel free to stay in the guest room that was first assigned to ye. We do so hope that ye all will stay on for a fortnight until the Coronation. I will be seeing ye tomorrow for the breakfast feast. King Lore may not attend depending upon his condition. He tends to dine in his chambers more often than not." Then without delay the royal servants and Prince Lars helped the aged King to his feet and taking his arms gently led him out of the ballroom.

Their voices could be heard echoing off the Castle walls as they traveled through the hallways. Bjork feeling quite tired himself after the long evening rose from his chair and paid his respects to his Nimbus fairy friends. He bowed to the Queen Fairy and looking about the room he said, "Geneva, Nimrod, and all my comrades I will be turning in myself. Will we be staying for the Coronation?"
"I am anxious to see my homeland and my dear husband and daughter, yet I don't wish to insult the good King. After all it was because of him and his Captain that I was rescued from Leprechaun Isle," Geneva said. "Bjork, in answer to your question I must say, yes we will be staying on for the Coronation." Then Bjork strode off down the dim lit hallways and passages, lit by the flickering torches on the walls in search of his guest room. He was pleasantly surprised to find it

was much easier to find on the return trip. He opened the door and seeing that his bed had been turned down and a fire lit in his hearth, he closed the door. On the table near his bed was a book. Upon closer examination he could read the title, "The Tales of The Wimpet King." Oh my how convenient he thought that the very book he was reading at home would be lying in his guest room. He would enjoy this stay at the Vashing Castle and he could catch up on his reading also. An eerie thought came to mind, could it be that the King had a wizard that had read Bjork's mind? (a wizard with powers to conjure up a copy of his favorite book?) Nah, he thought I'm an old tired Hork letting my imagination run off with itself. Then he disrobed and climbed into the comfortable bed, blew out the candle on the table and fell into a deep and blissful sleep. A sleep filled with old memories from his homeland, days of yore when he was but a Hork lad and Naomi was his new love.

CHAPTER 14.

A NEW JOURNEY

Bjork was pleasantly surprised when he awoke to the familiar voice of his friend Nimrod. "Must you sleep life away? We have things to explore in this Vashing Kingdom. So up with you now, I'll be waiting in the dining room. I know you well my friend and you need a good breakfast to start off the day." Then Nimrod left and Bjork rose and got himself dressed and his face washed.

He lifted the window sash and looking outside he could just see the sun rising over the waters. It must be very early, no wonder I was still in bed he thought. It was a beautiful day though and he wasn't going to let Nimrod upset him. He did feel a bit hungry and so he was looking forward to a nice breakfast. He was soon walking down the halls leading to the dining room.

As he entered the dining room he could see his fairy men friends and Queen Geneva sitting at the table. There were servants scurrying in and out pouring hot liquids and carrying in steaming bowls of hot porridge. There were platters of fresh fruits. Bjork could see there were many different types of fruit, some of which he had never eaten. He drank from the steaming cup of hot tea, and quickly ate his steaming bowl of porridge only stopping every few minutes to blow on each spoonful before consuming it. He then ate a sample of each delicious fruit and washed it down with more tea. When he had finished he pushed his dishes away and rose. A good brisk walk and some fresh salt air would be just the thing to aid in his digestion he thought.

"Coming, Nimrod? He asked as he began to walk towards the front entrance hall. Nimrod hurried to keep up with him. When they reached the castle door Bjork said to the guards, "Good morning men, my friend and I would like to venture out for a bit of fresh air." "Do enjoy thy walk," the guard said with a smile as he motioned to the other guard to raise the door.

The ancient door began its ascension with the creaking of the gears. As it opened Bjork could see the sun was now higher in the cloudless sky and he could feel the cool chill from the ocean breeze. Together they stepped out upon the bridge that would lead to the stone path, the path which would bring them down from the cliff to the Vashing seashore. They could see the impressive long ships that were moored along with the cargo vessels from faraway lands. The decks of the cargo ships were full of busy crew members, loading and unloading wares. The long ship decks were mostly vacant except for the security and maintenance crews that were always aboard.

The ocean was calm as gentle waves rolled into shore when they finally reached the bottom and began to stroll along the beach. "I wonder what lies beyond this cove," Nimrod said. "We have many hours of daylight my friend. Let's find out the answer to your question," Bjork said as he began to walk in the general direction of the area which Nimrod had spoken of. Looking up the cliff sides they could see the growth of wild plants that had wedged themselves into the rocks. At the very top the land grew flat and they could not determine if there were wooded areas beyond the rim or not. The cove was protected by the cliff's wall which ran its length, but the end of the cove had a small well-beaten path that rounded the outside tip, leading to another side. What lie on the other side they did not know and this gave them a sense of exploration and anticipation as to what it could possibly be. It seemed to be a lot closer when they started, but after walking for a spell they realized it would be longer than anticipated before they reached the end.

The weather was pleasant enough and the ocean was calm as it rode into the shore bringing with it seashells and bits of seaweed. The seagulls were busy flying to and fro and the sandpipers were chasing the waves. Bjork had a very pleasant peaceful feeling of well being. He was also looking forward to Prince Lars coronation ceremony. Nimrod was in a cheerful mood as well and Bjork found it a bit difficult to keep up with him. "We have plenty of time my friend, please do slow down a bit, you are wearing out this old Hork," Bjork said. Nimrod hearing this laughed and said, "Very well Bjork, we can go at an easier pace," as he leaned against the cliff wall waiting for Bjork to catch up to him. Soon he reached Nimrod's side and they began to travel slowly toward the outside tip of the cove. The position of the sun told Bjork that it was late in the morning when they finally reached the well-beaten path.

Nimrod stepped out first and then swung his head around the edge of the cliff to see where the path was leading. He then stepped back and with a smile said, "It leads to a long barren beach that has mossy hills with large trees behind it. "There is no sign of inhabitants from here, but way down the beach I see smoke rising, perhaps from a campfire", Nimrod said. Then they both continued on the beaten path around the edge of the cliff until they stood on the sandy beach. Behind Bjork rose the backside of the tall cliff that had separated the sheltered cove from this side of the island. He could see way off down the shoreline the smoke of which Nimrod had spoken. As he looked to his right he could see the many tall rolling moss covered hills that were covered with smatterings of rock and pine trees. They had passed the cave entrance that led to the land of the Cyclops long ago on the other side of the cliff. Now Bjork wondered if this too was the Land of the Cyclops and they had only found another route to bring them there. The cave had traveled deep underground and its paths had turned and twisted along the way, so he couldn't really say which direction it had led him. Now he felt a sense of apprehension as he and Nimrod continued down the seashore heading toward the smoke. What would they find when they reached it? Would it be friend or foe? Neither one of them had come armed, Bjork did have his cloak and the book of spells were still tucked away in the inside pocket. He determined to not get too close until he was sure that the smoke came from a friendly campfire. He felt as though he was being watched out in the open, yet turning around he couldn't distinguish any evidence that he was. Still he kept on guard as they were now getting very close to the smoke and could see clearly that it was indeed a campfire. Strangely enough there was no one near it. There were some clothes hanging from a makeshift line between two pine trees nearby. They stopped and began looking and listening in all directions. They could hear some rustling in the wooded area upon the hill to their right. So they stood perfectly still and waited. Bjork's heart was beating very fast as the rustling became louder and with the bending of the tall brush a shape appeared on the downside of the hill.

A short stature portly fellow emerged with a
red scraggly head of hair. Seeing Bjork and
Nimrod he stopped and looked behind him as
if he was about to run off. Then another man
appeared looking similar in stature and age,
perhaps brothers, Bjork thought. This man
upon seeing Nimrod and Bjork said, "We are
shipwreck survivors, we meant no harm, just
a bit of fire to dry our clothes. We apologize for
invading the beach." Nimrod threw back his
head and laughed, "Sir we don't own this
beach we are visitors as well. I'm Nimrod and
this is Bjork the Hork we are pleased to meet
your acquaintance."

The strangers began to tell their tale of being
held captive aboard a handmade raft by the
notorious One-Eyed Jack. They then were
banished into the sea before the raft was
smashed up on the rocks near an island. They
had managed to swim ashore and stow away
aboard a vessel moored on the other side of
the island. They were unfortunately found by
the crew members the next day, whom were a
very accommodating bunch of Leprechauns.
They agreed to take them as far as the
Vashing Kingdom as they were off on a trip to
Skull Island to do some trading. By the
description of the vessel, it seemed to Bjork
they had been dropped off in port by the crew
of the Muirin. What a small world Bjork
thought, small indeed. Nimrod and Bjork filled
in their new friends with the information
about the capture of One-Eyed-Jack by
Syncore the Sailor. They encouraged the two
men to follow them back to the Vashing Castle
where they would have much better chance at

gaining employment on one of the King's vessels, or perhaps working in his Kingdom.

The sun was getting lower in the sky and they knew they must turn back now as it was at least a couple of hours before they would reach the Vashing port. They doused the fire with seawater and then gathered their meager belongings rolled them up in old clothing and slung them upon their shoulder. The air was crisp and a gentle ocean breeze kept them cool as they hiked their way back around the edge of the cliff to the other side. The ocean was still gently bringing its waves into shore, the sandpipers still running along the water's edge and the seagulls soaring above, nothing much had changed except for the shadows cast upon the shoreline from the cliff above. It made for a cool walk back to the Vashing port. They could see the fine vessels gleaming in the rays of the setting sun as they finally reached the end of the shoreline and began the ascent to the Castle's bridge. This had been an enjoyable day and Bjork knew the evening too would be full of more interesting conversation along with a delicious feast. He was suddenly very ravenous, realizing he had not eaten in many hours.

The guards still stood waiting as if they were permanent fixtures. He knew it took great discipline to keep at a post for so many hours. How they did it without going mad from the monotony Bjork did not know. He was not aware of the fact that they entertained themselves with strategic mind games and memorization of historic Vashing events and dates to keep themselves sharp. He would find out much more later when the guards were relieved by their warrior substitutes for the Coronation. The Kingdom would be on high alert during the ceremony and only the strongest and most accomplished warriors were allowed to guard the bridge and the castle's great door.

They reached the door just as the last of the sun went beneath their view and darkness fell on the Vashing Kingdom. The guard was cheerful and inquired as to their day, whether they had enjoyed themselves. They were careful about allowing the strangers to gain entrance, but trusting Bjork and Nimrod's recommendation the guard opened the castle door. It began its creaking ascent and they squinted at first to adjust their eyes to the flickering light of the wall torches. One of the guards inside the door excused himself saying for them to wait until the King gave his permission for the strangers to enter into the main reception area. Bjork and Nimrod waited as well even though they were told they could enter. A few moments later the guard returned along with Prince Lars. "Welcome to me father's castle gentlemen, please follow me, servants are waiting to take ye to thy chambers, where ye can freshen up before tonight's supper is served. Bjork, Nimrod, I hope thy day has been a good one and our hospitality has met thy expectations. I do look forward to speaking with ye tonight, please join father and I at our table." Then he promptly left and walked off down the hall with the two strangers taking up the rear.

The evening was full of good food and conversation as Bjork and Nimrod sat with King Lore and his son Lars filling them in on the details about the new strangers. "What may their names be?" Nimrod asked Bjork. "That's odd but I don't remember them introducing their selves to us", Bjork said. "Well then Bjork call them over here for a proper introduction," said Lars. Bjork rose and quickly walked to the table where the two strangers were sitting. "Excuse me sirs, but the King wishes to meet you, please accompany me to his table."

The two young men rose and soon they were standing in front of the King's table with Bjork. "Your Highness these are the men I spoke of. I apologize sirs, but I don't know your names, to properly introduce you," he said glancing over his shoulder at them.

The taller of the two stepped forward first, "Thy majesty I am Drake Mclandish and this fellow is me younger brother Harold, then they both bowed in unison. We hail from Wimpet Island which is ten days passage across the seven seas near the Bay of Bewilderment. We had been in port with our comrades aboard the Marauder doing trade with thy merchants, when one night we noticed thy splendid vessel, the Ægileif in harbor. We asked the crew members left on board if we could come aboard to admire her more closely. It was then that a despicable pirate One-eyed-Jack took possession and forced us at dagger point to assist him in sailing her away from the Vashing Kingdom. It was a pity that the Captain had left her in the hands of only a few young waifs. The warriors of the crew and the Captain were onshore. Through a turn and twist of fate the Ægileif was lost, we were banished to the sea by the evil pirate and after being rescued by another vessel we were brought back to this very port. We were in hiding on the other side of the cliffs, afraid that the evil pirate would find us, or we would be blamed for the fate of the Ægileif. We humbly apologize for any hand that we may have had in the theft of thy splendid vessel. We offer our services to ye to repay this terrible deed."

King lore and Prince Lars listened intently to Drake Mclandish, then King Lore spoke. "Gentlemen ye were not responsible for the demise of the Ægileif. Ye also were victims of the dastardly scoundrel One-Eyed_Jack. He lies in shackles in me dungeon now awaiting his fate. Do make me Kingdom home for as long as ye wish. If ye seek passage to Wimpet Island I'm sure another of thy vessels shall be in me port before the year's end. I do so love the aromatic spices that wonderful island has. I'm always in need of more. Now enjoy the evening. I'm afraid being an old King I need to retire for the evening." Then he rose and Lars being a loyal and loving son, grabbed his feeble arm and carefully led him off down the halls to his chambers.

Bjork finished his delicious dessert, and rose himself. "Good evening everyone," he said. Bjork then began his walk back to his chamber. Wimpet Island he thought, how small this world is, why that is the very island I have been reading about in The Tales of the Wimpet King. He was anxious now to continue his conversation with the Mclandish brothers tomorrow. He was very intrigued and curious as to what knowledge he could glean from speaking with these two young men. Perhaps they knew the very Wimpet King whom Bjork was reading about. He remembered fondly his displaced Wimpet friends who lived in the Troll forest, relatives of those on Wimpet Isle. He also remembered the wise Methezdah who had given him his copy of The Tales of the Wimpet King. He remembered its inscription reminding him to believe in miracles.

This adventure had now woven itself into his past experiences with the Wimpet people. Bjork was a believer in fate and he now knew that he was placed here at this moment in time to meet with two true inhabitants of Wimpet Isle, to learn more of these people and their history. He reached his chamber and removed his outer clothing and crept into bed. Too tired to read tonight, he closed his weary eyes and fell into a fitful sleep full of strange dreams.

Upon arising in the early morn, he dressed quickly and washed the sleep from his face. Then he ran a comb through his sparse hair and headed out down the hall toward the dining room. He could smell the wonderful scents of breakfast as he entered the room and spying the Mclandish boys he approached an empty seat nearby. "Do you mind if I join you?" he inquired. "By all means do join us Bjork we are eager to get to know ye better."

Through the sampling of the morning fare and sips of hot steaming tea, Bjork familiarized himself with the Wimpets. He told them of his past experience with the Wimpets of the Troll Forest and the great wise Wimpet Methezdah whom had given him the book, "Tales of the Wimpet King." "Ah yes we have heard of Methezdah, they said. It is told that he was lost at sea many years ago with his family. We also know of the book which ye are speaking of. It was written by our King in the year of the Wimpet Wars. Many years before our father was born. It is a vital part of our heritage. Our reigning King would be that King's great great grandson. In Wimpet years we speak, years which number far more than human kind. Me brother and I are but humble peasants and servants of our King. We served him for many years by tending his crops and livestock, most recently by working aboard his trade ships. He is a fine and honorable King, King George. When we return to our homeland we will have much to tell him, and hopefully we may bring back some rare treasures from King Lore in trade for the spices he requires."

It was only a few days more until the Coronation and the Castle servants were busy making preparations. The great hall would be fully decorated and the Prince would be fitted for a new wardrobe complete with a flowing robe. The crown along with its many gems would be polished carefully. The cooks would be planning a magnificent feast like no other before. The tailors were busy sewing new upholstery for the throne and the matching curtains in the Throne Room. The last act of King Lore would be the decree of punishment set for One-Eyed-Jack. The castle had been filled with gossip of when this would occur. It was just this morning that Bjork had overheard the King's aides speaking of this taking place soon, perhaps this very evening. He was anxious to see what the fate of the pirate would be. He knew King Lore was more than fair with his decrees, and he also knew that the Ægileif had been his favored vessel for traveling to distant lands in the days when he was younger and more agile.

Bjork was in the mood for a long walk as the weather was splendid. He had noticed how nice it was from his chamber window this morning. So not wishing to disturb his fellow Nimbus fairy friends whom were busy with parlor games with the Wimpets and Queen Geneva, Bjork decided to strike out on his own. He did ask King Lore's aides if he could accompany Sulton on his daily walk.

Sulton was a handsome dog of pedigree. He was a perfect specimen for a Norwegian elkhound. He also held the title of The King's finest hunting dog. Bjork was fond of dogs and although at the present time he did not own one himself, he did enjoy being in their company. He also felt safe with this trusty dog by his side. He promised the chief aide Beauregard that they would stay on the east side of the cliffs and only walk the shoreline. He would return in a few hours, in plenty of time for the noontime meal. The guards quickly let him pass as they recognized the King's hunting dog. They did stop for a brief moment to pet Sulton though, which thoroughly enjoyed the attention. Soon Bjork and Sulton were across the bridge and descending the stone path to the beach. Sulton was enjoying the ocean breeze upon his face and keeping in close stride with Bjork. Bjork noticed there were many vessels in port now. There would be even more arriving from distant lands to attend the Coronation. He was pleased that he would be staying on to meet the interesting guests and to admire their splendid ships. Geneva had been very gracious in accepting as Bjork knew she really longed to be at home in the Fairy Meadow with her husband Calliope and daughter Naomi. It was a sacrifice on her part to stay on to pay her respects to the Vashing people and their new crowned King.

Bjork's thoughts were wandering now to Horkland and his own sweet home, his family and his friends, he now missed very much. He missed the comfort of his own humble abode and his soft down feathered bed. Sulton and Bjork walked on, the salt air crisp in their lungs and the smells of seaweed upon their nostrils. The ocean was a royal blue today and she was not quite as calm as she had been when he went on his last walk. The tide was coming in, so they had to hurry along the narrow shoreline where the beach was a thin strand before the cliff. Even so from time to time a large wave would roll in and wet their feet and the hems of Bjork's trousers.

Bjork had removed his shoes a while back and was enjoying the feeling of the ocean waves upon his bare feet, and the way the ocean tried to pull him out with her as each wave ebbed. He was oblivious to time and sooner than anticipated they reached the end of the beach. He knew he had promised the aide they would not go beyond this point, even so he was quite tempted. So he stopped for a bit to pick up a seashell and then to his dismay he noticed that Sulton was at the edge of the cliff with his head looking around the rock to the other side. "Sulton come here boy," Bjork called gently. Sulton promptly obeyed and then they began the long walk back down the beach. Perhaps I'll explore the other side before we leave this Castle, I'll see if Nimrod and the others would like a bit of adventure. I'll ask them today at noon meal, he thought. He had been a bit afraid when it was only he and Nimrod, but if the rest of the Nimbus fairies came along too, especially if the deep thinker Jeziah was along for the trip, he would feel less anxious about what they may encounter on the west side of the cliff.

When he reached the path which led to the bridge he was feeling content, it had been an enjoyable walk with Sulton and now he had worked up a bit of an appetite. The guards were friendly as always and soon Bjork found himself entering the familiar reception hall. The King's aid was busy talking with the tailor, when he noticed Bjork he promptly excused himself and began to lead Sulton off in the direction of the King's chambers. "Come along Bjork the aid called," the King wishes to speak with ye before the noon time meal is served.

Bjork had never stepped foot inside the King's chambers so he was a bit hesitant at first, until Sulton tugged at the hem of his shirt. He followed dutifully and was led to two large swinging doors which opened out onto a large veranda. The King had a huge courtyard outside of his veranda and this was where he often would spend the daylight hours. Here Sulton loyally took up post at his side.

It was a beautiful day with a crisp ocean breeze which rustled the leaves on the tall oak trees inside the courtyard. The courtyard was enclosed on all side by tall well trimmed hedges, giving it more privacy and security.

King Lore was sitting on a stone bench shaded by a large oak. He was reading from a scroll of some sort when Bjork and his aid approached. Hearing their footsteps the great wise King lifted his grey head and motioned to Bjork to sit next to him on the bench. Bjork was curious as to what the King would want with a simple Hork such as himself.

Taking his seat near the King he waited patiently as King Lore finished reading the scroll and then carefully rolled it up and handed it back to his aid. "Bjork, I have been thinking it would be rude for me to not invite Queen Geneva's husband and daughter to the Coronation. I also know that traveling from their meadow to the Vashing Kingdom could be dangerous. There for I am asking ye me friend to accompany Syncore on this expedition. Ye are to bring along this royal invitation and two of me finest warriors will accompany ye as well. If the Nimbus fairy King and his daughter wish to attend, which I am sure they will, (after being informed that the Queen and Nimrod are here), then I am instructing ye to bring them back safely. Me warriors will bring along duffel bags, as well as ye and Syncore, this will disguise ye as vagabonds. The Nimbus fairy king and his daughter will use these duffel bags to hide from any adversaries along the way. The Coronation is in five days. If ye leave tomorrow morning this gives ye two days to travel there and two days to travel back. Me dear friend will ye do this for me?" King Lore said.

"I would be honored to do so; I will prepare to leave at once," Bjork said. "Very well Bjork, God speed to ye, thy traveling companions are preparing as we speak. I would like to thank ye for taking Sulton on a splendid walk today, he doesn't get the opportunity to do this much anymore. Ah but he did in me younger days."

The King handed Bjork the scroll, as Bjork bowed in respect and left. He went straight to his chamber and carefully packed the scroll in his duffel bag which the King's servant had provided. Then he walked off whistling down the hall to the main dining room. He was very happy just thinking about seeing his Naomi again and telling the King of the good news of his Queen and the grand invitation to the Coronation of the New Vashing King. He was very happy indeed, he felt safe in knowing he would be accompanied by the King's finest warriors and none other but Syncore himself. He had forgotten all about the decree being read for One-Eyed Jack. It wasn't long though and he was reminded by the strangers and the Nimbus fairies at the noon time meal. News traveled fast among the Castle, and he was amused and glad to find that he would hear the decree read tonight, before he left for the Fairy Meadow.

That evening there was the sounding of horns being blown in the Grand Hall. Bjork had retired to his chamber after noon meal for a bit of an afternoon nap. He had opened the window sash and fallen asleep upon the comfortable bed with the gentle breeze blowing in over his body. He now was fully awake as he listened for another blast of the horn. He waited for a few minutes and when the sound was not repeated he rose and went to his door, thrusting his head out the crack into the hall, he was startled by the appearance of his friend Nimrod standing there about to knock. "Do pardon I hope I haven't startled you,"

Nimrod said. "I have come to escort you to the Grand Hall. King Lore is announcing his decree before supper."

Bjork excused himself briefly while he washed his face, ran a comb through his thinning hair and slipped into his boots. Then he left his chamber and hurried toward the Grand Hall. He was not surprised that Nimrod and he were the last of the guests to be seated. The King was upon his royal throne and his son Lars was sitting on a large stuffed chair near his father's side. The King's aid stood dutifully at the right of the throne with a large scroll that was rolled and bound in hand.

The King cleared his throat and in a raspy voice said, "Very well then bring the prisoner before me." The aid relinquished possession of the scroll to the King, bowed and with a nod hurried out through a large wooden door. When the aid had opened the door Bjork noticed many stone steps leading downward. He assumed the steps led to the Castle's underground chambers and dungeon.

The King sat up and tapping his chalice lightly he said, "I have invited ye me honored guests to the decree reading for the acts of piracy committed by One-Eyed_Jack against the Vashing Kingdom. Proceeding the decree supper will be served in the Main Dining Room. I wish to announce that I have extended a royal invitation to the Nimbus fairy King Calliope and his daughter Naomi. This will be hand delivered by a chosen few, namely Bjork the Hork, Syncore the Sailor, and two of me finest Vashing warriors. Upon acceptance they will escort the Nimbus royalty back to our Kingdom. In five days the Coronation ceremony will begin with the celebration of me son Lar's birthday." Then he cleared his throat and leaned back clutching the arms of his throne with his hands.

It was clearly apparent that Geneva and Nimrod were well-pleased that Calliope and Naomi would attend the Coronation. They had no doubt that the King would graciously accept. The guests were busy conversing in their seats when the sound of shackles rattling up the steps became louder. The large wooden door swung open. The aid appeared with One-Eyed-Jack in tow and with another dungeon keeper as his assistant. They brought the struggling and muttering pirate forward across the marble floors. When they reached the floor just in front of the throne and about three feet away, they stopped. The King began to unbind the scroll and then carefully unrolled it with his gnarled fingers. Then looking straight ahead at One-Eyed-Jack the King spoke, "Prisoner, ye are charged with the act of piracy of the Ægileif, which caused her to be lost at sea. In light of the great cost incurred by me Kingdom for the vessels dispatched and the crews that manned them while searching for the Ægileif, I find it a fair decree that ye will be held in the Vashing Kingdom in servitude working on the vessels she employs for a period of three years. Ye will be shackled at all times, unless ye are aboard a vessel at sea. Ye will be staying in the servant's area of the castle and will take meals when they do. After three years ye will be unshackled and given thy freedom."

One-Eyed-Jack grumbled and snickered, "I can do that standing on me head." Then he was led away by the King's aids.

"Well now on with the evening repast and let us enjoy the night. Tomorrow and the next few days will be busy ones, I have many new guests arriving and the Coronation preparations wait." Then he slowly rose and Lars taking his arm gently led him off down the hall heading toward the Main Dining Room.

Bjork was surprised to find such a lenient decree, and admired the King for his generous spirit. He was also surprised that he wasn't hungry, but rather excited about the journey to his homeland. He had queer butterfly feelings in his belly and was anxious to see the King and Naomi again. He also was hoping for a bit of time to stop by his humble abode. That was not of utmost importance to him though, so he pushed that aside and determined to enjoy this journey and tonight's feast.

The evening meal was more delicious than he expected and the excitement from today's events sparked the conversations. Nimrod was at first a bit disappointed that he would not be returning home with Bjork and Syncore, but after his mother wisely reminded him that his place was at her side, he settled into the evening feast.
Syncore had taken a seat near Bjork and they were pleasantly discussing their plans for departure. Neither of them knew which two of the King's warriors had been chosen to accompany them. So this would be an added surprise to tomorrow's adventures. They agreed to turn in early as they would be getting a very early start in the morning. They would rise four hours before dawn and meet

for a quick breakfast before disembarking. The King had informed Syncore that the warriors would be ready by daybreak and waiting in the Dining Room. So after a small dish of bread pudding and a cup of hot tea, Bjork excused himself from his dinner companions and began his walk to his chambers. Syncore followed suit and Bjork heard his boots on the marble flooring as he strode off in the opposite direction.

In no time Bjork was in his chambers, preparing his duffle bag for his early morning departure. He looked around the pleasant chamber, glancing at the book, The Tales of the Wimpet King, wondering if he would ever have the opportunity to finish reading it. Then he stepped out of his clothing, and crawled in between the sheets. He fluffed his down pillow and lay back. His mind was a million miles away in Horkland when he finally dozed off to sleep. The sound of his loud snores were barely audible through the large wooden door as Nimrod passed by hours later on his way to his chamber for the night. "God speed Bjork," Nimrod whispered as he walked down the hall.

CHAPTER 15.

RETURN TO THE FAIRY MEADOW

The morning came with a tapping at his door. Bjork sat up and answered, "Come in". The door swung open and there stood the King's aid. "Sir Syncore is waiting for ye in the Main Dining Room." "Very well, thank you tell him

I'll be there in a flash." The aid nodded as he closed the door.

Bjork sprang into action and in no time he was washed dressed and heading down the hall, duffle bag in tow.

When he arrived at the Main Dining Room he found Syncore at a table with a steaming mug in his hand. There were fresh breakfast rolls on platters and the baker instructed them to eat their fill and take what they could for their journey. They were provided with water pouches as well. Now the only thing missing was the two warriors. Just as Bjork was about to inquire about them to Syncore, he heard a back door open and two men strode in. Much to his surprise it was the two guards from the bridge. The two brothers whom Bjork had found so likeable were the King's best warriors as well.

Darell and Jarell were not wearing their guard uniforms but instead had donned tunics and trousers, with walking boots. They each were carrying large duffel bags as well. Darell proudly showed Bjork and Syncore their concealed weapons.

They were equipped with daggers in the top of their knee high boots, as well as flintlocks in the inside pocket of their tunics. These weapons had been commandeered from pirates. Traveling on foot it would be too difficult for them to carry the typical Vashing weaponry of battle axes, spears and bow and arrows. These warriors were experts in weaponry and adept in using all pirate weapons as well.

Syncore was aware of their talents and had known the brothers for quite some time, so there conversation turned to tales from days gone by. Bjork was feeling a bit left out as he couldn't relate to any of their conversation, but could only nod his head. They proceeded to consume the steaming cider and then the rolls, packing a few for later consumption in each of their duffle bags. Then Darell spoke, "We should leave now we have three hours before the sunrise and perhaps we can manage to sneak by the sleeping Cyclops during the day."

"The caverns are long and in the dark how will we find our way?," Bjork asked.

"Caverns Jarell chuckled, me friend we won't be traveling that way, we will be traveling to the edge of the cliff and then around the path to the other side. Going this way is safest and the path is straight, no turns or twists, we shall reach Cyclops land going this way in about two hours. If we travel across the middle of their land where the forest is the thickest we can reach the outer borders of Horkland before the sun reaches the top of our cliff. The cliff has been a blessing to us in this way. It keeps the Cyclops sleeping a bit later. The forest too is very dense and full of shadows, and we can travel the beaten paths and be in Horkland by early morning. Darell knows a clan of woodsmen there with Wolverine Banshees. The Cyclops are no match for them and they will protect us until we reach the border."

"I am familiar with the Banshees," Bjork said. Then Bjork proceeded to tell them about Windor the King of the Dwarves, as they passed through the darkness out of the Castle door, only pausing to receive permission to cross from the substitute bridge guards. Then Bjork and his entourage proceeded across the large bridge and down the stone path to the beach.

It was a pleasant enough day and the conversation with his new comrades was quite enjoyable. Syncore was quieter than usual today. It seemed to Bjork that he was a bit distant as if in deep thought. Other than that the morning air was cool and the journey to the end of the cliff seemed shorter than on the other day when he had taken the King's prize hunting dog Sulton for a stroll. They took the beaten path that led to the other side and then were suddenly cast into an eerie darkness as the sun had not yet reached above the top of the cliff and this side was covered in darkness. They wasted no time getting to the edge of the grassy knoll and following Darell and Jarell they quickly found themselves in the very midst of a huge dark forest. Bjork stumbled along trying to focus his eyes in the absence of light. After a short while he became accustomed to the darkness and could easily see the dirt path that wound through the area of large ancestral trees. He could hear the rustling of leaves and foliage as the forest creatures went about their daily business. He was careful to not fall too far behind Darell and Jarell as Syncore took up the rear.

It seemed like an hour or so had passed when they came upon the scent of a camp fire. Then the path took a sharp turn and began its steep descent. As they traveled along the smell grew stronger, until a small clearing appeared and there a large hollow tree trunk, which had been constructed into a wooden cabin. From the top of it's chopped off trunk grew moss and thatch and a crude smoke stack made of clay and stone rose. Smoke was billowing out of the stack. It smelled fragrant and reminded Bjork of his own hearth at home.

Darell approached the crude abode and knocked upon the outer wall, which now swung open revealing a hidden door. Out stepped a rather brawny short woodsman, accompanied by two large Wolverines. The man was dressed in deerskin and beaver pelts and wore a large unruly dark moustache. His hair was dark as well, shoulder length and a bit wavy. His face was ruddy from the fire and his hands were large and callused. His arms were very muscular, the arms of a woodsman indeed, from many days of swinging axes. He was pleasant enough though and seeing his friend Darell he clasped him roughly by the shoulders and grinning broadly said, "Welcome me friend, it's been a long time since I've seen ye face at me door. What brings ye to me neck of the woods.? Pardon me bad manners, do come inside along with ye traveling companions, have a cup of hot tea and then ye can answer me question."
The group went inside and closed the hidden door. It was quite nice inside, all the comforts of home and a large hearth with a table placed before it. They were glad to rest a spell and the tea was quite good. Their host introduced himself as Lee Vancleif. His brother and he lived in the woods and made their living by floating newly cut lumber down the river for sale near the town of Lost Mine. This town was nestled at the foot of the mountains beneath the dense forest and was secluded and protected from the Cyclops by the

woodsmen and their Wolverines. Merchants came down the river form near Horkland and beyond in order to purchase the lumber for use in their homelands. His brother had a wife Nell and they lived just beyond the next ridge. Bjork found the man to be genuinely interesting and was not concerned with how long their visit would last. Syncore on the other hand reminded his friends Darell and Jarell that if they wished to escape the Cyclops they needed to be on their way. The Cyclops were frightened of the woodsmen and their Wolverines, but they were foragers in the daytime and were known to enter the forest as well.

"Let me escort ye to Lost Mine," said Lee, from there ye can catch a ride on one of the river vessels traveling to Horkland, I have made a few friends with them over the years and they won't mind giving ye free passage as a favor to me, for a better deal on their purchase." This was agreed to instantly with thanks all around. This would save them even more time in getting back to Horkland. A man can travel faster on water than on foot.

Bjork had never ridden the river so he looked forward to this as a new experience. Syncore who felt more at home on the water also approved, and of course Darell and Jarell as well, for nowadays they rarely got to travel by water as the King's loyal guards in charge of the Castle bridge. It appeared to Bjork that this journey would be less perilous than he thought, at least on the way to Horkland. He hoped everything would go as smoothly on their return trip to the Vashing Castle.

So off they went with Lee and his Wolverines down through the winding forest path past his brother's simple abode and beyond to the banks of the river and the town of Lost Mine.

It was late afternoon by the time they reached it, and there were few vessels at dock. There was a large river boat with two oarsmen and it was here that Lee stopped. The man on the boat looked up; he was a swarthy fellow, ruddy complexion, whiskered face, bushy dark knit together brows and weathered wrinkled skin. He wore a felt cap and when he smiled there was a gap in his teeth, from an old brawl no doubt. Although he was aged he was muscular still and it was apparent he was no man to reckon with. He smiled at Lee and said, "Morning, I'm looking to purchase some choice pine for a set of table and chairs." Lee scratched his chin and then he began to make his proposition. "Hector McDill, if ye will take me friends here as far as ye are going on the river I will sell ye lumber at half cost." The man looked a bit puzzled as he took into assessment what Lee had offered. "Me boat is large enough to seat four men comfortably with cargo. Seeing as its only one more man, I can make do. The little old fellow can ride with me up near the prow, he said referring to Bjork." So it was decided and so it went.

The rest of the afternoon was spent loading the pine and making ample sitting space on the deck. Then they were off down the river with only the sounds of the birds and the animals nearby and the river itself flowing over the rocks in her bed. There was a cool breeze off the river and Bjork was well pleased with how this day had gone so far. He hoped the evening would be as pleasant. The river was tranquil and their conversation turned towards Horkland. Syncore had a few tales of his recent visits to Bjork's homeland. Darell and Jarell had not ventured there so this was indeed a new experience for them. They had traveled the river long ago but not taken her as far as Horkland. They had also camped in the shelter of the trees near her banks and even done a bit of fishing. They were content now in just listening to Syncore and watching the scenery pass them by. Bjork could hear the sounds of the wildlife that followed along the river's course. There were many species of birds that sat in the large oak trees that lined her banks. It was sheltered from the setting sunlight by the trees on either side and as the evening wore on the bank's foliage was lit up by thousands of fireflies. The boatman lit his oil lamp and hung it above her prow. There were strange sounds now that came from the edge of the river. These were the sounds of splashes in the water. This alarmed Bjork a bit so he asked Hector, "What is making the splashes? what type of fish may that be?" Hector crinkled his face into a deep grin and then he said, "Me friend that is the sound of the river's caretakers, they work mostly at night keeping her banks from overflowing the land. They swim rather well but are not fish; they are the beavers of this river. They build dams to keep her flowing along her natural course, and protect the landlubbers who live near her banks. They are friends of the river men. Their only foes are the trappers who come with their hearts full of greed killing the gentle creatures for their beautiful pelts, with no understanding or regard of what harm the river will come to, if the beavers are not allowed to live here and continue their work."

Bjork had heard of beavers but had never seen one, and was now intent on trying to catch a glimpse of one along the river bank. There was a fair amount of moonlight, and the oil lamp let off its pearly glow upon the waters as they continued their travel downstream. He was just about to give up on ever seeing a beaver when he heard a rustle in the foliage to the right of the boat and there in the moonlight he saw not just one beaver but two as they gracefully dove into the water. They were larger than he had imagined and they seemed to be at home in the cold dark river waters. He kept watching to see if they would pop up out of the water for air, but after awhile realized they had drifted quite a distance from where the beavers had entered. Someday I will camp near the banks of this river he promised himself. Then he sat back and suddenly feeling a wee bit tired he closed his eyes.

Syncore had finished his tale and Darell and Jarell were on guard, a habit they had acquired from being in the King's service. They kept watch throughout the night as the river boat made her trip downstream toward Horkland. Hector kept watch and using his oars skillfully pushed her away from the shallow waters and rocks. He had no need for rowing as the flowing river moved his boat along at a pretty good clip. Every mile or so the river grade changed a bit and they were constantly moving downhill. When the boat reached her destination they would be once again at sea level.

Hector did not intend to travel all the way to Horkland at first but after getting to know his passengers better he decided he would take them all the way. It would only be an extra hour out of his time to do so. He also enjoyed their companionship as well as listening to their stories. He didn't travel far these days and had very little chance to meet new friends from other lands. He calculated that they would reach Horkland before daybreak. Bjork looked to be asleep so Hector started a bit of a conversation with Darell asking him about the Vashing Kingdom. Then he skillfully took his boat along the river as the new tales came flowing from the Vashing warriors, enjoying every minute of this journey. A journey he had taken so many times alone, now seemed different, being shared with his companions, it was a very pleasant turn of affairs. He was glad his friend Lee had made this offer. It seemed to Hector that he would have paid full price and then some to have the company. It was in that moment that he realized how lonely the river could be. He determined to bring his grandson along the next time. He was ten years old now, (plenty old enough to learn the river man's life.)

As the first rays of the sun brightened the sky Hector finished the last leg of his journey with his new friends. He was nearing the end of the line and the end of the river, as he came into the last stop. There were a few river boats moored at the dock near the Horkland Trading Company. He recognized one as belonging to a swarthy fellow that dealt in the fur trade. For the life of him his name escaped him and no matter how he tried he couldn't conjure it up. He hoped the man wouldn't notice his boat as he tied her off and nudged the sleeping Bjork. "Ye are home lad, be off with ye now and good tidings. Safe travels to ye and thy comrades. If ye ever need a ride down this river again be sure to look me up." Bjork scrambled to his feet along with Darrel ,Jarrel and Syncore. They grabbed their duffle bags, and with Bork's, "Farewell Hector God speed to you," they stepped off the boat and headed toward the Trading Company.

They were hungry and needed a few provisions to tide them over until they reached the Fairy Meadow. They had finished off the last of the provisions that they had brought from the Vashing Kingdom. Looking about the shelves Bjork saw some dried berries and purchased these. The others also bought a few supplies and then they were on their way.

It would be a bit of a walk, perhaps three hours before they reached the Fairy meadow. Now that he was in Horkland Bjork could transport himself there instantly with the use of his cloak. Today he decided he would rather accompany the Vashing warriors and Syncore. The weather was pleasant and Bjork felt the need for a long walk, time to reflect on things and prepare himself for the evening's events. He knew it would be a tremendous celebration once they reached Calliope with the news of his wife and the invitation to the Coronation. He also knew he would see Naomi again and this made his heart happy. She would be so pleased to know that her mother was safe. He needed time to think of what he would say to them all and this long walk would give him that time.

He needed a place to tidy himself and not being familiar with this route he didn't realize how close it would come to his home.

As the day wore on he began to realize that the surroundings were taking on a familiarity. Then he noticed an area in the woods where he often came to gather wild huckleberries. He jumped for joy when he recognized the beaten dirt path that would lead to his door. "Men follow me. We are in my neck of the woods now. We can stop to rest and freshen up a bit. Then we will continue on to the Fairy Meadow. It isn't far from here now, but only a stone's throw away." The men didn't argue, and by the looks on their faces they were pleased to do this. So Bjork led them down the path and soon he was standing outside his very own door.

He fumbled around in the hedges nearby and produced a key which he put in the lock. Then he held open the door and said, "Welcome to the home of Bjork the Hork."

His home was just as he had left it. There was no sign of entry and the note he had written was still lying unread upon his table. "Make yourselves at home. I'll be making us some tea."

Soon there was hot tea and the men consumed the rations they had purchased at the Trading Company. Then they proceeded to wash their faces and groom themselves for their meeting with King Calliope.

Bjork also changed his clothes and put on fresh trousers and a vest along with clean socks and boots.

Syncore and the Vashing warriors changed their clothes also with the clothing they had brought in their duffle bags. Then feeling refreshed and with renewed strength they left and locked the door behind them.

Bjork was whistling a familiar tune as they walked off down the winding dirt path which wound through the forest and the flat lands until it ended at the Fairy Meadow. The sun was high in the sky, and the shade from the large trees that enclosed the path was welcome to the travelers. This would be a wonderful evening, Bjork mused.

Within the hour they came upon a break in the trees and the foliage changed to that of berry bushes. They were on the outskirts of the Fairy Meadow now and Bjork knew they could not gain entrance without permission from King Calliope. He had strengthened his security measures ever since his wife Geneva came up missing. Bjork was the exception to the rule and had free access at all times. He now turned toward the Vashings and Syncore and said, "My friends please wait here I must gain permission from King Calliope to allow you to enter his Kingdom." Then clutching his cloak and lifting his arms he vanished into thin air.

This both amused and puzzled the men. "I knew there was something peculiar about that little fellow," said Syncore. "He is an odd sorts but he does have a tendency to grow on you after awhile. He's a friendly sort though and wouldn't harm the hair of anyone's head unless to save his life. So we shall wait just as he asked."

Then they proceeded to pluck ripe berries from the bushes and eat them while they waited patiently.

Bjork was instantly transported to the center of the Fairy Meadow, and at first was unnoticed. Then out of the corner of his eye he spied her, it was his dearest Naomi. She seemed a bit down, not her normal cheerful self. She was sitting upon a satin cushion in her open chamber. Her curtains were drawn open wide and tied back. She was busy weaving her long hair into a tight braid to place upon her head. He took pleasure in watching her delicate fingers as they gracefully wound her golden hair. Then he remembered his friends were waiting for his return, so he prepared himself to speak and walked closer toward her.

He cleared his throat then and nervously fidgeted with the hem of his cloak.

Naomi looked up and seeing him, dropped her braided hair and sprang to her feet. Her face lit up at once, "Bjork!, Father Bjork is back." Then looking around with a puzzled expression on her face she kinked her head to the side and asked, "Bjork, where is my brother Nimrod?"

"Never fear Naomi, Nimrod is well, I bring very good news for you and your Father. I will tell you as soon as he arrives."

Calliope had heard his daughter's cries and soon arrived through her chamber doorway. Upon seeing Bjork he too was elated and stretched out his hand in a warm welcome. Then he too inquired about Nimrod.

Bjork carefully withdrew the Vashing King's invitation. Then holding it toward Calliope he said, "I bring you good tidings your majesty. Your wife Geneva has been found alive and well. Your son Nimrod is with her as I speak. They are guests of the Vashing King. He has sent me here to give you this message." Then he handed the neatly rolled invitation to Calliope.

The King was smiling now broader than any smile Bjork could remember and Bjork noticed tears of joys in his eyes.
Bjork cleared his throat, "Your majesty I am not alone as I was accompanied here by two of the King's finest warriors and Syncore the sailor. We are to bring you and Naomi safely to the Vashing Kingdom if you accept his invitation. I have left them outside the meadow, waiting for permission to enter."
Calliope hardily shook Bjork and exclaimed, "You have given me the best news I could ever hear and of course they are more than welcome." Then looking about he called out to two of his servants, "Men go to the edge of the meadow and bring back the Vashing warriors and Syncore the sailor for tonight we celebrate! My dear Geneva is found! We have a Coronation to attend! We have the safe return of our friends and so much to be thankful for."
"Excuse me Bjork; I'll leave you two alone now so you can give my daughter the wonderful details of your travels. I must tell the cook to prepare for our special guests."
Then just as quickly as he appeared he disappeared and Bjork began to tell Naomi all about his adventures as she continued to carefully wind and braid her golden hair.

The evening was more splendid then Bjork had imagined. The Nimbus fairies had outdone themselves as far as drink and feast. There were exquisite foods from far off lands to tempt the pallet. The fairy brandy was absolutely delicious and the music was extraordinary and magical as fairy music is. There were the sweet sounds of the harp strings and flutes that no other clan could match. The evening wore on and soon it was time to retire for the evening. King Calliope graciously provided comfortable accommodations for his new guests. They would leave the day after tomorrow at dawn to make their journey back to the Vashing Castle. It was still undecided as to which route they would take.

Bjork left that decision up to the Vashing warriors and Syncore who had far more experience traveling than he.

CHAPTER 16

THE PERILS OF THE FOREST

The day had passed quickly and now they were making preparations to leave at dawn for the Vashing Kingdom.

Bjork was hoping their return trip would be as pleasant as the trip getting here had been. He was looking forward to the Nimbus King and his wife reuniting and the grand Vashing Coronation. He also missed the company of the Nimbus fairies. He had grown quite fond of them all. He reached into the inside pocket of his cloak and checked its contents. The list of spells was safely tucked away. He felt quite safe being accompanied by the Vashing warriors and Syncore and was sure that they would reach their destination without any harm coming to Calliope or Naomi. He was wondering though if they had decided on the route they would travel. He was determined to ask them before retiring this evening. He had enjoyed spending time with Naomi and the weather had been truly magical inside the shelter of the meadow. The Nimbus fairy meadow was protected by their fairy magic and the temperature remained comfortable and the sky remained clear. There was plenty of morning dew to feed the lush grass and the many beautiful flowers. He had been gathering fresh berries for the evening feast with Naomi and the cook was now busy preparing them. Perhaps baking them in a pie, or cooking them in a pudding. He had gone to his chamber to retire for a spell and upon awakening from his nap he decided to wash his face and go out in search of the others.

He found the warriors and Syncore sitting outside sipping berry nectar and playing an ancient fairy board game.
Walking up to them he asked, "Care if I watch?" In unison they replied, "Do as ye wish". Then he sat down on a nearby stump that had been fashioned into a chair. Above them was a canopy of woven tree branches that were densely covered with leaves providing shade to all. Interlaced between the branches were beautiful climbing flowers of all types. It was most pleasant and when Naomi announced that supper was ready and that they would eat in the courtyard, they all immediately left their game and followed after her.

There were two wooden tables in the courtyard that contained fresh fruits and nuts and plates of steaming delicacies and beyond these stood a large long wooden table with wooden stools. Each place setting held a freshly picked flower and a cup of fairy nectar. The men quickly filled their plates with the food and sat down to eat. After this King Calliope came and sat at the head of the table. Then before anyone could begin he said, "I would like to give thanks to God for bringing this wonderful news to us. I want to make a toast to these men who have found my beloved Geneva. May God grant us safe passage as we travel to the Vashing Kingdom. Eat hearty for we leave at dawn." Then grabbing his nectar he drank and sat down. Instantly his servants began to bring him plates of food.

The food was more delicious than Bjork remembered although he was feeling very hungry and had hardily eaten the day before. He was glad to have this special time together and looking forward to coming to the end of this journey. Then he remembered what he wanted to ask and after the meal was finished before the men rose to return to their game, he walked up to Syncore and asked, "Have you decided the route we will take?" Syncore answered, "The Vashings have decided we must not return by river, unless word has reached anyone of our travels. We will be going over the Marshlands into the Winding Desert and enter the Vashing Kingdom through the edge of the forest of the Cyclops. We are traveling light so if we leave at dawn we should reach the forest by dark. We should arrive at the Vashing Castle before daybreak."

Bjork didn't like the sound of this, he felt it was taking unnecessary risks, but he didn't say anything out of respect for the Vashing warriors. He tried to remain high spirited as he watched the men playing their game. Then finding his mind was wandering he excused himself and went to his chamber to think. He doubted he would sleep much as this was a worry to him. He lie down and thought, at least I can close my eyes for a bit. Then he fell into a fitful sleep, tossing and turning.

He was soon awakened by the sounds of voices as the others gathered together getting ready for their expedition. Then he felt a cold clammy sweat fall upon him as he lay in dread of the path that the Vashings had chosen. Bjork did feel some comfort in the fact that Calliope had asked the good Lord to bless their travels. He knew the fairies were spiritual creatures, and although he himself was not as spiritual as he had been as a young lad, he did believe much in the power of prayer.

So as the darkness still lay upon the fairy kingdom, he crept from his bed and knelt beside it, calling upon The Creator to remove his fears and to provide them safety in the days ahead. Then he slowly gathered his belongings, washed his face and ran his stubby fingers through his unkempt hair as he ran to meet the others.

The sun was just beginning to make its presence known to them as they began their journey. Calliope and Naomi were safely stowed in the Vashing guard's bundles. As an extra precaution they had decided after every four hours the bundles would be swapped with the nearest traveler, so that they never were in anyone's sole possession for the entire trip.

The Marshlands were a bit damp and they had
to be careful to not leave the beaten path as
there were areas of deep quicksand on either
side. Everywhere there were the sounds of
buzzing insects, flies, mosquitoes and others.
At times in the morning air they would find
themselves surrounded by thick clouds of
them, yet they pushed on.
Bjork spent much of his time swatting them
away with his chubby hands, as they flew into
his face along the trail. The Vashings and
Syncore seemed to not even notice them.
Although as Bjork well knew the stature of a
Vashing Guard was to stand absolutely still
until spoken to, never speaking or even
swatting away an insect. They were highly
trained in this so as to catch any unwanted
guests off guard.
Syncore perhaps had acquired this skill from
his companionship with the Vashing Fleet. At
any rate Bjork felt out of place in his gestures
and attempted to ignore the pests to no avail.
He was indeed relieved when at last they left
the Marshland behind them.

The winding desert now lay ahead of them. In
the mid morning heat it was uncomfortable
and foreboding. The sweat dripped down
Bjork's bushy brow and found a path into his
eyes where it stung and blurred his vision.
He felt an enormous thirst and was wishing
for just a wee bit of shade, to hide him from
the oppressive rays of the hot desert sun. They
were careful as they stealthily moved along,
watching for the snakes and vermin of the
desert floor which slithered all around them.
Light of foot and ears in tune for the sounds of
a hissing asp, they moved in graceful unison.

After what had seemed like many hours to Bjork they came upon a cragged cliff of barren rock which cast a cool shadow upon their path. Looking straight up to the top Bjork could see a vulture sitting upon a lone barren branch of an old withered tree. As soon as he spied it, it rose off the cliff circling the area with its large wings spread.

It was magnificently beautiful in a most eerie fashion and Bjork almost tripped over a stone in his path, which reminded him to not take his eyes off his feet. The group came to an abrupt halt when Darryl stopped dead in his path. He turned and said, "Let us take a bit of water and rest a spell in this cool shade." So they all took his advice and soon were refreshed from their thirst, being fed and the absence of the unbearable heat upon their bodies.

It was nearing late afternoon now as Darryl spoke again, this time with a bit of urgency. "We have tarried long enough we must hurry now to reach the end of this miserable desert. We will be traveling through the forest of the Cyclops by nightfall. We are making good time and should arrive at the Vashing Castle near dawn."

The weary travelers arranged their bundles upon their shoulders and resumed their journey through the high desert. As they climbed they noticed the landscape was changing and there was evidence of new plant growth and foliage. The ground itself was changing also from dusty sand to a darker color of clay. The air felt a bit cooler now as the sun was lower in the sky and there was a pleasant breeze. They kept up the winding path that led to the uppermost peaks and the edge of the Cyclops forest. It was a long climb and they stopped once again just before nightfall to take a bit of food and drink.

Bjork took a deep drink and capped off his water pouch. He wiped his wet mouth with his sleeve and took a deep sigh.

He had been worried about the path his companions had chosen and now after coming this far for the first time he thought his instincts to be in error. They had managed to get this far without even the slightest mishap. Perhaps his prayer for safe travels had provided them all with good fortune. At any rate he was feeling his age and looking forward to getting to the end of this journey. The men swapped their bundles as they had been doing at regular intervals and then began the last leg up the path to the uppermost desert. The sun was now barely casting a red glow as she dipped into the horizon.

By the time they reached the top the sun had sunk beneath the horizon and they could now see the edge of the forest which lay to their north. They had slowed down their pace and were wary of the Cyclops that lay sleeping ahead. By the time they reached the forest the sky had darkened and they could now see by the light of the full moon.

Once they began their journey inside the forest they would be in total darkness.

The forest was black as pitch and Bjork could see the glowing eyes of her inhabitants as they stared back at him from their lofty heights. Darryl had assured them that he knew his way well through these woods and that they must keep on the path. If they swayed from the dirt path, they would become disoriented and lost among the eerie darkness of this vast forest.

They kept a steady pace now, looking over their shoulders with their ears intently listening to the sounds of the night. Bjork could not see his companions but he could hear the sounds of their feet as they traveled along the winding path. Every so often they came to a small clearing where the moon's beams shone down upon the path and then Bjork could glimpse the backs of the Vashing warriors that had taken up the lead. In the distance Bjork could hear the sounds of water trickling. He didn't realize that they were swiftly approaching the community of the forest imps. He had been told that the forest imps were wee in stature as the elves and the fairies, only they were more of an evil nature. They were allies with the Cyclops and had dwelt along side of them for many centuries. They had been known to trick innocent bystanders into falling into the hands of the Cyclops, which many had and the horror of their demise was well known by the lucky ones who escaped death at their hands.

The sounds of the forest creatures as they rustled the leaves startled Bjork and his companions, but they were careful not to cry out. The vastness of their surroundings made Bjork feel claustrophobic as if he would never reach the end of this black forest. He felt this must be what it is like to be blind as he carefully moved his feet along the path, searching with his toes for rocks and fallen branches that may lie beneath his feet upon the forest floor. His eyes had adjusted a bit more to the dark and he could barely make out the forms of his leaders as he followed along closely.

The path took a sudden turn and Bjork found himself gazing upon the source of the trickling water. The opening in the forest canopy above gave room for the moon beams to shine upon the small winding stream that lay to his right. It was here that he first heard the sounds of hushed whispers. At first he thought it came from Darryl, Jarryl or Syncore, but then as the sounds became more audible he distinctly heard the wee voices of the imps. He wondered if the others ahead of him also heard. They were too far away for Bjork to inquire without speaking too loudly, so he simply picked up his pace to follow in closer behind them. Then he leaned forward and tapped Darryl upon his back.

Darryl jumped and turned to face Bjork with a stern look upon his face. "Do you hear them?" whispered Bjork.

"Aye, said Darryl, "They be the imps of the forest, pay them no mind for they will not dare to cross the path of a Vashing warrior."

They continued on their way as Bjork mustered the courage to follow along behind not paying heed to the murmurs of the imps that surrounded the path. They had to keep a steady pace in order to reach the edge of the border and cross over onto Vashing land. The Vashing land began a short distance from the edge of the forest and was protected on all boundaries by the clans of the lowlands. These clans were a stout and swarthy type, fearless and pledged to King Lore's service as warriors. They were allotted by the King plentiful rich acres of land and modest country cottages in return for their service and protection of the boundaries of the Vashings. They were the Brute's to the north, the Serfs to the south, the Mason's to the east and the Claussens to the west. They were all highly skilled in armed and non armed combat.

Darryl began to whisper to Bjork and tell him of these clans and to be wary of them as they were sworn to protect the King's land and they could pounce upon them at anytime.
"If they approach us let me do the talking, Darryl said. "I speak their dialects and can dissuade them from any unnecessary confrontations."
Bjork was more than happy to do this as he had no intentions of trying to persuade any of the King's warriors.
It was much to their surprise as they crept through the darkest areas of the forest that there was an eerie silence, no rustling of leaves, no eyes glowing back at them. It was as if the forest here was uninhabited. Bjork was puzzled at this as well as the others. He also had a very distinct feeling that they were being watched.

Meanwhile......
She gazed into her crystal ball that sat upon the wooden table. Then with a cackle and a scratching of the long whiskers on her chin she said to her comrades, "I believe we have visitors, seek them out and bring them to me the Cyclops will reward us dearly and perhaps they have something more valuable for me."
Then she turned and her shadow danced eerily upon the inner walls of the chamber. The room was lit by the fire that consumed the logs in the fire pit.

Hagatha had taken up residence in the tree trunk after her narrow escape at sea. She still wondered what had become of One-eyed Jack. "Well be off then, she snapped, and don't tarry, I don't like to be left waiting."
She opened the door and pushed the three imps out into the dark forest. She waved her hands and murmured an inaudible chant as she transformed the imps into simple woodsmen. Then she hastily closed the door.

Hagatha went to the fire pit and stirred the coals. She began to place a large cauldron over the flames. Now what potion shall it be, she said to herself. She reached up and grabbed the thick book upon the top shelf of her bookcase and with a long boney finger she ruffled through the pages until her finger came to rest on the book of sleeping potions. With a wicked smile and a chuckle she thought to herself if I put them all to sleep, I can search them for valuables and when they awaken they will be in the forest in broad daylight, a breakfast feast for the Cyclops.

Bjork couldn't shake the feeling of being watched as he slowly followed the Vashing warriors and Syncore through the forest. They had come close to a clearing now and Bjork could make out three indistinct shapes coming towards them. His heart leapt into his mouth as he wondered, friend or foe? Darryl whispered, "Halt, beware we have come upon three travelers. I will do me best to convince them we mean them no harm."
So the four weary travelers were stopped in their tracks.

Jarryl, Syncore and Bjork waited as Darryl approached the three, who now upon a closer look took on the appearances of three woodsmen.

"Hail men, we are weary travelers who have lost our way. We are searching for the Vashing Kingdom. We wish ye no harm only clear passage. Perhaps ye would be so kind as to point us on our way," Darryl said.

The three woodsmen stopped their approach and began whispering amongst themselves. Then two of them pushed the other forward. This woodsman took a bow, and waving his axe in the direction to their right he spoke, "The path to the Vashing Kingdom is beyond this clearing to thy right. If ye follow it ye should reach there well before daylight.

We don't often meet up with strangers, so forgive our inhospitality. Perhaps ye would like to join us for a cup of hot tea. We have left a large pot of the brew setting on the fire. We won't let ye tarry long; but don't fear ye have plenty of time before the dawn. Our humble cottage is nearby, it is the very least we can offer."

Darryl not wishing to offend these men humbly accepted.

"Let me return to me men and tell them of thy generous offer." Then hastily he went not wishing to lose time, knowing very well that the dawn waits for no one.

Soon the seven of them were making their way into the clearing leading to the tree home. The imps were grinning to themselves as they anticipated the demise of the four weary travelers. Not many did travel this way so it had been quite awhile since they had been able to witness the capture of unwary travelers by the Cyclops. In return for these men the Cyclops would allow the imps and Hagatha free reign upon any intruders and allow them to keep any valuables which they held in their possession. These were the terms which Hagatha had agreed to in order to have sanctuary in the forest.

Bjork could not explain his feeling of apprehension. He knew these woodsmen seemed to be pleasant enough by appearance and speech, yet he didn't trust them. He also knew that the King's warriors were well capable of defending them if an altercation occurred. So he brushed off his uneasy feeling and picked up his pursuit. Soon they reached a large tree that was situated in the midst of the clearing. By the moonlight Bjork could see that its branches reached out far and wide above them and entangled themselves into the forest canopy on all sides. It appeared to him that the clearing beneath was the after effect of many years of shade beneath its branches. One of the woodsmen stepped forward and rapped upon the trunk of the immense tree. To all of their amazement a hidden door swung open revealing a beautiful young maiden.

"Ah this be our dear sister the woodsmen said, do come in and have a cup of tea with us."

" We have plenty to share," the young girl said with a smile.

It seemed harmless enough but Bjork knew he would not rest until he questioned his cloak for an answer, so he excused himself claiming he had dropped something outside and promising to return promptly.

Once outside and a few feet away from the tree home Bjork, unable to read his instructions by the dim light, forced himself to remember the words to speak to the cloak for revelation of good and evil. I mustn't tarry long he thought, and it was at that moment that he remembered. "Cloak of fairy wisdom and splendor, tell me if they be foe or friend here. Let me see them as they are with all powers diminished and let me evoke a spell to counter theirs until our journey is finished."
Then Bjork turned and walked back to the tree and rapped upon the trunk three times as he had witnessed the woodsman do.

The door immediately swung open and to Bjork's horror he now could see Darryl, Jarryl and Syncore about to sip their hot tea, which was being handed to them by a horrible witch and three ugly disgusting twisted forms of creatures, with long boney hands and feet and large pointed noises. Their eyes were sunk far back in their heads and their skin was a pasty rancid green color.
Gone were the three woodsmen and the beautiful young maiden.
He realized that the others could not see what he could, so he leapt at them and with one swoop of his cloak he dashed the tea mugs to the ground as their hosts now became frozen as if made of stone or wood.
Darryl, Jarryl and Syncore gasped in unison. Then Darryl spoke, "What have ye done Bjork, what magic has turned these woodsmen into imps and the maiden into a witch."

Bjork began to explain how he had been given the cloak many years ago in return for a good deed, and that its powers were for good and not evil. "My cloak revealed their true character, just in time before you drank whatever potion they had conjured. I dare say I would not like to guess what plans they had for the likes of us. There is no time to waste, I will tell you more upon our arrival at the Vashing Castle."

They all agreed that it was best, and thanked Bjork profusely for his saving them from certain doom. Then they gathered their bundles, after checking to make sure the Nimbus Fairy King and his daughter were still safely tucked inside. They made haste out of the tree home and into the night.

"I can't trust the directions the woodsman provided us either, considering he was an imposter," said Darryl.

"So there for I am going to trust me instinct .We will head in the direction of the east wind, this should lead us back to the Vashing Kingdom."

The four of them began the last leg of their journey. Bjork made it a point to stay in the middle letting Syncore take the rear and Darryl and Jarryl the lead. The breeze began to change and Bjork could now feel a drop in the temperature as well. He knew from past experience this could only mean one of two things. Either a rain storm was on its way or they were getting nearer to the ocean. He preferred the later as he was not prepared to be soaked by a blinding rain. It was to his pleasant surprise that the terrain took on a different appearance now as the trees became thinner and the ground beneath his feet felt softer, almost like a sandy loam. Then he realized the change in the air, the scent of the ocean was becoming very strong. It was still

quite dark as they reached the familiar path that he had taken on his first journey to the Vashing Kingdom. The path intersected with three others, and in the dim light Bjork could not be sure which path he had originally taken that led him to this point. He was happy knowing that just a few more feet down the path it would take a certain turn and lead them to the mouth of the caverns.
He recognized how the trees lined both sides of the trail and was now greatly anticipating their arrival and the reunion of the Nimbus King and Naomi with his wife and son Nimrod. This was to be a very happy occasion. Also the alliance with King Lore and the Coronation of the new King made for many other reasons to celebrate.

It was not long before Darryl and Jarryl reached the mouth of the cavern and stood waiting for Bjork and Syncore.
Bjork smiled and said, "I've taken this path before, it brings back many memories." Then the four of them began their winding twisting descent into the caverns as the sounds of the oceans waves grew louder. Yes indeed Bjork mused this would be the best celebration he had attended yet. What a blessing for him to be part of this re-union and of the new King's coronation. He would write this all down in his journal at home as soon as he returned. He couldn't wait to record it so it would be read for generations to come. He had wished for an adventure and this so far had been the grandest. As they carefully made their way through the maze of twists and turns letting the ocean's waves guide them, Bjork begin to fantasize as to how it would all unfold and found himself humming a familiar hymn.

CHAPTER 17

THE NIMBUS FAIRY REUNION

The dawn was breaking when at last the four
weary travelers and their royal companions
tucked safely in their pouches stepped out of
the caverns onto the beach.
The Vashing fleet stood enchanted at port,
their wooden hulls and decks gleaming in the
sun. The Vashing King had ordered them
polished and upon each deck was a large crew
of workers carefully inspecting each nook and
cranny.
The Coronation was to be soon and many
ships from foreign lands were soon to be
docking in port. The King wished that they
would find his fleet to be impeccably
maintained. He took great pride in the
Vashing vessels.

Nimrod and Geneva had risen early and were
in the main dining hall partaking of the
morning feast. They were unaware of the fact
that Bjork and his entourage were scaling the
steps to the Vashing Bridge and soon would
be entering the Vashing Castle with Naomi
and King Calliope in their possession. They
were busy with idle chatter when the King's
son, Lars entered with his father King Lore.
Geneva noticed that the King looked more
weary than usual these days. She hoped in
her heart that he would live to see his son's
coronation.

The king's servants made busy setting a fine
plate of the best the kingdom had to offer in
front of the prince and his father. They were

also given mugs of steaming cider. They both
were enjoying their meal when the sound of
footsteps walking across the hallway became
nearer and nearer and then the King's
messenger arrived. His stride was a quizzical
harried fashion as he quickly approached King
Lore and then bent over and whispered into
his left ear.

Then the King in return leaned over and
whispered into Lars' ears. The dining room
had become absolutely still as each diner and
servant waited to hear the King speak. Lars
finished his meal, pushed his plate away from
himself and rose to a standing position.

"The King has asked me to make an
announcement. He has learned that Bjork and
the others have returned from the Fairy
Meadow. They along with their royal company
are now freshening up after a long night. They
will be joining us very soon. Me father has
also told me that tonight we will be holding a
party in honor of the Nimbus fairies."

Geneva was beside herself with joy as she felt
her heart leap in her chest. She felt tears of
happiness run down her face and drip into her
lap. How long had it been since she had seen
her dear Calliope and her precious daughter
Naomi? Her mind was still confused as she
had no real memory of the past. She knew it
was probably for her best that she had
forgotten it, and pushed it aside. I will make
new memories she thought as she smiled.

She found it very difficult to sit still and could
not finish her meal. She reached across the
table and firmly grasped her son Nimrod's

hand. "Oh I am so nervous son, how long has it been, do I look alright?" she said as she nervously brushed her auburn hair away from her face.

"You look beautiful as always Mother," Nimrod said as he firmly squeezed her hand.

"Come and walk with me son to the outer garden, I can't bear to sit a minute longer," Geneva said. They both rose and excused themselves from their table companions. They then turned and began to cross the great dining room, when they noticed the sounds of voices getting nearer coming down the hall. In an instant Geneva recognized Calliope's voice, "It's your Father!" she said with anticipation. Then they stopped in their tracks and waited as the voices came louder even still and then came the appearance of a royal messenger. He strode in to the King and his son and then taking a bow he announced. "Thy Highness I wish to announce the arrival of the fairy King Calliope and the princess Naomi, they are accompanied by thy two loyal guards, Darryl and Jarryl and the dubious Bjork the Hork."

Within seconds the King and Naomi appeared arm in arm with the guards and Bjork taking up the rear.

Geneva ran and collapsed into the King's open arms weeping tears of great joy. She then turned to her daughter and hugged Naomi to her breast.

Bjork felt blessed to have been a part of the reunion of the Nimbus fairy royal family. He was deeply moved by the love that these fairies had for each other. He was proud to have been one of the few chosen to find the fairy Queen and return her to her people. This had been a very noble adventure indeed.

The dining room was full of a spirit of glee as the King's addressed each other. "Tonight we celebrate the fairy kingdom's good fortune, King Lore said." Then he gave orders to his servants to prepare an abundant feast of celebration, and to assemble his fine musicians. Then he retired to his quarters leaving his well capable staff overseen by his son Lars to finalize preparations for the evening.

The dining room slowly emptied as each guest and servant made ready for the evening's events. Bjork returned to his guest chamber for an afternoon nap, suddenly feeling very weary from all of the past events. He was fantasizing about the night celebration and looking forward to spending time enjoying the splendid feast and the magical musical performance. Perhaps he would do a bit of his Hork jig tonight, he mused.

The evening began with a splendid feast one of which there could be no comparison. King Lore never ceased to amaze his honored guests by providing the sumptuous delicacies of their native lands. In this case he had gone to great difficulty and expense to have his royal chefs create a Nimbus fairy feast resplendent with all their traditional celebratory entrees. There was an array of festive flowers that took center stage at each and every dining table. The linens were of the King's finest and the napkins were finely embroidered with the King's monogram. At each table setting there was carefully placed a name card along with the King's finest silverware and china. Each guest was given a traditional silver goblet and a carved wooden ale stein.

The smells were so intoxicating that Bjork found himself salivating. The Fairy Meadow herbs and spices were of abundance and he mused as to how the King had managed to have them in stock, seeing as they were only found to grow within the confines of the Nimbus Kingdom.
As the dining room began to fill with guests Bjork noticed the Nimbus fairy royal family were all seated at a table of honor placed directly perpendicular to the table of King Lore and Prince Lars. Next to their table sat Jeziah, Mahew, Jacor and Ryob. The tables quickly filled with guests until there was no vacancy, it was at this time that the royal families entered the dining hall and took their assigned seats.

The room was filled with silence as King Calliope tapped lightly on his goblet with his silver spoon. It echoed off the walls and a deep hush fell over all as the Nimbus King rose to speak. He then turned to address the Vashing King.
"Your majesty I feel that this evening gives me a great opportunity to show my deepest gratitude to Your Highness for aiding in the reunion of my family. We have always been allies with the Vashing people, but now more than ever I am offering you our loyalty. We will serve the Vashing people above all other clans. We shall strive to protect the Vashing royal family at no expense to our kind. Our homeland will be as your homeland and we will be forever indebted to your people." Then

he stood back and took a deep and gracious bow toward the King and his son. "May your King forever rule in times of peace and war."

The King stood to his feet along with Prince Lars. "May it be so that our peoples are as one from this day forward," King Lore said. Then he looking upon the occupants of the dining hall scanning each table, reached out his goblet to his servant who poured the Elderberry wine. "Let the festivities begin," he said with a smile as he raised his goblet. Then looking at King Calliope he said, "To us dear brother." He then sat down and began to clap his hands summoning the musicians.

The entire seven course feast was served to the subtle music of the Vashing musicians. When the last dish had been cleared from the tables the long aged Vashing ale was served and the musicians picked up the tempo. They played a medley of Vashing warrior dirges and then fairy meadow flute and harp. Bjork was surprised as to how well they played the Nimbus fairy instruments. Perhaps the King had been preparing for this occasion for some time. At any rate he didn't know if it was how beautiful Naomi appeared with her cheeks rosy from the elixir, or if it was the effects it had upon himself, but he found himself whirling upon the dining room floor, dancing his Hork jig.
Nimrod soon followed suit and before the song had ended most of the seated guests had paired off with the Vashing women in attendance. The King had seen fit to invite most of the local Vashings to the festivities, including the crews of his Vashing fleet. There

for there was a large mix of folk from all walks of life participating in the celebration.

The music went from Nimbus fairy to Vashing maritime and the captains and their crew entertained the guests with their own sort of jig. It was a rare delight to see Syncore's fancy dance steps.

The evening was a huge success and new friendships and acquaintances were formed by all. Bjork thought how can the King out do this grand event? He knew though that the Coronation would be of far more splendor. There were many vessels due into port from far off lands. These were cultures that Bjork had only heard tale of. The feast would include entrees from all and the musicians would play songs from every land.

The Coronation Celebration would last for three days in order to give representation to all foreigners in attendance. Of course the solemn Coronation would precede these festivities. He was looking forward to this time of enlightenment. It would be splendid to communicate with these foreigners and learn about their heritage. He was thinking about his return home and how he was glad that it was delayed. He missed his people this is true, yet he thoroughly enjoyed the Vashings. He would miss Darryl and Jarryl and his friend Syncore. He would miss being in an adventure. He had no way of knowing if he would ever have another. He was getting on in years although Horks did live a fairly long life, two hundred years to be exact.

The evening wore on and Bjork after much ale and dancing found himself growing weary. He approached the Nimbus family and bowed, "I wish to bid you all a good evening, I'm afraid the festivities have worn this old Hork out. Until tomorrow then", he said with a smile and he turned and began the long walk through the winding halls to his guest room. Once inside he closed and latched the door, removed his outer clothing, turned back his bedding, climbed in between the sheets and fell into a deep sound sleep.

His snoring was loud but within the confines of the thick castle walls was virtually inaudible to the other occupants.

Bjork woke early the next morning and after a quick wash he dressed and went out into the hall. The halls were busy with servants running to and fro carrying fine linens and cleaning supplies. The floors were being polished and Bjork was given strict warning to be careful of slippery areas. He continued on amused by the activities. When he reached the dining room he was surprised to see that there was a group of the King's finest chefs holding a meeting. They were busy making a menu for the Coronation feasts.

The other guests were still asleep so Bjork found himself alone at a table as a servant girl brought him a mug of hot tea.

"Pardon sir, I'm afraid our breakfast has been delayed, "she said as she looked over her shoulder toward the table where the chefs sat. "I am at liberty to bring ye some fruit and muffins with fresh jam if ye desire," she said with a bow and a cheerful smile.

"Why you must have read my mind missy, I have been craving a bit of fruit and muffins. The jam will add just the right touch," Bjork said as he gently patted her arm.

She hurried off and returned quite quickly with an assortment of fresh fruit and fresh baked muffins. She also brought a container of fresh huckleberry jam.

In short time Bjork made himself a plate of each and began to sample the muffins. At this time the chefs rose from the table and retreated to the kitchen area. No sooner had they left, the dining hall began to fill with the guests of the Vashings. Syncore arrived in tow of a bunch of the Vashing fleet crewmates. They were busy discussing the conditions of the various vessels in port. Bjork not wishing to intrude upon the conversation but very interested turned his ears in their direction. Then he thought he heard a strange comment. He heard Syncore ask for the young crewmate to repeat his sentence. Yes he had heard it correctly. That sly and crafty old pirate, (One-Eyed Jack) had escaped in foot shackles by cutting the lines to a survival dingy and dropping it into the water sometime during the night. The night watchman of the vessel had fallen asleep at his post. The Captain of the vessel had given strict orders to not divulge the information to the King until after the Coronation. Syncore was in argument and was stating that omitting this fact could lead to the piracy or capture of the foreign vessels due into port. He slammed his fist on the table and said, "I will not be silent in this matter, I will deal with this Captain myself, but as of this moment I am summoning audience with King Lore". He then rose and stormed out of the dining room.

So the pirate had escaped and now when all these foreigners were traveling to port. Bjork knew that Syncore was right, that a crew of

warriors must be dispatched immediately in order to re-capture One-Eyed Jack. The Coronation would go on as planned, and Syncore aimed to see to it that none of the King's guests would be in peril.
Syncore quickly found the King's messenger and asked him to request a visitation with King Lore immediately since this was a matter of security.

The King quickly responded to the request and within one hour Syncore was assembling some of the King's finest and bravest warriors as a crew. "Prepare the Drakkar to set sail , we must leave at once, before the tide's turn we must find this evil pirate and put an end to his plans," Syncore bellowed. Then as quickly as they had assembled the crew dispersed with Syncore in the lead.

Bjork finished his breakfast and began to anticipate the arrival of foreign vessels. He tried to take a stroll in the inner gardens, but his curiosity could not be put to rest. He decided to take a stroll down on the beach near the Vashing sea port.
It was a chilly morning that greeted him as he stepped though the Castle gate and approached the bridge sentry. He was pleasantly surprised to see that Darryl had taken up this post. "Good day Bjork," Darryl said with a comical smile."Yes it tis a fine day for a long walk," Bjork replied.
Then Darryl stepped aside to allow Bjork access to the bridge. He could smell the scent of salt in the air which had a rather fishy odor today. The breeze was pleasant enough and he was glad his cloak was tightly wrapped

around him when he stepped out on the other
side of the bridge to wish Jarryl a good day.
"Going for a walk me friend?" asked Jarryl.
"I believe the ocean air will do me some good
and I am curious to watch the King's crews as
they make ready for the arrival of other
vessels. Perhaps I will see a new one in port",
Bjork said as he hurried down the stone steps
which led to the beach.

He could see the Vashing fleet as she lay
gleaming in the new day's light. The decks and
hulls had been highly polished and the crews
continued to prepare for the festivities.
It was customary to allow the Captains of
foreign vessels to board the Vashing vessels to
admire the fine craftsmanship.
Bjork was a bit disappointed when he noticed
the Drakkar's empty berth. There was no sign
of her on the horizon so he knew she had set
sail a few hours prior to his decision to leave
the confines of the castle.
He felt a twinge of envy considering the
adventure that lay ahead for Syncore and his
crewmates. Yet he knew he wouldn't have
missed the grand Coronation celebrations
either. So he decided he had made the right
choice in staying behind. Although Syncore
had not invited him along, he assumed he
would have been welcome if he had asked.

Bjork spent the morning walking the shore
line and enjoying the crisp salty air. Then he
made a hasty return back to the castle for a
bit of lunch.
The castle once again was abuzz with chatter
and planning for the beginning of the young
King's reign. The Coronation was to take place

the day after tomorrow after the last of the King's invited guests arrived.

Throughout the course of the day Bjork noticed more and more foreigners being led to their guest quarters, they came in all ethnicities, shapes and sizes. He was intrigued by their traditional wardrobe and their native tongues were unfamiliar. As to be expected that evening the dining room was filled almost to capacity. Bjork was astounded by the abundance of foreign foods and beverages that were being served. The aromatic scents of spices that he had never savored made him ravenous.

Soon he found himself indulging in the feast and idle conversation with the Nimbus fairies that had chosen to sit nearby. It pleased Bjork to see how happy Geneva and Calliope appeared, together once more. Naomi and Nimrod were more content than Bjork had seen them in quite a while.

The conversation was about the different clans attending and the preparations for the Coronation. The King's servants seemed more serious than ever and a bit in a dither about serving such an enormous crowd. It was to their credit that the entire meal went off perfectly without a hitch. Every guest was fed and drinking their beverage of choice along with a wonderful choice of desserts.

Bjork could not imagine the effort that went into preparing such an elaborate feast. It gave him much appreciation for the King's chefs and servants. I must show them my gratitude before I leave he thought.

Then an idea occurred to him, so tapping upon his mug with his spoon until the dining room fell silent, Bjork arose to a standing position. "Pardon me if you do not understand my language but I hope that you will join me in applauding the wonderful feast that the King's servants have provided."

To his pleasant surprise everyone in the dining room stood to their feet and began to applaud.

The King's servants wondering what the commotion was entered the dining room from the kitchen. Bjork turned in their direction and applauded. The servants and chefs beamed and blushed with pride and then slowly backed into the kitchen.

Bjork said his good evening to the Nimbus fairies and then left the dining room. He felt a bit like reading this evening he thought. So he returned to his room, lit the fire and settled in the cozy chair beside it with "The Tales of the Wimpet King" upon his lap. He opened the book to where his bookmark lay and began to read.

The fire was comforting and the book was captivating as usual and soon Bjork found himself deep within its pages. He didn't notice how late it was getting but as the fire started to dwindle, he rose and went to his bed, set the book down on the night stand, removed his outer clothes and slipped between the sheets. He fell into a very deep and sound sleep dreaming of the Wimpet King.

CHAPTER 18.

THE NEW KING

The next day was met with the rising sun and the sounds of hustle and bustle as more guests arrived into port. Bjork had risen early and after a quick breakfast he retired to his guest room to prepare for the Coronation. He was disturbed that he didn't have any proper attire for this grand event. So when he reached his room and found a splendid suit of clothing laid out upon his bed and a pair of polished boots, he was pleasantly surprised. The suit consisted of a pair of deep blue trousers with a darker vest and a waistcoat to match. Beside the suit was a white dress shirt. The King's servants had taken care of every detail. He decided he had time to take a stroll through the castle garden as the Coronation would begin after the noon meal in the Grand Hall. So he opened the door and walked down the hall to the large door which led to the King's Garden. Then he stepped outside and took a deep breath of cool salt air. The sun was shining down upon the beautiful flowers and he could hear the birds singing in the trees. This would be a splendid day for the Coronation.

New ships had arrived in port and Bjork could not wait to meet the foreigners they carried. He thoroughly enjoyed the stroll around the Garden except for one brief period of time when he got a bit confused and lost his way in the maze of perfectly sculpted hedges. He was surprised when he returned inside the Castle doors to smell the strong scents of food. The halls were strangely silent now and as Bjork made his way closer to the dining room he could hear the din of many folks engaged in idle chatter. He couldn't understand many of the foreigners, but he knew that time for lunch had arrived. So he walked inside and searched about for an empty seat. He was once again pleasantly surprised to see that Naomi had left a seat open next to her.

This had perhaps been the longest he had seen the Nimbus fairies at his size. They had taken on this appearance to make it easier for them to spend time with the others. When he thought of how small they were he chuckled to himself imaging the lot of them standing together upon a cup saucer. He sat down next to Naomi and began to eat. He felt nervous inside as if he was expecting something odd to occur. Surprisingly for him he had a lack of appetite and was not able to eat much of the food on his plate.

The other guests were busy chattering away when Bjork decided to return to his room and prepare himself a hot bath. The Coronation was only two hours away and he wanted plenty of time to get ready. So he excused himself from the table and made his way back to his room. On his way he ran into one of the King's chamber maids and asked her if she could draw him a hot bath. She obliged and he asked her to let him know when it was ready that he would be in the King's Library.

The King's Library was across the hall from his room so he conveniently retired there. He sat upon a comfortable chair placed in front of the hearth and leaned back. The warmth of the fire felt comforting in the cool drafty library and soon Bjork found himself reminiscing of the past.
He was startled when the chambermaid appeared and announced his bath was ready.

So once again he returned to his room, went inside and latched the door. Then he proceeded to enjoy the comforts of a hot and sudsy bath. The bath tub had been placed in front of the fire to keep the chill from Bjork when he grabbed the towel provided to dry off and get dressed.

He then looked into the mirror and noticed how sparse his hair had become and the lines of age upon his face. He grabbed a comb from the dresser and carefully ran it through his hair, mustache and bread. He felt disappointed at the reflection that looked back at him. Naomi was still young and beautiful and he had become an old wrinkled Hork. Yet when he was with her he felt as young as she looked. It made him sad to realize that his days would come to an end soon and she would live on, youthful as ever for many years to come. Then he realized when he had let her go, it was the most loving thing he could do for her. She had protested and sobbed, but he had known it would come to this, that they could never be content. He would grow old frail, weak and uncomely. They would never grow old together. He was surprised that this thought brought him closure and that he could let go of his past.

He made the final checks on his attire and confidently strode down the hall to gather with the others in the Grand Hall.

When Bjork reached the Grand Hall he was overtaken with the immense crowd gathered there. So many different peoples from all over The Lands of Nod and beyond were in attendance. Each one of them dressed in their traditional finest. The din of their voices, mixed tongues, and the servants calling out

orders made it difficult for Bjork to hear the voices of his friends as they called out to him. Then he saw the frantic waving of the arms amid the crowd and his eyes came to rest upon Nimrod and Naomi. They had left a seat open for him in between them.
He made his way down the row of guests careful not to jostle them and took his seat.

They were busy looking around and admiring the fine decorations and the beautiful statues and paintings of the Grand Hall when the trumpets were sounded.
Standing at the doorway, one on each side, were the King's trumpeters. Each instrument bore a banner of the King's Herald. They held the trumpets to their lips once more and blew and then they stopped. They stepped out of the doorway and King Lore and his son the Prince entered.
The king was dressed in his finest robes, wearing the Vashing crown and holding a scepter. Prince Lars was also dressed in fine robes bearing the Vashings colors.
They took their places, the King on his throne and the Prince kneeling in front of it.
The King's Royal messenger strode up the red carpet to the throne and then unraveled a scroll and turned to the crowd. "Welcome guests of the Vashing Kingdom. The time has come for our great King Lore to hand over his crown to the royal heir Prince Lars. May we all serve the new King well."

Then the King rose and slowly walked to his son and with the royal scepter he tapped lightly on one shoulder and then the other. Then he removed his crown and carefully placed it upon the Prince's head. "I dub thee

King Lars, long may ye live and blessed be thy reign."

The king had tears of pride in his eyes as he took his seat next to the Throne and King Lars rose to his feet.

Lars took his seat for the first time as King upon the royal throne. Then the crowd lay in hush waiting for him to speak.

"I wish to thank me guests for attending and do hope ye find all accommodations pleasing. As me first order for the day I say to one and all we must recognize me Father for his years of service and may we all celebrate his reign today. I can only hope to be as wise a King as me Father has been. I am humbled to be in charge of this grand Vashing Kingdom. May the festivities begin."

Then the crowd began to clap so loud that it hurt Bjork's ears. When they ceased to applaud the King said, "Father choose thy entertainment."

The retired King whispered to the messenger who then went to the musicians and gave them the request. Soon the hall was filled with the melodies of different lands. There was a medley of all traditional folk music for the foreigners that were in attendance.

The Celebration lasted well into the night and was not finished until long after the retired King had went to his chambers.

The next couple of days were spent enjoying the different foods from many cultures and the entertainment never ceased to amaze Bjork. The Magicians were astounding as well as the musicians. The poetic recitations were impeccably performed and there was such a sense of camaraderie amongst the many guests. What was not understood with language was understood by hand motions and nods of the heads. Bjork was simply fascinated by how many different languages the King's servants understood and spoke fluently.

The Nimbus fairies and Bjork spent the evenings together as the celebrations wound down and the time for their return to the Fairy Kingdom drew nearer. He knew he himself would be returning home to his humble abode and felt a sense of regret that this adventure was coming to an end.

On the last evening at the Vashing Castle he was gathered in the King's Library conversing with the Nimbus fairies around the warm fire. They were making preparations to leave the Vashing Kingdom the very next morning. Nimrod had inquired if Bjork would be accompanying them. Bjork shook his head and said, "I believe I will tarry here for perhaps one more day. I wish time to rest up from the festivities before the long journey home." He felt a bit tired and in need of some rest and relaxation.

Now that King Calliope and Geneva had been reunited their fairy powers had grown capable enough to where they could sprinkle fairy dust among themselves which would instantly transport them all back to The Fairy Meadow. They had no need for a guardian or protector as long as they stood strong together. Geneva had vowed to never leave the Fairy Meadow without King Calliope and Bjork knew when a fairy made a vow it was never to be broken.

They spent the greater part of the evening discussing the Coronation and the grand celebrations and then the Nimbus fairies and Bjork bid each other farewell, leaving Naomi behind. "May the Lord bless you with safe passage Bjork," Naomi said. Then she blew him a kiss and left the library.

Bjork soon retired himself to another night of blissful sleep filled with fond memories. The fire in his hearth danced shadows upon the chamber walls and the sounds of his even breathing kept rhythm. All was well in the Vashing Kingdom. The new King had been crowned and the celebration had been met with huge success.

The next morning Bjork took a stroll to the King's Garden. He felt strangely invigorated as if the night's sleep had totally refreshed his body and mind. He was deep in thought walking amongst the flowers and hedges when he was startled by a gruff voice. "Why hello Bjork, it's been quite a spell since I lain me eyes on yer face." Looking up he found Drake Mclandish larger than life standing right in front of him. He had a broad grin upon his face and held out his hand to firmly grasp Bjork's. "I heard tell that ye were here but I searched the faces at the celebrations and ye must have gotten lost in the crowd. I'm here with me dear brother Harold on orders of King George. Our King is a bit under the weather so he sent me brother and I in his place. We had informed him of the information ye had provided us about the whereabouts of the Wimpets of the Troll Forest. He has sent us to attend this Coronation and then with God's speed to hasten to the Troll Forest to bring our lost clan safely home. We are quite unfamiliar with this Troll Forest so the King has asked me to give ye this message."

He then reached inside his waistcoat and brought out a rolled up scroll tied with string. He handed this toward Bjork, who hesitated for a moment and then grabbed it from his hand.
Slowly Bjork unrolled the scroll and was pleasantly surprised to see it had been penned in his native tongue. It read" His Royal Highness King George would humbly request thy service by accompanying his servants Drake and Harold Mclandish on their journey to the Troll Forest. It has been brought to the King's attention that ye are highly familiar with this territory. Of course upon return to Wimpet Island ye shall be greatly rewarded, as long as the lost clan has been brought safely home along with His Highnesses royal and trusty servants."

Drake Mclandish stood solemnly waiting for Bjork's reaction. Bjork smiled and he now understood why he had delayed his departure and why he had felt this strange sense of anticipation. Could it be he had been blessed with another adventure?? He felt his heart leap in his chest and with great excitement he said, "When do we leave, I need to prepare my belongings and bid farewell to the Vashing King." Then Drake grabbed Bjork's hand once more and shook it vigorously. "Welcome Bjork, we will be as one clan, (forever allies.) We shall return to our ship at dawn to give our crew strict orders to not set sail but stand guard over our vessel until our return from the Troll Forest."

"We must travel through the Troll Forest under the cover of night as the Troll's suffer from night blindness. They are keen on smell though, but if my memory serves me correctly some raw fish oil will take care of that," Bjork said.

"Very well Bjork we shall be leaving tomorrow afternoon, I will see to it that we bring along a bit of fish oil. We will meet ye after the noon meal in the King's Library. This will give ye ample time to prepare thy belongings and say thy farewell."

Then Drake and Harold bid Bjork a good day and left hastily to make preparations for the journey. Bjork realized it was late morning now and although he did enjoy the Garden he retreated to the Castle to summons a meeting with the new King.

King Lars and his father were gracious in accepting Bjork's request and agreed to meet with him in the Royal chamber. They were intrigued with Bjork's plans to travel to the Troll Forest and inquired of him as to if there were warriors accompanying the Wimpets and Bjork. Bjork replied he was not sure who would be joining with him and the Mclandish brothers. King Lars tapped his finger lightly upon his chin and then said, "Speak with the Mclandish brothers Bjork and tell them we have long been allies with King George and the Wimpet people. Tell him that I will send along four of me finest warriors to aid in this expedition. He is not to refuse this as the Troll Forest is a dark and sinister place, as well ye know. I will have them ready and at his

disposal by tomorrow mid morning. God speed Bjork may thy life be long and prosperous."
Then Bjork knelt briefly in honor to King Lars and then slowly turned and left the chamber. As he left he looked over his shoulder and was surprised to see King Lars smiling fondly back at him.
Bjork would spend the rest of the day preparing his belongings and catching up on a bit of the Tales of the Wimpet King.

The next day began uneventful as Bjork rose to a delicious breakfast. His belongings lay carefully packed in his room. He noticed how empty the dining room had become as many of the King's guests had already departed. He felt alone this morning as his Nimbus fairy friends had returned home and there were no companions at his table. At the same time he felt invigorated by the possibility of another grand adventure. It had been quite awhile ago that he had conversed with the Wimpets of the Troll Forest. He wondered how they would react to seeing him accompanied by some of their own kind from the far off Wimpet Island. He remembered his first encounter with Damien, Vincent and Hector. It had been a pleasant memory. The Wimpets secret home in the underground caverns, the wonderful feasting and music, the enjoyable conversation with their wise and old Methezdah, (his dear friend whom had given him the book The Tales of the Wimpet King.) It would be a much welcome visit. He knew at the same time that there were many dangers in the Troll Forest and that he and his Nimbus fairy friends had been extremely fortunate to escape without misfortune.

Knowing that King Lars warriors would be added to his comrades on this journey did give him a sense of peace.

The Vashing warriors were highly skilled in all forms of hand to hand combat, and were excellent marksmen with their weaponry.

Bjork was startled from his deep thoughts as he heard voices in the outer halls. He decided he had spent enough time in the dining room and would now gather his belongings and retreat to the King's Library. Perhaps he could read a few more pages in the Tales of the Wimpet King before his fellow travelers arrived.

Bjork retreated to his guest room and with the fire aglow and so inviting decided he would read the Tales of the Wimpet King here. This way he could return it to the nightstand where he had found it. He would read for about an hour or so and then forego lunch, as he felt quite satiated from his large breakfast.

So sitting down in the comfortable chair by the hearth he picked up the book and began to read where he had left off. The book became completely engrossing and Bjork soon had read through three more chapters. He then set the book down upon the nightstand realizing he should see what time it was. It was at that moment he heard a clanking out in the hallway and decided to gather his belongings and head to the King's Library.

True to the King's word the Vashing warriors were gathered together in the King's Library when Bjork arrived clutching his gear. He was a bit disappointed to see that they were not his old friends, Darryl and Jarryl, (the keepers of the bridge).

These were larger and more stoutly built men with muscular frames. There were four of them total. They were dressed in the finest Vashing warrior apparel. They wore lightweight leather armor with a fine lightweight chain-mail beneath and each carried their weaponry of their choice. Their long reddish blonde hair was pulled into one long braid which hung on their backs. Their heads neatly tucked under their helmet.

Bjork barely had time to introduce himself to them when in strode Drake and Harold Mclandish. They too had their packed belongings. Introductions were made all around and Bjork learned the names of the Vashing warriors. Ari was the tallest, Brandt next tallest, Gunnar and Hallvardr were equal in height. None of the warriors were related to each other, so their faces bore no resemblance. Gunnar had a rather rough red bristly beard and a face with a broad nose and noble chin. Brandt had a more thin facial structure with high cheek bones and a long roman nose. Ari had a youthful face blonde beard and moustache and red rosy cheeks. Hallvardr had a round face with a large nose scruffy beard and mustache. Together they made a fierce group, each with their own bold and fearless attitude. Bjork was instantly sure that they were in good hands.

It was early afternoon when the group of miss-matched travelers bid farewell to the Vashing Kingdom and began their descent down the Vashing stone path that led to the beach. They would take the cavern route which would bring them into the land of the Cyclops by mid afternoon. It would be quite a long hike before they reached the Troll Forest and the sun would have been set far beneath the horizon.

Bjork prepared himself for the long journey ahead as he followed behind the McLandish brothers. Two Vashing warriors took the lead and two Vashing warriors took the rear. They had vowed their protection to this strange group of wanderers, even unto death. They took the royal commission of King Lars as a sworn oath forsaking all others. They would not fail their King in this quest and would safely return the Wimpets to their Island home. Then they would return to their homeland in triumph and victory.
Bjork wondered how long this new adventure would take, where would it lead them and when he would finally return to Horkland for a joyous reunion with his people. He mused he would be a hero of some sorts to his people. None other but Bjork had traveled so far away from the safe confines of Horkland. The young Horks would anticipate his story telling around the community fire. Ahh but that would be a long time from today. Bjork also wondered if this would be his last adventure. He knew in his heart he was getting on in years, but he also knew he could never turn down an offer for adventure. He thrived on adventure it was something that flowed through his very veins, something he could never give up easily.

The travelers came upon the mouth of the caverns and Bjork looked over his shoulder and wondered if this would be his last glimpse of the splendid Vashing Kingdom. He shrugged it off and then pushed the fear

aside. He knew he had a purpose in this life and his purpose now was to rescue the Wimpets of the Troll Forest. He would see the day when they arrived back safely to board the Mclandish vessel and set sail to Wimpet Island. It was ten days passage across the seven seas near the Bay of Bewilderment to reach the shores of Wimpet Island.
Then he wondered what had become of Syncore and his crew as they traveled in pursuit of the escaped prisoner One-Eyed Jack. Perhaps in the future their paths would meet again.
Bjork positioned his satchel upon his shoulder stepping inside the twisting caverns, winding further and further away from the sounds of the sea.

To be continued..............

18011367R00140

Made in the USA
Charleston, SC
11 March 2013